# Delphi Station

## Delphi in Space
### *Book Three*

## Bob Blanton

## Cover by Momir Borocki
momir.borocki@gmail.com

# Table of Contents

# 1    DIBS

Marc McCormack had just finished explaining to his team why they needed to build a massive floating airport to accommodate a fleet of Oryxes, a C17 knockoff that could reach Low Earth Orbit. Everyone was staring at the rotating image of the massive space station, trying to absorb the enormity of what he had planned. His thirteen-year-old daughter, Catie, had just called 'Dibs.'

"What do you mean, dibs?" Blake asked.

"I get to be the pilot," Catie said.

Blake looked at Catie like she'd lost her mind, "Of a space station?" he asked, pointing at the image on the screen.

"No, dummy, of the Lynx."

Marc raised his eyebrows and tilted his head down at Catie. "So, you know what I have in mind."

"Oh yeah, I know," Catie said.

"This is all too much," said Samantha Newman, the legal counsel for MacKenzie Discoveries and Marc's girlfriend. Learning that her boss, Marc, and his brother, Blake, had discovered an alien spaceship almost one year ago had come as quite a shock, now his wanting to build a space station was pushing her over the edge.

"What does he have in mind?" Blake asked his niece, Catie.

"He's got to go get a couple of asteroids," Catie said.

"What? Why?"

"You can't afford to lift that much mass into space. It would take too many ships and too much time," Catie explained. "He needs an iron asteroid and a carbon one to have enough material to build the space station."

"How is the Lynx going to be able to tow two asteroids to Earth?"

"How is the Lynx going to *find* two asteroids?" Fred asked. Fred Linton, another member of MacKenzie Discoveries and a pilot, was coordinating most of their production activities.

Marc nodded at Catie, signaling her to continue her explanation.

"The Lynx can easily accelerate at one-G in space. With a constant one-G acceleration to the halfway point and then a constant one-G deceleration after, it's only like four days to the asteroid belt that's just beyond Mars. Then you spend a few days cruising around until you find an asteroid you like, slap a fusion reactor and three gravity drives on it, leave a comm probe so ADI can steer it, and voilà, Asteroid Deliveries R Us starts operation."

"And this digital intelligence . . ." Samantha started.

"Autonomous Digital Intelligence," Catie corrected.

"Yes, this ADI can steer the asteroids?"

"Sure, she's a ship computer, she's designed to steer things in space."

"Why not just send the Sakira?" Blake asked. The Sakira was the alien spaceship that Marc and Blake had found earlier under the ocean. It was the source of all the technology they were exploiting, and the Lynx was its captain's cutter.

"That's a bit like using a sledgehammer to swat a fly. And I don't want to risk exposing the Sakira."

"Okay, so how long will it take to get the asteroids here?" Blake asked.

Marc nodded at Catie again.

"Ummm, depends," Catie said. "Moving something as big as an asteroid would suggest low acceleration and lots of caution." Catie paused as she closed her eyes and thought. "You'd want to aim it so that it hits the orbit you want at a tangent at just the right speed so it will get captured by the sun. Then you could bring it up to Earth and parallel the orbit. Would you bring it into Earth orbit?"

"What do you think?"

"People would go nuts if you put it in Earth orbit. I'd put it in the same solar orbit as Earth, but leading. Then I'd bring a third ice asteroid so we'd have plenty of water to fuel a fleet of Oryxes to bring the ore in for us," Catie said.

"Why leading?" Marc asked.

"Easier and faster to accelerate while empty, you can use the Earth to help slow you down when you come back loaded."

"Okay, so how long?"

"You don't want to waste a lot of time and energy," Catie said. "Bringing it into orbit at just the right speed would be best. You fly it at thirty kilometers per second to get here, so seventyish days plus half of the time it takes to accelerate up to speed, so I'd say add another fifteen days and plan on two-thousandths of a G acceleration."

"Pretty good for a girl that used to complain about her math homework," Marc said. "But?"

Catie put her hands on her hips and looked at her father in a huff. "I only complained about having to convince the teacher that my answers were right when they gave me extra assignments that they didn't understand."

"But?"

"You'll probably need a couple of months to get them into the leading position, depending on where I find the asteroids we want."

"Really good."

Catie smiled at her father. "So, do I get the mission?"

"Who's your copilot?"

"I don't know, I figure I can have my pick," she laughed.

"Who's going to lug the gravity drives around?"

"They won't weigh anything; you just have to deal with the mass; the EVA suits in the Sakira have jetpacks so anyone can do it. But I'll take a beefy guy if you'll give him clearance."

"Wait! You're not giving it to her?" Blake said.

"Come on, Uncle Blake," Catie said with her little girl voice.

"She's figured it out in five minutes," Marc said. "Seems like she's the one to lead it."

Blake gulped a couple of times like a fish. "Damn that brain of hers."

"But wait, that's what you're planning?" Samantha asked, looking around at everyone. Liz and Fred nodded their heads in support of her question.

"Pretty much," Marc said.

"You are crazy."

"I've heard that before," Marc laughed. "What's next?"

"I've got to figure out how to build a floating airport fast," Blake said as he poured his third shot of scotch.

"I've got to figure out what Catie wants for the copilot slot," Fred said as he left the room laughing.

"Hey, what about the rest of us!" Liz yelped. Liz Farmer was one of their pilots and also doubled as Catie's personal security.

"I think the copilot thing will work itself out," Marc said. "Liz, do you want to help me figure out how to build the space station? The hull has to be formed in orbit."

"Why is that?" Liz asked.

"Not having to lift the material for one. And that's the difference between the polysteel we made down here and the Lynx's hull. The Lynx's hull absorbs any EM energy; it has a superconductor matrix under its skin that directs the energy into the batteries for storage. The space station will do the same thing, that way most of its power will come from the sun," Marc said. "Of course, we'll have a fusion reactor up there, but we need to do something with all that solar energy hitting the shell. We'd also like it to be stealthy."

"That sounds like fun," Liz said.

"Wait, can't I help?" Catie asked.

"You're our jet person, so why don't you work on the Oryxes," Marc said. "We'll see how the workload goes. We have to keep our other projects going. We need money; we need an airport; we need planes; we need to be prepared for someone who wants to take any or all of that away from us."

"Ohhh," Samantha said.

"Sam?"

"That's why you wanted the contract with the Cook Island government structured like a treaty," Samantha said as she gave Marc a very knowing look. "You are so devious."

"What?" Blake asked.

"He's planning to declare the space station a free nation," Samantha said.

"Just thinking about it," Marc said.

Samantha's head jerked with a start as she realized what else Marc might be planning. "What about Delphi City?"

"On the list."

"Sir," the captain knocked on Admiral Michaels' door.

"Come in," Admiral Michaels said. "So, we have more on our friends."

"Yes, sir," the captain said as he entered the office. He stood in front of the admiral's desk at parade rest.

"Relax, sit down."

"Yes, sir."

"So, what have our friends been up to now?"

"Quite a bit, it seems. Our man in New Zealand reports that they have submitted the specs and necessary documents to certify a new executive jet design."

"Why is that of interest?"

"It's supersonic."

"Oh, so it is their jet we heard about before."

"Yes, sir, but there's more."

"What?"

"The specs are very similar to what we picked up from the incident with the Chinese carrier."

The admiral made a rolling motion with his hands to tell the captain to continue.

"It specifies a top speed of Mach four, and they say it doesn't produce a supersonic shockwave."

"No shockwaves!" the admiral repeated, his eyes wide in surprise. "Do they explain how they accomplish that?"

"No, sir, the documents specify that it is proprietary technology, but they will demonstrate it during the qualifications."

"I think we have to brief the secretary on this."

"I would agree, but there is one more thing you should see first."

"Okay."

The captain opened his briefcase and pulled out a folder of photos, he laid four photos side by side on the admiral's desk.

"What am I looking at here?" Admiral Michaels asked. "It looks like an offshore drilling platform."

"That's what the analyst thought, too, but if you look at the dimensions, sir."

"Just tell me."

"It started out two hundred fifty meters by two hundred fifty meters, sir. That's three times bigger than a typical oil platform. It has since been expanded to six hundred fifty meters by six hundred fifty meters, and they've started to duplicate their production on it."

"That is big," the admiral said, nodding his head as he studied the pictures.

"It's not done yet," the captain said. "It looks like they're planning on another three sections, making it about sixteen hundred by sixteen hundred meters, that's almost a square mile."

"These people are ambitious."

"Yes, sir. We also have these photos from our man on Rarotonga," the captain added four more photos. They showed one of the pontoons being lowered into the water and two provided shots looking straight at the structure from the side.

"Okay, what am I supposed to notice here?"

"The spans are two hundred meters."

"There are braces here," the admiral pointed to the angled braces from the columns to the beams.

"Yes, sir; even with those, you have a one-hundred-meter span. Also, note the size of the columns."

"Okay."

"They're only five meters in diameter. Our engineers say it's impossible for them to support the structure."

"But they seem to be doing so."

"Yes, sir, possibly related to the material that the executive jet is made of."

"What material?"

"They call it polysteel," the captain said. "The specs they gave New Zealand make titanium look like plastic."

"That good?"

"Half the weight and twice as strong, at least that's what the documents they gave the Kiwis say."

"Okay, are we ready to call a briefing?"

"There's more, but it can wait for the briefing."

The admiral buzzed his assistant, "Meg, please set up a briefing with Secretary Barrows and General Wilson."

"Yes, sir, when do you want to hold it?"

"At their earliest convenience, and invite Director Lassiter as well."

"Yes, sir."

"Gentlemen, I apologize for the late hour, but this was the earliest time we could get all three of you together," Admiral Michaels said as he entered the room. It was 10:30 p.m. EST in Washington D.C. Seated at the table was Secretary of Defense Jerry Barrows, Director of the CIA Bill Lassiter and National Security Advisor General John Wilson.

"Couldn't this wait until tomorrow?" Secretary Barrows asked.

"Possibly, but I felt that sooner was better given the stunning nature of the data."

"Okay, give it to us."

"Please be seated. Would anyone like some refreshments?"

"Not yet. Get on with it."

"Sirs, you all probably have been briefed on the incident in the Philippine Sea in March."

"Yes, where the Chinese pilots claimed some super jet took them down."

"That's correct. We have an application to New Zealand for the certification of an executive jet that closely matches the claims of the Chinese pilots."

"How so?"

"It specifies a speed of Mach four, is made of a new material called polysteel that is half the weight and over twice the strength of titanium."

"Wait," General Wilson said. "How is this possible, Jerry?" he asked, looking at the director of the CIA.

"We have no data showing that the Russians or any of our major allies have anything like that," Director Lassiter said.

"That is probably correct," Admiral Michaels said. "The application comes from a company called MacKenzie Discoveries. It's run by Dr. Marc McCormack, who is the same fellow we purchased the new sonar technology from that we're now installing in our submarine and surface fleets."

"Aren't they the ones who discovered that Portuguese shipwreck?"

"Yes, the Las Cinque Chagas," Admiral Michaels said.

"Hold on here," Secretary Barrows said. "Can you lay this out from beginning to end? I'd like some perspective here."

"Yes, sir, I can. Does everyone agree? It's a long list."

"Then, I definitely agree," General Wilson said as he sat back in his chair. "Start at the beginning."

"Yes, sir. Dr. Marc McCormack has a PhD. in mathematics. He wrote his dissertation on signal processing. He made some significant advances in the field, was offered, and accepted a department chair position at MIT. He was twenty-nine at the time."

"Smart guy."

"Yes. He worked at MIT for four years. We first became aware of him when he consulted with the DEA on a project where he modeled drug smuggling in an attempt to identify which vessels were actually smuggling drugs. It was his analysis that led to the series of big drug busts three-and-a-half years ago. Everyone was shocked at how much they recovered. He wound up getting the yacht and about two million as his commission. He and his brother, Commander Blake McCormack, repaired ..."

"Commander McCormack?" General Wilson interrupted. "The one who was awarded the Navy Cross?"

"Yes, sir."

"I thought I recognized the name. Please go on."

"As I was saying, he and his brother restored the yacht over the next eighteen months. They then shipped it to Hawaii. Dr. McCormack left MIT and formed Hyperion Sonar. He and the commander moved to Hawaii, where Dr. McCormack developed the sonar system, and the commander did private charters on the yacht. A year later, Dr. McCormack contacted the Navy along with several major defense contractors to invite us all to review his new sonar technology."

"I remember this," Director Lassiter said.

"Yes, this is the first time that I met Dr. McCormack. When he showed us the technology, I declared it top secret, and we eventually bought his company."

"This is all interesting, but how does it lead us to the new jet?"

"I'm getting to it; you asked that I start at the beginning, and it is important for you to see the pace of discovery here."

"Yes, we all agreed we wanted the whole story," Secretary Barrows said. "Go on, Admiral."

"It was barely ten weeks later that they raised the Chagas. They accomplished this without any prior experience, and apparently without ever doing anything but cruise around the Azores."

"What, and how would you know this?"

"The technology jump on the sonar was so dramatic that I thought it would be worth keeping an eye on Dr. McCormack. I had some of my assets follow him after we were briefed on the sonar. I kept them following him when he was in the Caribbean, the Azores, and Portugal."

"You were taking a lot of license with your position," General Wilson said.

"I know, but it was a minor cost, and I was worried he had help with the sonar, possibly foreign help."

"Okay, so that explains how you know what he was doing, but explain about 'just cruising' a little better."

"Dr. McCormack, his brother, Blake McCormack, his daughter, Catie, and two ex-Marines went to the Caribbean and cruised around for two weeks. They did quite a bit of diving during this time but never in the same area. They then flew to the Azores on a private jet that Dr. McCormack had leased. While in the Azores, they lounged around the island, went to the beach, essentially waiting until their yacht, the Mea Huli, arrived. When it arrived, they moved aboard it and started cruising around the islands. They went out for two days; they came back to the hotel for one; then they went out for three days. When they came back, they sailed the Mea Huli to Lisbon. Dr. McCormack, his daughter, and former Marine Captain Elizabeth Farmer met with the Portuguese Minister of Antiquities, where we presume, they discussed the Chagas. During this time, the commander and former Marine Staff Sergeant Kalani Kealoha met with a chemical company where they specified and ordered a foam compound, which was a completely new formulation with properties that had never been engineered before. This foam was used to help raise the Chagas. Any questions?"

Everyone shook their head, "Go on."

"While Dr. McCormack, his daughter, and Captain Farmer stayed in Portugal to negotiate with the government, the commander and Sergeant Kealoha sailed the Mea Huli to Casablanca."

"Wait, they sailed to Casablanca?" Director Lassiter asked. "Around the eighteenth of August?"

"Yes, sir."

"Why is that date important?" Secretary Barrows asked.

"That was when Omar Harrak, a notorious arms dealer and smuggler, went missing."

"Yes, and his nephew, Muzah Harrak, who happened to work for the Portuguese Minister of Antiquities, also disappeared about that time," Admiral Michaels added.

"A coincidence?" General Wilson asked.

"I generally don't believe in coincidences," Director Lassiter said. "Please, continue."

"After spending two days around Casablanca, the Mea Huli sailed back to the Azores, while Dr. McCormack and the other two finalized their agreement with the Portuguese. They then flew back to the Azores. While there, the crew from the jet they were leasing joined the rest of them on the Mea Huli. Again, they seemed to just sail around the islands, staying out for five or six days at a time. Like before, the yacht was never in the same place for more than a few hours. On the fourteenth of September, they met up with a small flotilla from the Portuguese Navy; they then set sail to a set of coordinates about three hundred miles southeast of where they met the flotilla. When they arrived, the five Americans went diving. They stayed down for several hours, then they and the Chagas surfaced."

"Unbelievable," Director Lassiter said.

"I would agree, except that it happened," Admiral Michaels said.

"Keep going, we're still not to the jets."

"At this time, things got quiet. They received 2.6 billion dollars for the Chagas; their company was registered in the Caymans, undoubtedly for tax purposes. They eventually shipped the Mea Huli to Rarotonga in the Cook Islands. While there, they enlisted the help of a top international lawyer, Samantha Newman, who negotiated an agreement with the government to give them a fifty-year lease on Manuae, an uninhabited island within the Cook Island system. In exchange, they agree to pay the government fifty million dollars per year over the term of the lease and to invest another one billion dollars in the economy, setting up local industries and also setting up a high-

15

end medical facility for research and treatment of chronic diseases. Cook Islanders are to receive free treatment."

"Magnanimous of them."

"Yes. On the sixteenth of November, Dr. McCormack brought his daughter's great grandparents to the islands, accompanied by his ex-wife. Also accompanying them were Dr. Leo Zelbar and his wife Nikola, both of them are specialists in material science; Dr. Tanaka, a nuclear physicist, and his daughter; and Dr. Nakahara, another nuclear physicist. All of the doctors, except Mrs. Zelbar, were reported to be suffering from Alzheimer's."

"And you're going to tell us that Dr. McCormack was able to treat them," Director Lassiter said.

"Dr. McCormack's ex-wife is a medical doctor, a brain surgeon actually, but the treating physician was a Dr. Metra Kumar according to our source. After three weeks, the McCormacks and the grandparents returned to the U.S. The others stayed behind. According to discreet inquiries, the grandparents are both extremely healthy and leading a completely normal lifestyle."

"Are they treating others?" Secretary Barrows asked.

"They are offering to treat others. It has been very discreet; our sources say they are charging five hundred thousand dollars for treatment; they have also brought in a few more old codgers from various scientific fields who were treated and are continuing to stay with them," the admiral continued.

"Five hundred thousand dollars, my god, that's a fortune."

"It costs upwards of fifty thousand dollars a year to take care of an Alzheimer's patient," Admiral Michaels said. "And the people who are getting the treatment are the wealthiest of the wealthy. We've had trouble verifying the success since there is so much secrecy around them. But they're treating over twenty-five people a month. It should go up as the new clinic comes online. Right now, they're using a hospital ship they've leased."

"That's over twelve million dollars a month!" Secretary Barrows said.

"Yes, it's a nice chunk of change," the admiral said.

"The jets," General Wilson interrupted.

"Yes, sir, the jets, getting there now," Admiral Michaels said. "In February, our asset noticed that China and Russia both had spies in place on Rarotonga. He indicated that they didn't seem to be having any more luck gathering intel than he was. On March ninth, our asset reported there was a huge stir. Dr. McCormack, his daughter, his brother, Sergeant Kealoha and Captain Farmer boarded the Mea Huli and left Rarotonga. They were gone for two days, came back for two weeks, then everyone except Dr. McCormack disappeared again for a week. The Chinese incident occurred in the middle of that last week."

"Finally, the jets," General Wilson said.

"Yes, the jets," Admiral Michaels said. "The communications we intercepted show the Chinese pilots reporting that they were being attacked by one jet. They said it was almost impossible to get a radar lock on, and that at times, it was flying at over Mach five. They said it actually outran their missiles. Two Chinese jets were shot down in a matter of minutes. The Chinese launched two more jets, after which a second unknown jet joined the fight. It shot down the second pair of Chinese jets while the first jet apparently attacked the carrier. The carrier Liaoning returned to port with its flight deck severely damaged."

"Also, during this time, several ex-Marines and ex-Special Forces soldiers have been recruited to join the team in the Cook Islands. Most of the Marines and Special Forces guys are amputees."

"That's a strange recruiting pool," General Wilson said.

"I agree," Admiral Michaels said. "Most of them have been isolated on Manuae since they arrived. Now somewhat mundane but significant, McKenzie Discoveries just introduced a revolutionary battery into the market. They are now providing all the batteries for Tesla Motors, and they have signed an exclusive deal with Apple to provide batteries for their laptops and phones. These batteries reportedly never age, recharge four times faster than lithium-ion, and hold over five times the charge. They have purchased Johansson Motors and started production of electric motorcycles with them. They are apparently negotiating with Honda Motors to purchase the rights to produce an all-electric version of the Honda CRV."

"These people are really ambitious," Secretary Barrows said.

"Oh, it gets better." Admiral Michaels turned to the big screen in the room, which was now displaying the pictures of Delphi City.

"How does it get better? And what is that thing?" asked Director Lassiter.

"Our engineers assure us that this is impossible to build without it collapsing in on itself. The platform is eight hundred fifty meters by eight hundred fifty meters; it is floating on pontoons and columns. The columns are impossibly small, the span between columns is two hundred meters, and based on information from our asset, they plan on expanding it to sixteen hundred fifty meters by sixteen hundred fifty meters. They're duplicating their production of the polysteel from the island of Manuae on the platform, and moving their battery production there," Admiral Michaels explained.

"Okay, we need to know a lot more," Secretary Barrows said. "I'll give the president a brief synopsis, but he's not going to be happy. We need to get real intelligence on whatever they're doing," he said while looking at Director Lassiter.

"I'll get my best people there immediately. Admiral, I'll need the info on your assets."

"I'll send it over right away."

"Good work, Admiral," Secretary Barrows offered his hand.

Everyone shook hands and left. Admiral Michaels turned to Captain Johnson, "Well, we've lit the match. I hope we don't get burned."

"Yes, sir. So do I."

# 2    Design

Catie walked into Marc's office and gave her father a cautious look. "Daddy, I have a question." She sat down in front of Marc's desk.

"Sure, what's up?"

"Don't take this the wrong way, but why rotate the station for gravity? Wouldn't using artificial gravity work better?"

"Have you read up on the theory?"

"No, but the Sakira uses it."

"Only when in deep space," Marc said. "If you use it around a gravity well, then it starts fighting the gravity there. It starts acting like a gravity drive and creates acceleration. Hard to maintain an orbit while you're accelerating; and if you want to maintain a fixed position, you have to balance the forces, so you wind up sitting in place with guess what?"

"No gravity," Catie answered.

"Right. Besides, it takes an enormous amount of energy; the Sakira only uses it at one-tenth G except for a short time each day when it's set it to full gravity for the crew's health."

"Oh, I guess it would only make sense for a deep-space station then."

"Right, maybe someone will figure out how to get around the problems," Marc said. "But until then, we have to live with it. Do you have everything you need to design the Oryx?" Marc asked.

"ADI does, she's doing most of the work; I'm just figuring out what parts we can buy from other manufacturers and convert them instead of having to print them all," Catie said.

"I hope you're working on the engineering too."

"I'm only thirteen," Catie said.

"Funny, I don't recall you mentioning that when you called dibs."

"Okay," Catie sighed. "I am working on it as much as I can, but I can only learn so fast, and I don't want to slow things down. I've got the lift on the wings figured out, but I don't have the math to figure out how to avoid the sonic shockwave. I'm just trusting ADI on that."

"I don't have the math for that either," Marc said. "We're going to need to get a real theoretical mathematician somewhere."

"Oh! I know just the guy," Catie said.

Marc shook his head in surprise, "You do?"

"Yeah, I came across him when I was reading up on gravity theory for a class," Catie said. "Einstein's model, the one that works for orbits and such."

"I'm aware of it."

"Anyway, he has a PhD. in mathematics and was working on a second PhD. in astrophysics. He submitted a dissertation on gravimetric waves, and it got rejected," Catie explained. "He was only eighteen, and he's been arguing his case since. He's teaching at some junior college in Ohio now. ADI says his theory is mostly right."

"So why should we hire him?"

"He's super smart; he' can't get a decent job because he's being shunned by the scientific community; he seems to know something about the gravimetric waves that the gravity drives use; he's a bit isolated so he should be easy to get. And, he's young enough that he'll probably be willing to wait to publish and get his revenge until you're ready."

"Good points. Send me his info, and I'll look into it."

"Okay. Bye, Daddy."

"Bye, Sweetie."

Samantha knocked gently on the door jamb, as she stuck her head into Marc's office. "Marc, gotta minute?"

"For you, I've got all the time in the world."

"I'll remind you of that when you're saying uh-huh to everything I say while you're buried in that HUD of yours."

Marc removed his HUD, and turned to face Samantha, "I'm sure you will. What's up?"

"I'm looking at our investment numbers. We're overcommitted. Where is all the cash going to come from?"

Marc grimaced, "Oops."

"You forgot to tell me something else. What, another spaceship, a new alien species, you can turn lead into gold?"

"Sorry," Marc said while looking as apologetic as he could. "ADI takes care of the shortfall."

"How?"

"We opened a few trading accounts; seeded them with twenty-five million each. She's built them up to about one hundred million each, and now she returns about one hundred million a month."

Samantha leaned forward in her chair, looking very worried. "How does she do that?" she asked.

"It appears that ADI can sift through all the economic data faster than anybody else, and she predicts the market movements, both stock and futures."

Samantha bit her lip, "Aren't you cheating?"

"Everybody uses computers to predict the markets, ours is just faster. Besides, her trades have the side benefit of stabilizing the markets."

"Stabilizing the markets?"

"Sure, she buys big and early when it looks like the market is undervalued. It forces the price up, keeps it from undershooting too much; same thing when it's overvalued."

"But you siphon off a big chunk."

"Of course, think of it as a stability tax."

"So, when I tell you that Johansson wants five hundred million to close that deal with Honda to license the CRV design, you're going to be fine with it?"

"ADI?"

"Yes, Captain. I have 1.2 billion in the accounts."

"Thank you, ADI," Marc said. "Seems, we're good."

Samantha reached across the desk and slapped Marc on the arm, "I want a raise."

"Hey Liz," Catie said as she walked up and gave her father a hug. "How's it going?" Catie synced her comm up to theirs so she could watch the three-D image of the project they were working on in her HUD as well.

"We've figured out how to form the pieces to make the hub," Liz said.

"You're going to build it in pieces," Catie said; clearly she didn't think that was a good idea.

Liz raised her eyebrows and looked at Marc, "Sure, what else would we do?"

Catie ducked her head a little and shrugged her shoulders, "Oh, I don't know."

"Go ahead, Catie," Marc said. "We want this done right more than we want to be right."

"Well, I assumed you would extrude it," Catie said.

"How would we do that?" Liz asked.

"At first, I thought you'd form a foam base and spray it on, but that seemed a little unwieldy. Then I realized you should just extrude it like Uncle Blake makes the columns and beams. He's modified the form. Now, it has little wheels that push the beam out of the form as it's being made."

"How does that help us?"

"You make the form and fit it with a plasma torch to deposit the polysteel. Put it all on the end of an arm that you can rotate around the center. Some big mass attached to the center to keep everything stable, a magnetic bearing to let the arm rotate. Plumb the mix and power out to the plasma torch," Catie said.

Liz and Marc nodded their heads as they followed along.

"Then you start rotating it, the speed sets your extrusion rate, then you start pushing the shell down."

"Wow, that might work," Marc said. "You just keep pushing it until you're done."

"That's what I thought."

"What about the rings?"

"You should extrude those too," Catie said. "Set it up just like you do the hub, but rotate the whole thing around the hub. You probably should do it in quarter sections; otherwise, you'll be extruding it for months."

"What happens when you reach the start of the last section?"

"Put a taper on the inside form, put all the hardware on the outside form, then just let the inside form go into the other quarter section. You'll have to cut the inside form into pieces to get it out of the ring, but that won't take all that long."

"That wouldn't be so bad," Liz said. "You can cut it with a laser so you can reassemble it for the next ring."

"What about the holes for the elevator spokes?"

"You slide a foam plug into the form when you want a hole. It'll get pulled in by the wheels, and then the plasma gun won't deposit there. Support it on the inside of the form. You can pop it out later when you're ready to add the spoke. You might want to go back and put a thin coat on the outside, so you're airtight until you want to add the spoke to the next ring."

"This should really speed up the project," Marc said. "I was really frustrated at how long it was going to take."

"I think each shell for the hub will take three or four days to extrude," Catie said. "That's assuming you use four plasma guns."

"What made you think of this?" Marc asked. "You didn't just come up with it here, did you?"

"No," Catie grinned. "I was trying to figure out if there was a better way to form the Oryx's wings. Those things are huge. I was trying to figure if there was a way to extrude them. But the wing shape is too complex. We are going to extrude most of the fuselage, but we have to form the wings in two pieces by spraying them on a foam base. Anyway, that led me to think about what you were doing and how nice it was that you had such normal geometric shapes."

"Really?" Liz said.

"What can I say, I was a little bored one night."

"Yeah, why couldn't you have come by last week before we did all the work on the hub?" Marc said.

"I was busy catching up after playing with this idea," Catie said. "Oh, and don't forget to attach the superconductor matrix while you're extruding the shells. I'll send you the details of how we're doing that for the Oryx's fuselage."

"Thanks," Marc said. "Now, get lost. I'll see you at dinner."

"Bye."

"Damn, she's smart," Liz said.

"I know, try being her father," Marc said. "At least you can take your frustrations out when you're working on self-defense with her."

"I sure can, and we're going to have a really tough lesson tomorrow," Liz laughed.

"Toss her on the mat once for me."

"Okay, so what are you thinking?" Liz asked.

"I'm thinking I'm in over my head," Catie replied.

She and Liz were standing on quad one of Delphi City, looking at the expanse of polysteel that had been laid down by the construction crew. The crew was busy assembling the first manufacturing plant over in the corner of the quad.

"Why do you say that?"

"Reading a few articles about adding greenbelts to planned development and actually doing it are different things. I've never been much of a gardener."

"Well, you're not being a gardener," Liz said. "You're being a city planner. We'll hire the gardeners."

"Okay, one of the first things they say is not to create wind tunnels," Catie said. "We're going to have streets every one hundred meters. The streets will be fifteen meters wide, six meters for a lane and sidewalk on each side, and three meters for the median. That makes the blocks eighty-five meters square."

"And you want something like thirty percent green area."

"But I don't want to chop it up into tiny pieces. We need something big enough that you can play soccer or baseball in. Then some area big enough for big community events."

"So, how big?" Liz asked.

"I think if each quad had two parks that were four blocks each, plus another two one-block parks, then everybody would be close to a nice green area, and the small community would have a couple of big parks, so baseball people could go to one and soccer people could go to the other."

"That sounds nice. What about when we have a whole section up?"

"Then I think you put a big park in the middle of it. A park that is sixteen city blocks will break up the space and give a really nice area for the community to gather." Catie was painting the image in her HUD and giving Liz access to it.

"Are we going to get bigger than that?"

"Yeah, Dad is planning for at least four sections," Catie said. "I think when we have four sections, we put a huge park in the middle, one that is sixty-four city blocks. Eight hundred meters on a side."

"Wow, why so big?"

"Because it's gotta have a big saltwater lake in the middle of it and beaches around it."

"Beaches?"

"You can't have a city in the middle of the ocean and not have beaches," Catie said. "The kids are going to want to play at a beach."

"How are you going to make a beach and a saltwater lake?"

"We'll pump the ocean water up and circulate it," Catie said. "Bring in fresh seawater and create waves. I'm sure we can figure something out. We can put a nice resort hotel along the beach. But I want to keep that secret until it's done."

"I can keep a secret. It sounds pretty nice, what does that come out to percent wise?" Liz asked, sure that Catie had exceeded her budget.

"It's for the four-section city, it's only two hundred fifty-six blocks of park space. That's only twenty-five percent. The medians along the streets should bring us up to the thirty percent target."

"Oh, it sounded like so much more and looks like so much more on my HUD," Liz said.

"That's because it's all clumped together. All those other blocks are chopped up by roads and such, so they don't look as massive."

# 3    Board Meeting – April 29th

"This meeting of MacKenzie Discoveries' Board of Directors is now called to order."

"Drinks are on me," Blake said. He pulled a bottle of scotch out and started passing out glasses.

"Really!" Marc said.

"Trust me, you're going to need a drink," Blake said.

Marc just blew his breath out and decided to live with it. "Why am I going to need a drink?"

"Labor shortage," Blake said.

"What?" Marc looked at Kal. "You're our director of labor, what's up?"

"We're growing too fast," Kal said. "The islanders would rather work the jobs being created on their home island than come out to Arutanga, Manuae, or Delphi City."

"Can't we just pay them more?" Samantha asked.

"Really doesn't work that way with islanders. It would draw a few, but we really need hundreds, especially if you want to start production of those Oryxes," Kal said. "We're ramping things up much faster than we originally planned."

"I realize that," Marc said. "Can we bring in labor?"

"From where?" Kal asked.

"Guatemala, Honduras, any place with refugees," Marc said.

"Those people are going to want to bring their families," Kal said. "They're refugees because they're fleeing their homes due to violence, they want jobs, but they're really looking for a safe place to live with their families."

"We're building a city," Marc said. "It needs families. Just make sure we get at least one English-speaking refugee for ten non-English speakers, same language of course."

"What about skills?" Kal asked.

"We need cooks, gardeners, housekeepers as well as manufacturers. A lot of the manufacturing work is semiskilled. We train them. Move the Cook Islanders into the higher-skilled jobs and pay them extra to stay on and be crew bosses; they'll like that for a while."

"Preference of where they come from?"

"I'd focus on the UN refugee programs first," Samantha said. "They'll have vetted the people from the various camps, and have a structure in place that you can use to vet them again. You'll have to set up your own infrastructure to interview and vet people from Central America if you try to recruit there."

"Make it clear that there will be no Sharia law here or other religious restrictions. They're welcome to bring their religion, but individual rights will trump religion every time," Marc said.

"I'll contact them today," Kal said. "We need about three hundred new workers right away."

"That will mean about twelve hundred people," Samantha said. "Unless you were counting the support staff in your three hundred."

"No, just manufacturing," Kal said.

"Okay, put together a team to set up the process," Marc said.

Samantha clicked her nails on the tabletop. "You should probably hire a refugee coordinator from the UN, someone who's set up a camp before and is experienced in working with refugees."

"That makes a lot of sense," Marc said as he smiled at her.

"Of course," Samantha laughed. "I've got it."

"Catie, how are your greenhouses coming along?"

"I've got it down to a process now," Catie said. "But we should really get a real horticulturalist if you want to ramp up production to support that many people."

"Sam?"

"On it."

"We'll need more doctors and nurses," Dr. Metra said.

"Doctors are not as easy to recruit," Samantha said, "but money will work there?" She gave Marc a look.

"Whatever it takes, we need to make Delphi City a paradise so we can attract more talent," Marc said.

"To do that, you need to have Lynxes running back and forth, so people don't feel so isolated. Being able to be in Sydney or Wellington in less than an hour will do wonders for people, much less being about three hours from New York City or Paris." Samantha gave Marc a knowing look when she mentioned Paris.

"Got it, vacation in Paris for the Lynx's maiden flight to France," Marc said. "Liz, how are you doing with our gaggle of scientists and engineers?"

"Gaggle is right," Liz said. "I should have known when you foisted this off on me that it was going to be difficult."

"They're not that difficult," Marc said, knowing full well how much those scientists demanded. "When I was handling them, they were just asking for more lab facilities and test equipment. That wasn't that taxing." Marc ducked a little as Liz threatened to throw her comm unit at him.

"Not when you've got someone else looking after them," Liz said. "Anyway, the design team on the trucks is doing great. They've modified a semi-truck with all the changes and are now running it through its paces. Because that's a bit hard to do on Rarotonga, I've arranged for it to be shipped to Australia where they can run it any which way they want.

"Now I'm looking into how to start manufacturing them," Liz continued. "We could try to start a factory ourselves, but I think licensing the design and selling the fuel cells and batteries is a better bet. Tata Motors of India is the world's biggest supplier of big vehicles; they're aggressive, and they're everywhere."

"I agree," Marc said. "Sam?"

"Adding it to my list."

"What about manufacturing the fuel cells?" Marc asked.

"We can make the membranes here in the city, then send them to Rarotonga for assembly. At least until we max out the labor population there. After that, we can just send them to wherever we're manufacturing the vehicles and let them set up a plant to assemble

29

them," Liz said. "That way, we don't overload the labor force here. We can just throttle it to whatever the Cook Islanders want to have local."

"I like that," Marc said.

"Good, so does Fred take this over now?" Liz asked.

Fred nodded, "Adding it to my list."

"Next, we have my favorites, the nuclear physicists," Liz continued. "Although they seem to spend most of their time arguing, they've now started asking for some very big and very expensive equipment."

"Anything we can't afford?"

"No, just sharing my pain," Liz said. "And Dr. Zelbar has started to work on transparent polysteel."

"How did you manage that?"

"I had Catie ask him why, if polysteel was so much like diamonds, it wasn't clear like a diamond."

"Clever of you," Marc said. "See, I knew you were just the person for the job."

Liz glared at Marc before she continued. "Our plasma physicist is excited about the potential to make a big plasma torch so Blake can use it as a weapon, and Dr. Nikola Zelbar has cracked the fuel cell nut. She did that mostly on her own, ADI only had to add a little nudge."

"That's a good thing since we're getting ready to start manufacturing those things in Mexico," Sam laughed.

"Anything else?" Marc asked as Liz sighed and gave him a look.

"No, that's it for now."

"Okay. Blake, how's construction going?"

"We've got the first quad done," Blake said, "dormitories are finished, and we have a couple of apartment buildings up; they need furnishings and such, but we can start putting people in them. We won't need as much dorm space if more of the workers are going to be living in the apartments. We've got the second quad built up to the subdeck and are starting to add infrastructure. Quad three has the basic frame done.

We'll be adding the subdeck soon. The construction workers seem to love the three months on, one month off routine, so no issues there."

"How's our airport coming?"

"We'll start producing pontoons and columns for it next week. It'll be a while before we have capacity available for the decking or beams."

"Okay. Catie, how are the Lynxes coming along?"

"I took the new baby up yesterday. It handles as well as the first one did. With the governor engaged, it tops out at Mach four. Without the governor, it gets up to Mach five. Not as good as a real Lynx, but we don't have its engines."

"When do the Kiwis start evaluating it?"

"Next week. Liz and I will fly one over to Wellington, and give it to them to evaluate. It's going to take a while; people are really nervous about the Mach four thing."

"Okay, how about the Oryx?"

"Design's done, I'm still tweaking the manufacturing process with Uncle Blake, but it should be ready when we have a plant to build it in."

"Alright. Sam?"

"We've inked the deal with Honda. I have a little homework to do with the parliament here to make sure we're good to bring in refugees. We covered immigration as part of the original deal, so probably just smoothing some ruffled feathers. I also have a long list of people I'm supposed to hire. The exclusive deal with Apple ends in two months, so we're negotiating with Samsung and the big laptop companies to add them to the deal."

"That's great. We can use the extra cash."

"And best of all, our car plant in Acapulco will be ready to start production in two weeks. I think you're going to have to do a press conference for the opening."

"No!" Marc said, dropping his head into his hands.

"I'm afraid so. You're going to get some hard questions about why it's not in the US, what you're going to pay, greenhouse gases. You'd better study up." Samantha was obviously enjoying Marc's discomfort

**31**

at having to give a press conference. She knew he hated public speaking, and he'd been avoiding any public meetings or press conferences since she'd joined MacKenzie Discoveries, forcing her to do them instead.

"Why do I feel like I'm being set up?"

"Probably because you are," Blake said. "Now, do you want that drink?"

"Sure," Marc said as he reached for a glass. "Okay, on a lighter note, Liz and I, with a little help from Catie, have the base design and manufacturing process for Station Delphi. We just need some Oryxes and an airport to start construction."

"And a few asteroids," Catie added.

"Soon, Sweetie, soon," Marc said. "Kal, how's the security team doing?"

"Despite the A-team kicking their ass, the new guys are excited and training well."

Catie stood up and did a little dance, "Who's the big dog in town?"

"We are!" Liz, Blake, Kal, and Catie shouted together.

"Children," Samantha groaned and laid her head on the table. Dr. Metra reached over and patted her arm.

"Dr. Metra, how are we doing with the new facilities?"

"They're coming along nicely thanks to Cer Blake's efforts. I am looking forward to leaving the Virginia Henderson and being in a real facility," Dr. Metra said.

"You do realize you'll still be floating," Blake joked.

"I know, but the platform will be so much more stable than a docked ship, and at least I can go outside and walk around on some grass, thanks to Catie," Dr. Metra said.

"How are the patients doing?" Marc asked.

"Dr. Sharmila has been doing wonderful work. The surgeries are going smoothly, and the patients are getting into physical therapy quickly. Our Alzheimer's patients are doing well; we've got that down to a science now. Their families will also appreciate the new facility.

There will be much more room, and they'll be able to go outside easier. We've started treating more patients with muscular dystrophy, but that's much slower since you're wanting to keep that treatment under wraps and the patients will be going home."

"And your research?"

"We're working on a cure for diabetes, and I actually think I can have that one ready for trials very soon. We've begun characterizing coronary artery disease; that looks like it will require regular treatments until we're ready to introduce medical nanites or genetic engineering to the general public. And I've started work on a generic virus treatment."

"What's a generic virus?" Liz asked.

"Maybe that's the wrong term. I'm working on a treatment that will just kill any virus in your system. It reads your DNA and kills all the RNA running around that doesn't match."

"Wow, that would be nice."

"It relies on nanites, so it will have to wait or be done in-house," Dr. Metra added. "Your world's problem with antibiotics is troubling. ADI and I feel that the best thing to do would be to pick a couple of the teams that are close to a solution and push them along with some carefully placed hints. We're focusing on the government programs and non-profits to avoid it just becoming a moneymaker for big pharma."

"Good, anything else?" Marc asked. He looked around the table and didn't see anyone wanting to add something. "Alright, Kal, we're getting a lot of visibility, so we're counting on you. Back to work, people."

◆ ◆ ◆

It was Thursday after the board meeting when Samantha tapped on Marc's office door. "Do you have a few minutes?" she asked.

"Sure."

Samantha came in and closed the door behind her.

"Uh oh," Marc said. "Something serious?"

"A little," Samantha said.

Marc took a deep breath, "What is it?"

"Do you know what you're doing?" Samantha asked.

"Mostly."

"Don't get me wrong, I'm in one hundred percent, but a space station, a spaceship, alien technology, my head is swimming. I just want to know if you have a plan."

"I do," Marc said, "it's a bit sketchy, but it is a plan."

"Care to share?"

"Yes, maybe you can help fill it in," Marc said. "I think you're the best strategic thinker we have in the group."

"Thanks," Samantha said as she rolled her hands, signaling Marc to continue.

"Okay, here goes," Marc said. Then he took another deep breath. "I'm concerned about two things."

"Only two," Samantha said with a snort. "Sorry, go on."

"One, that the Paraxeans will come to Earth before we're ready for them."

Samantha nodded her head, agreeing with him.

"And two, that before they come, the Earth will be a remnant of what it is today, smoldering in the ashes of World War Three."

"Oh my, you do pick the big problems. The first I understand, why don't you elaborate on the second."

"Climate change is going to continue to get worse; it will destabilize the political situation as it creates more refugees. The growing need for energy will continue to pit the major powers against themselves as they vie for control of critical resources. As the people realize how devastating climate change is, their reactions and protests will further destabilize the political situation. With that kind of powder keg, just one match will set it off. Then with all those nuclear weapons we have floating around, someone is going to decide to call everyone's bluff and use one."

"Succinctly put," Samantha said. "So, what do you think you can do about it?"

"We've already introduced the batteries. Once we get the fuel cells into the mix, we'll dramatically reduce emissions from vehicles. Especially once the trucks start coming out of Tata's factories."

"But all that power has to come from somewhere," Samantha said. "And that's guaranteed to be mostly fossil fuels."

"True, but it's about efficiency," Marc said. "The more efficient you are at turning those fuels into energy, the lower the carbon footprint. Besides, I want to introduce fusion reactor power plants."

Samantha gave a start, "I thought you said something about a fusion reactor, but that was when I was wondering if you were a madman."

"And now?"

"Still wondering," Samantha gave Marc a smile. "So, a fusion reactor."

"We've got two of the best nuclear physicists working on it. They've got one of the best plasma scientists helping them, and we know the answer."

"Then why not give it to them and let them reverse engineer it?"

"That leads to the obvious question of *'where did you come up with a working fusion reactor,'* which would lead to the Sakira," Marc said. "Then we'd have World War Three as the nations around the world start fighting for control of her."

"So, you want a plausible explanation of how you came up with it."

"Right. ADI and I are carefully guiding them along the path. Nuclear fusion really isn't that difficult, it's creating a sustainable reaction that's hard. Part of the problem is the plasma field you have to create and maintain, part, the incredible temperatures the containment vessel has to withstand. Polysteel is the answer to the second, the answer to the first is just better management of the plasma field and fuel as well as more efficient magnets and better superconductors."

"Won't there just be competition over the fuel?"

"No, deuterium is relatively abundant and easy to extract from ocean water."

"I thought it was rare."

35

"It's only point-zero-two percent of the ocean's water, but there's a lot of ocean water out there, and we can eventually mine ice asteroids for deuterium."

"Oh, so no shortage of fuel," Samantha said.

"Nope."

"So, you want to remove the competition for oil and natural gas from the mix."

"Exactly. First, it will remove tension from one of the world's biggest powder kegs, the Middle East. Second, it will allow developing nations to get a leg up. With cheap, plentiful power, they'll be able to improve the lifestyles of their population dramatically, start manufacturing more of their own products."

"But, won't that start another cycle of competition as everyone vies for markets for their exports?"

"It will, but when you remove the cost of power from the equation, or at least reduce its impact, you lower the price of goods. With developing nations improving their standard of living, you create more markets."

"I'll buy that, but you still have to distribute that power."

"That's why the batteries and fuel cells are so important. They can cover the areas that are hard to get power to, while the fusion reactors cover the areas that have distribution. A large fuel cell can power a village, add solar power to the mix, and you have a solution to the distribution problem. The fusion reactors are safe and can be placed inside of, or closer to communities so you will reduce the complexities of the distribution system."

"But you have to build all new power plants."

"Nope, the reactors are small enough that you can just replace a power plant's existing boiler with the reactor. You keep all the turbines and power distribution that's already there."

"Okay, how do you decide who gets them, and how do you keep them from just taking them from you?"

"That's why we need a space station. If we can move our operation up there, then they can't get to us. We have the high ground, and we'll be able to protect it."

"Can't they just come up after you?"

"You've seen the Lynx; it can fly up to the space station in a few hours. Their multi-stage rockets are nothing compared to the Lynx or the Foxes. We can control what gets into space. We just need to get there first."

"Okay, I see the urgency. You're worried that you've already attracted too much attention, so you're running to the high ground."

"Correct."

"How do you control the technology once you share it?"

"We don't think anyone can control a fusion reaction accurately enough without high-temp superconductors and computers far more advanced than we have today. Nobody can build those now, but once we're in space, we can copy the computers from the Sakira, and we can build the superconductors."

"Why do you have to wait until you're in space?"

"You have to be in space to make the high-temperature superconductors, and in order to combine them with integrated circuits, you also have to build the integrated circuits in space," Marc said.

"Okay, how do you sell the technology?"

"We give them the design, and we license the use of the technology on a sliding scale based on national income level," Marc said. "We set it up so we have to reenable it every year to keep them honest."

"So, the capital investment to switch over is minimal."

"Yes, they'll make it up in the first six months."

"Then who?"

"Coal burners," Marc said.

"Not the best choice of customers from a political situation."

"Well, China is the problem.  India and Indonesia will be easy, they're reasonably stable governments.  We can address Eastern Europe as well."

"But you have to get to China if you want to impact climate change."

"I think there will be enough internal pressure and economic incentive that they will come around."

"But they would be putting their entire energy production into your hands."

"That's the crux of the problem.  I haven't figured out how to address that without giving it away.  But I think we'll come up with a solution."

"If you are the supplier of the key components, you would have the leverage of building the next plant to keep them in line," Samantha said.  "That plus maintenance might be enough."

"It might," Marc said.  "I guess I'm not really trying to protect the revenue stream for forever, so that might be enough."

"Good, now, are you taking me to dinner?"

# 4    Press Conference

The ceremony to celebrate the opening of the Fuerza Motores S.A. was finally wrapping up. Now Marc had to face the press conference. It began with Karl Johansson speaking about how honored he was to be given the opportunity to run such a groundbreaking car company.

Herr Johansson explained that they would be providing two versions of each model, one that would be pure electric with the new MacKenzie Discoveries' batteries and a mixed-fuel one that would also have a fuel cell to provide electricity when the batteries ran low, and a charging station was not available. He described their first model, based on the Honda CR-V. He promised to deliver a more upscale model based on the Honda Pilot within six months. He explained that seventy percent of the production was destined for the United States and Canada, while thirty percent would be for domestic consumption. Then he introduced Marc as the president and CEO of MacKenzie Discoveries, the parent company of Fuerza Motores S.A.

"We at MacKenzie Discoveries are happy to partner with the government of Mexico to bring this plant into operation here in Acapulco," Marc said. "We believe the people of Mexico, Fuerza Motores, and MacKenzie Discoveries bring an unbeatable combination of skills, knowledge, dedication, and talent to deliver the best cars to the world market. We will set a new level of performance and economy in transportation efficiency without compromising luxury, safety, or reliability. Now I'd like to open up for questions."

Marc pointed to a reporter in the first row.

"Why did you choose Acapulco as the site for this plant?"

"Herr Johansson, MacKenzie Discoveries, and the Mexican government worked together to select a location that would provide a great talent pool; that would help the Mexican economy by creating quality jobs in a region that had the talent, but insufficient jobs; and would be able to export to the US efficiently as well as deliver cars to the Mexican market. Acapulco was hands down the best location," Marc pointed to a second reporter.

"Are you planning to pay the sixteen dollars per hour specified by the new NAFTA treaty?"

"First, let me clarify," Marc started his answer. "The NAFTA treaty requires that cars that export to the US have forty-five percent of the content of the car come from plants where the workers make an average of sixteen dollars per hour. There is a five-year phase-in period for the rules, and with the provision that forty-five percent of the vehicle content can come from outside of NAFTA countries, the rule actually doesn't impact wages paid in Mexico by very much. However, we are starting our workers out at eleven dollars per hour and will raise that based on their productivity improvements as they become trained. That is significantly higher than today's eight dollars per hour average, and we are not subcontracting our work to smaller manufacturers here in Mexico that pay substantially lower wages. We expect that within four years, our average wage will be above fourteen dollars per hour and that we will be setting the bar for automotive wages paid in Mexico."

"Aren't you just taking advantage of the rules to pay lower wages?"

"We are paying wages that are substantially higher than the prevailing norm. We are encouraging the workers to improve their skills and productivity by offering wage incentives and free schooling and training. As a company, we owe it to our shareholders not to throw money away by paying over-market pricing. But we temper that with what Henry Ford proved: if you pay higher wages, you raise the wages not only of your workers but of the community as a whole, thereby increasing the ability of the community to purchase your products. We look forward to seeing more of our products sold here in Mexico, and seeing the Mexican economy improve and grow along with us."

Marc pointed to another reporter who was pushing hard to be noticed. "Next question."

"What about climate change? By offering the fuel cell option, you're encouraging people to continue to burn fossil fuels instead of going all-electric."

"First, you need to realize that most electricity is produced using fossil fuels. This car is designed to maximize the efficiency of the fuel, be it electricity or diesel that it uses to propel itself. Many people would run the risk of running out of electricity based on where they live and where they need to drive. Having the diesel fuel cell encourages them to switch to electric, and we predict that more gas stations will start to provide charging stations. The battery charges fast; it would only take five minutes to charge the typical car, less if they haven't run the battery down completely. People who can, will plug their car in overnight. Many will use less than one hundred gallons of diesel per year. Others, who don't have the convenience of available electricity where they live and drive, will have the advantage that the car converts all braking energy back into electricity, further reducing the use of carbon fuels. Summing it all up, it gets fifty percent more miles per gallon of diesel than current diesel cars and one hundred percent better fuel economy than a gasoline-powered car. This car also satisfies the driver's desire for power, outperforming its gas counterpart in acceleration and braking. All in all, by providing a car customers desire that is substantially better at converting fossil fuel into miles driven, these cars will dramatically reduce greenhouse gases."

"Wouldn't it still be better for the climate if you only offered the electric model?"

"First: As I said, most of the electricity in the world is still generated by fossil fuels. What electric cars provide is the most efficient way to convert those fossil fuels to miles driven. Second: It's better for the environment if someone shifts to a fuel-cell car that consumes diesel at one hundred percent better fuel economy than the gasoline-driven car they currently drive than it is for that same person to keep driving their gas guzzler since the only option afforded to them is an all-electric car that they are unwilling to switch to because they find it too restrictive to satisfy their need for independence and mobility."

Marc pointed to another reporter, "Next question."

"How many jobs are being created by this plant?"

"The plant will employ four thousand people; we predict that there will be an additional two thousand ancillary jobs created in the community to support the plant."

"What do you say to people who accuse you of betraying your country by not putting the plant in the US and creating the jobs there?"

"MacKenzie Discoveries and Fuerza Motores are global companies. As such, they are obligated to their customers, workers, and shareholders to view the world as a whole. We are placing our plants where they do the most good for everyone. I'm a citizen of the Cook Islands, Herr Johansson is a German Citizen, and Ms. Juarez is a Mexican citizen. We cannot simply view the benefits of one country; we have to view the benefits to the world economy and quality of life."

"But what about the loss of jobs in the US?"

"Building this plant in Acapulco will create six thousand well-paying jobs here. That will reduce the pressure on the local population to migrate to where there are better jobs. The increased income will result in the workers buying better goods, some of which will be made in the USA. That's good for both countries."

"By that logic, you're only reducing the pressure to migrate to the US by six thousand people."

"I seem to remember quite a stir about jobs when a migrant convoy numbering five thousand, over half of them children, made its way toward the US border."

"But . . . but . . ."

"Next question."

# 5    Board Meeting – May 13th

"Let's start the meeting," Marc said. "Sam, how are we doing on critical hiring?"

"I've hired Margaret Hannaford to coordinate our refugee absorption. She's worked for the UN for several years, set up three different refugee camps, and she's currently heavily involved in managing their vetting process."

"She sounds perfect, when does she get here?"

"As soon as you go get her. She's in Lebanon."

"Fred?"

"I'll set up a flight that goes through Lebanon for tomorrow."

"Okay, I'll let her know to get packed. When you have a time, send it to me, and I'll tell her and copy you so you're in contact."

"Okay."

Marc looked at Samantha, nodding for her to continue.

"I've got four nurses arriving this week. The other nurses Dr. Metra has requested will take some more time to get here. For most people, moving halfway around the world isn't something you can just up and do in a week."

"Anything else, Sam?"

"The locals on Arutanga are thrilled now that the construction workers have moved onto the Sky Princess."

"How's that going, Blake?"

"We've moved all the male construction workers onto the Sky Princess. We've moved the women into the dorms on Manuae. I don't think any of them really wanted to be trapped on a ship with all their male co-workers."

"Smart women," Liz said.

"Any complaints from the men?" Marc asked.

"No, they're liking it. They have the cafeteria, a restaurant, and two bars with entertainment."

"Seems like a win," Marc said. "Construction?"

"Quad three will be ready for infrastructure by next week. Pontoons for quad four are going in now. With both the Manuae facility and the one on quad one, we've really accelerated production."

"Speaking of that, when would you be ready to shut down the facility in Manuae?"

Blake looked at his HUD and did some calculations, "I could start moving production next week. Our limitation is more labor than equipment, so by next week, our production capacity here starts exceeding our labor supply."

"Okay, we should go ahead and start moving it, then."

"And did anyone check out the new condos yet?" Blake asked. "We should be moving in this week. Better pick out the one you want."

"I want one that is far away from that landing strip you have planned," Samantha said.

"The landing strip is along the east edge; the condos are along the west edge of quad one. That's as far away as you can get until section one is finished. That will be six weeks, plus however long it takes us to put up new condos."

"Our airport?"

"We're spitting out columns and pontoons as fast as we can. We're still six to eight weeks away from having beam and plate capacity to start actually building it. We need more workers."

"I'm working on it," Kal said. "Starting up a new pipeline is slow. Margaret's not even here yet."

"Liz, how is our friend Herr Johansson doing?"

"They've started making cars, and they're ramping up fast. Fred will have to tell you about sales, I'm ready to hand this whole thing off to him."

"What about a second plant?"

"What do you think about Morocco for our next location? Ignoring our last problem there, it seems a good choice. They have the population to support the manufacturing, the government is only marginally corrupt, and it's perfectly located to export to Europe," Liz said.

"Sam?"

"Liz and I have been talking about it. You want a place that will take the immigration pressure off Europe, that needs help with income disparity, and has a relatively stable political environment, Morocco is it. The other choices would be Egypt or Syria, and their political situations are untenable."

"Okay, let's shoot for it. How does Herr Johansson like the idea?"

"It's closer to Germany, he likes that," Samantha said. "Casablanca is a nice city, at least in places, so he's game."

"So, you're going to start negotiating with the government?"

"First meeting is in two weeks," Samantha said.

"Catie, how's the Oryx design going?"

"We're almost done," Catie said. "We're down to selecting components and where we can get them. A lot of the interior is based on the C17, so Boeing is our friend, or at least their subcontractors are."

"And, how are your plans for the asteroid mission coming along?"

"I'm thinking that I'll have all my other assignments under control by next week, then I'll be ready to select and train the crew."

"Have you decided on your copilot yet?" Marc asked Catie.

"I was thinking Liz," Catie said. "I don't want to be stuck in a Lynx with just a bunch of guys."

"No fair!" Blake and Fred said together.

"I was thinking you might want an all-woman crew," Marc said. "Kal, don't you have a woman in your crew who can handle the heavy lifting?"

Kal was still stunned to learn that he didn't even have a chance to be the muscle on the mission. After a moment, he recovered, "Sure, Natalia Ortiz is as big and strong as most of the guys. She's got a level head on her shoulders and has a pretty good sense of humor. She was a cargo specialist in the Marines. But she's not cleared for duty for another week."

---

"If it's all girls, then how about the twins?" Catie asked.

"The twins, why would you take them?" Marc asked. He leaned back in his chair, trying to control his frustration.

"Come on, Daddy, the chance to be part of the first human space flight to go beyond the moon. You can't deny them that opportunity."

Marc sighed and shook his head. "If their mother is okay, I guess I can't see a reason why not."

"Then I'm going too!" Samantha said.

"What!"

"They need a cook and someone to look after the twins," Samantha said. She pointed to Catie, "Besides, what she said, *honey*." Samantha really stressed the honey.

"I thought you didn't do camping," Marc said.

"I'll make an exception this once," Samantha said. "Besides, Catie and Liz told me it wasn't that bad living on the Lynx."

"Marc, you're going to lose your man-card," Blake laughed, "by being the leader who authorized the first human mission beyond the moon and Mars to be an all-female crew."

"Hey, you men got to be the first in space, you got the mission to the moon, it's only fair that we women get the mission to beyond," Samantha said. "Consider it payback for Jerrie Cobb."

"Never argue with a lawyer," Blake laughed. "And who's Jerrie Cobb?"

"She was the first woman to be tested for astronaut training; she outperformed the men; then politics prevented her from joining NASA."

"Ouch," Blake said.

Marc waved at Samantha to get her attention, "And if Dr. Sharmila says no to the twins?"

"I'm still going."

"Alright, I give. Catie, you'll need to take everybody to the Sakira to get fitted for suits once you get the answer from Dr. Sharmila," Marc said, surrendering to the inevitable.

---

**46**

Samantha walked into Marc's office, "We need to talk."

"That doesn't sound good," Marc said.

"It's about Catie and this asteroid mission," Samantha said.

"Are you having second thoughts about going?"

"No, not that. I'd like to know why you're sending Catie. It's hard for me to imagine why you're sending your thirteen-year-old daughter," Samantha said. "Now don't get me wrong, I'm all for the all-girls mission and making up for Jerrie Cobb getting aced out of the space program, but you have to admit a thirteen-year-old in charge is a big stretch."

"I know," Marc sighed. "Since I realized I had to have the asteroids, I've been racking my brain for a way not to send Catie."

"Why don't you tell me why Blake is not the right guy?"

"Blake is a smart guy, and I love him, but he's more of a point and shoot type of guy. I'm not sure he could pull it off," Marc said. "Catie has run hundreds of simulations on the Lynx and the Foxes, she's done simulated space missions and planetary landings. I can't even begin to actually list all the things she's run a simulation on."

"But can't Blake do that?"

"Sure he could, but Blake's biggest weakness is he doesn't know what he doesn't know. He can build an entire plan with a gaping hole in it and not realize it. That's not usually a problem because he tends to know everything about the field he's operating in."

"And Catie?"

"Well, that hole looks like a blinking light to her. She sees it and fusses with it until she figures out what it is, then she fixes it," Marc said.

"What about you leading it?"

"I thought about that, but I'm not that flexible. I like to plan in straight lines," Marc said.

"You handle curveballs all the time," Samantha said.

"Sure I do, but I do it by sitting down and replanning," Marc said. "I can think on my feet, but not outside the bounds of what I know and expect. To do that, I have to sit down for hours. Catie can replan in a second, and that's what we need."

"Well, what are her weaknesses?" Samantha asked.

"She has two big ones," Marc said. "One: she doesn't realize that other people don't see what she sees. When something is obvious to her, she assumes it's obvious to everybody."

"And two?" Samantha prompted.

"She likes to plan in private, tie everything up into a neat package, and put a bow on it. I think that comes from having her teachers accuse her of claiming she solved a problem when they think she must have read the solution somewhere. She wants to prove she's not a little kid and can solve things on her own."

"So how does that not become a liability on this mission?"

"She and Liz make a perfect team," Marc said. "Liz is her friend, not her parent or some teacher, so when Liz asks Catie to explain something, she doesn't think she's being patronized. And then her desire to help her friend understand means she explains everything. And Catie takes direction from Liz and Kal, without even realizing she's doing it. They tell her to do something, it makes sense, so she just does it. When I try to tell her something, half the time she gets defensive."

"So, Liz will keep us from killing ourselves?" Samantha asked.

"Catie's pretty cautious, but yes, Liz will keep things grounded, if you can use that term for a space mission and not jinx it," Marc said, laughing a little as he thought about it. "Liz has been perfect for Catie, like a big sister. I hope they continue to enjoy working together."

"I suspect you're safe there," Samantha said. "Catie really cares about Liz and wants her to be successful. She's always reviewing stuff with her. Even more since the space station design thing."

"I've noticed. I like having them room together. It builds on that sisterly bond," Marc said.

"Linda would have a fit if she knew what you're letting Catie do," Samantha said.

"She might," Marc said. "We've talked about trying to hold Catie back from things she wants to do and can do. You can only say they're too young so often."

As Samantha left the room, Marc whispered to himself, "How does one keep a songbird from singing?"

"Dr. Sharmila, can we talk?" Catie asked.

"Of course, come on in," Dr. Sharmila said. Catie entered her office, followed by Dr. Metra. Dr. Sharmila gave Dr. Metra a curious look.

"I'm here for what Catie calls moral support," Dr. Metra said.

"Something serious?" Dr. Sharmila asked Catie.

"I guess you could say that," Catie answered. "I wanted to talk to you about a trip I'm getting ready to make. You know we're building a space station, right?"

"Yes, I've heard," Dr. Sharmila said. "Very exciting."

"Well, in order to build it, we need to go get some asteroids," Catie said.

"Why in the world do you need asteroids, and where would you get them?" Dr. Sharmila asked.

"We need them for the material to build the space station. And we would get them from the asteroid belt between Mars and Jupiter," Catie explained.

"You mean you're going to go into space, that is very exciting," Dr. Sharmila said, clasping her hands together and leaning forward on her desk. "I'm sure you'll have a fun time."

Dr. Metra suppressed a laugh, getting a sharp look from Dr. Sharmila. "I'm afraid to ask why my friend would think that was funny," Dr. Sharmila said.

"That's what I wanted to talk to you about, the space mission," Catie said.

"I don't know anything about space missions," Dr. Sharmila said. "Surely you should be talking to Dr. Metra."

"It not about medical advice," Catie said. "You know it's going to be a big historical event. Eventually, it will go into the history books."

"I would think so, the first mission beyond the moon, beyond Mars even," Dr. Sharmila said.

"Yes, and I'm going to lead it," Catie said.

"Oh, that will really be one for the history books then," Dr. Sharmila said.

"That's my problem," Catie said. "Your daughters are like sisters to me, and I think they're going to hate me if they find out I went on this historic trip and didn't take them."

"Well, children can't do everything. They will understand it is dangerous. In fact, I'm surprised your father is letting you go," Dr. Sharmila said.

"That's it, it's not that dangerous. We would be taking the Lynx, and it's very capable. We could take the twins if you would let us," Catie said.

Dr. Sharmila sat back in her chair in shock. "Take my girls into space? And you knew she was going to ask," Dr. Sharmila accused Dr. Metra.

"I did know, but just an hour ago," Dr. Metra said.

"So now they will hate me because I didn't let them go," Dr. Sharmila said.

"We can always blame my dad," Catie said. "But they're pretty smart, and they'll probably figure things out. I think they'll believe I should have asked to take them."

"But it's too dangerous," Dr. Sharmila said.

"I've had ADI analyze the risk," Catie said. "It would be pretty safe for the twins."

"Explain."

"Well, going there and back in the Lynx isn't that big a deal. It's designed to do that; ADI could actually fly it if necessary."

"And if something should happen to the Lynx?" Dr. Sharmila asked.

"We have the Foxes for backup. ADI could fly them out to get us if necessary, but she says the Lynx has a ninety-nine percent reliability rate. And we won't be doing anything unusual with it. The risk will be when we're working on the asteroids, and we would make sure the twins were aboard the Lynx while we were doing that. They would be safe then. Sam's going to come so she would be able to watch them," Catie said quickly.

"Who else is going to go?" Dr. Sharmila asked.

"Liz and a woman from Kal's team. She's experienced dealing with cargo and is pretty big so she'll be able to move the larger equipment around," Catie said.

"So, all women?" Dr. Sharmila asked.

"Yes, that's why I thought we should take the twins. They'll have a lot of fun," Catie said.

"I'm not worried about how much fun they would have," Dr. Sharmila said. "Dr. Metra, what do you think? This is insane even for you, isn't it?"

"I would have let my children go on a similar mission," Dr. Metra said. "But of course, I grew up with the technology and implicitly trust it, and I especially trust ADI's assessment."

"But if I let them go, they will know everything about Sakira and Dr. Metra," Dr. Sharmila said.

"They already know a lot," Catie said. "They've been around the hospital a lot, so they know about replacing people's limbs and stuff. I think they'll be able to keep it a secret."

"Yes, I've told them that everything we do here is a secret and sworn them to secrecy. They've been very good about it." Dr. Sharmila sat back in her chair, "What did I do to deserve such Karma?"

"I think it's good Karma," Catie said.

"You would, you're not the mother," Dr. Sharmila said. "I will think about it and let you know."

"Thanks," Catie gushed.

◆ ◆ ◆

"Hello, Natalia, I'm Catie." Catie extended her hand to the six-foot-tall woman who had just come to the door at the compound. She looked her up and down, realizing the woman must weigh two hundred pounds, and none of it looked like fat. Catie had just gotten word from Dr. Sharmila that she would allow the twins to go on the mission. Now it was time to get prepared.

"We're meeting in the dining room, come on in," Catie said.

"I know who you are," Natalia said to Catie as she followed her into the dining room. "Everybody calls me Nattie. Are you guys really going into space?"

"Yep, pretty crazy, huh."

"After your doctors replaced my left leg, nothing is crazy," Natalia said. "I just hope you decide to take me with you."

Catie led Natalia into the dining room. "Here are the other members of our crew, Samantha Newman, our cabin specialist; Liz Farmer, my copilot; Aalia and Prisha Khanna, our trainees, we just call them the twins."

Everyone waved hello to Natalia. The twins walked over and looked up at her, "She's so big," Prisha said.

"Prisha," Samantha scolded.

"Don't worry about it. I understand being big is why you're considering me for this mission. One of the few times in my life that being the big girl has been an advantage."

"I wish I was big," Prisha said.

Natalia knelt down, "You will be, little one. You just have to wait until you grow up," she said. "For now, I'll be big for you."

Prisha giggled, and she and Aalia ran back over to Catie.

"I'm good," Catie said. She looked at Liz and Samantha to see if they agreed.

"Works for me," Liz said.

"Welcome to the team," Samantha said. She walked over and shook Natalia's hand.

"That's it?" Natalia asked. "One minute and you've made up your minds."

"My mind was pretty much made up when Kal recommended you. I just wanted to be sure you didn't have two heads," Catie said.

"Nope, one head's all I've got. It's pretty hard, but there's still only one."

"Good, now let's do some basic planning," Catie said. "I understand that you're still under medical restrictions."

"That's right. The doctor says no strain on the leg until next week."

"Okay, now does anyone have any dietary restrictions?" Catie asked. "We want to make sure we're taking the right supplies along with us. There are no supermarkets up there that we can stop by to pick up something we forgot."

"I eat anything," Natalia said.

"I checked with Dr. Sharmila," Samantha said. "Besides the fact that they don't like broccoli, the twins don't have any restrictions."

"So, no broccoli," Catie said.

"Right!"

"As for me, no food allergies," Samantha said. "But I prefer to limit fat and sugar."

"Don't we all," Liz said.

"We don't!" the twins said.

"Not yet anyway," Liz laughed. "I'm good with anything. The Marines break you of any fussiness about food."

"Okay, we'll have chicken breast and filet mignon for meat," Catie said. "So, we need to come up with a set of menus for three weeks built around that as our source of meat. Sam, you volunteered as the cook, do you want to take that on, or was that just your way to get my dad to let you go?"

"I love to cook," Samantha said. "So, I'll work up the menus and create a shopping list for what we need. What do we have for freezer and refrigerator space?"

"We have a pretty big lower cargo hold that we're not using yet," Catie said. "We can split it up between freezer or refrigerator space however you want. I don't see any reason to limit your volume. Just pick what you want, we'll find room for it."

Samantha raised her eyebrows at the unlimited space, "Hmm, I'll come up with some nice menus then."

"We'll be wearing shipsuits for the whole mission; we'll get those made next week, so there won't be any other clothing requirements. Three shipsuits per person."

"Toilet paper," Liz said.

"Yes, we'll want plenty of that," Catie said. "Toothpaste, deodorant, soap, and no perfume, we have to share a small cabin, so no scents."

"Shampoo and conditioner," Samantha added.

"Oh yeah, can we all agree on a common set, or are we going to have to stock multiple brands?" Catie asked.

"I suggest you use your command authority to dictate one brand," Natalia said.

"Okay, Sam, you pick one, we'll all use it. Again, nothing scented."

"Got it."

"Entertainment?" Liz asked.

"You mean, you won't be entertained by the twins and my witty banter?" Samantha asked.

"It might get old after a while," Liz said.

"We'll have access to anything we have on the net down here," Catie said. "So, unless you think we should all work up a routine, I think we're good."

"Works for me," Liz said.

"Blankets, sheets, pillows?" Samantha asked.

"We'll be sleeping in our shipsuits; they pretty much regulate the temperature. So, unless you need a blankie, you should be good. Pillows are probably a good idea," Catie said.

"I don't need a blankie," Natalia said, "But I think you'll find you want a sheet anyway. It just feels weird sleeping without anything covering you."

"Okay," Catie said. "Sheets and pillows; Liz, will you get those? And Sam, why don't you make sure we have anything the twins might want with them." Catie was thinking that at ten, the twins might have a favorite stuffed animal or something they liked to sleep with.

"I already have a list of their special things," Samantha said.

The twins looked between Catie and Samantha, wondering what was on that list. They giggled and started whispering to each other.

"Cleaning supplies," Natalia said. "We want to keep things shipshape."

"I have a list from ADI of what we need. We'll get it when we get the shipsuits," Catie said.

"Razors, scissors?" Natalia asked.

"We have a depilation cream that works wonders," Catie said. "So, unless you're in love with your razor, that should cover us. Scissors we'll add. Do you need hair clippers?"

"Nope, scissors do it for me," Natalia said as she brushed her hand across her short-cropped hair.

Catie looked at Samantha.

"I plan on getting a haircut before we go, then I'll be good for three weeks."

"Same here," Liz said.

"Medications? Make sure you have whatever you take with you," Catie said. "I'll make sure we have the standard anti-inflammatory meds. Dr. Metra will outfit us with a first-aid kit so we'll be covered for cuts and bruises, even a broken bone or two."

"Ear-swabs," Samantha said.

"Boy is it hard to plan for three weeks without any chance to make up for what you forget," Catie said. "I'll add it to the list. If anyone thinks of something else, text me, and I'll add it. We should probably review the list with Dr. Sharmila and Dr. Metra just to see if she sees something we missed."

"I'll give you the list the Marines use for planning a weeklong recon excursion," Natalia said. "It's a pretty complete list."

"Thanks, anything else? . . . No, then we'll meet next week on the Mea Huli and go get our suits made and get what we need from the Sakira.

Until then, Natalia, you're moving in with Liz, so we're all in the same condo building. Now, we're all going out to the Flambé for dinner to initiate our mission."

"Sounds nice," Natalia said.

"Oh girl, you don't know how nice," Samantha said.

# 6    Commandos

"Cer Kal," ADI woke Kal up from a deep sleep. He rolled off of his bunk and hit the deck moving. He went to his nightstand to get his specs and comm unit.

"What's up, ADI?"

"Passive sonar has detected a submarine approaching the city," ADI said.

"Go to active sonar," Kal commanded. He had his specs on and was pulling on his pants. "All units check in!"

Kal's HUD started pinging, displaying the location of all the on-duty security personnel in Delphi City, their icons went from yellow to green as they checked in. As he was watching the icons update, the one for the guard on the pier went from yellow to red.

"ADI, red alert, number four is down!"

"I saw that," ADI announced. "RED alert, RED alert. Intruders on the pier," came over Kal's HUD and those of everyone else who was part of the security team. Kal grabbed his rifle and kit belt and headed out the door at a run.

"Cer Kal, active sonar indicates that the submarine is Chinese," ADI informed him. "It is circling to the west of the city at approximately fifty thousand meters."

"Over the comm, ADI."

"We have a Chinese submarine off the city. It is fifty thousand meters out," ADI announced for the rest of security.

"ADI, launch a Fox and put a mine on that submarine," Kal ordered. "Is Marc up?"

"I'm here," Marc said. "What do you want me to do?"

"Shelter in place," Kal shouted. "Liz should be there soon."

"Already here," Liz said. "I've got Nattie with me. We're locked and loaded."

"Keep us posted," Marc said.

---

"Team, use non-lethal force if possible," Kal said. "We want to talk to these guys, but if you need to put them down hard, then lethal force is authorized." Kal thumbed the selector on his rifle to stun. It was a knock-off of the M4A1 he'd used when he was in the Marines. The only real difference was the stunner selection and the small barrel under the main barrel that the stun bullets came out of. The stun bullets were built into the standard clip, so with a change out of a clip, another sixteen stunners were added. The stunners were essentially small capacitors that were shot at the target; two small barbed wires were flipped to either side on impact, forced out by the collision with the target. Then the capacitors discharged into the target just like a Taser, except there were no trailing wires to deal with, and it was effective at two hundred yards.

He was at the docks in one minute, since he and the rest of security were quartered there, the most likely location for an incursion.

"Report!" Kal yelled.

"I have movement on the lower dock next to the Mea Huli!"

"Number four's location was the upper dock!" Kal barked.

"I have her. She's dead, gunshot to the head!"

"Movement at warehouse three!"

"Team Bravo, converge on warehouse three. Team Alfa, continue to scout the docks! Team Charlie, you have backup, make sure nobody gets by us."

"A three-man squad is coming up the alley!"

"Take them out!"

POP! POP!

"Two down, one retreating back to warehouse three."

"I'm taking fire from warehouse three, front right window, top floor!"

"Use live ammo!" Kal ordered. "Lock onto the heat signature and shoot through the wall."

CRACK!

"Target is down, two more signatures in the warehouse."

"Bravo-three here, I've infiltrated the warehouse. Have visual!"

"Can you take them out with stunners?"

"Firing now! One down, one behind the forklift."

"Bravo-five, bravo-six, we're at the door!"

"Bravo-three, give them cover, bravo-five and six, you're cleared to enter!"

"Crack . . . Crack . . . Crack . . . Crack," the sound of the suppression fire came over the comms.

"We're in. I think he wants to give up."

"That's usually what holding your hands over your head means," bravo-three said.

"He's Chinese, are you sure?"

"Zài dìshàng, Zài dìshàng, on the floor" came over the loudspeaker in the warehouse, as ADI provided the proper translation.

The Chinese soldier lay down on the floor; bravo-five ran over and quickly wrapped him up with zip ties on his hands and legs. "We're going to have to carry him if you tie his legs."

"Well, I don't want to find out how good he is with his feet. Just get a cart, and we'll haul him over to the station."

"Alfa-leader here, we have their equipment. I count six sets of scuba gear here."

"Team Charlie, we have one missing."

"We copy," Charlie leader said. "We're continuing to fan out along behind you. No movement detected."

"Team Alfa, keep checking the docks," Kal ordered.

"Copy."

Marc and Catie were sitting in the dark with Liz while they listened to the action. They had their HUDs set to pick up infrared signatures.

"Where do you suppose the sixth one is?" Catie whispered.

"I don't know," Liz said.

"Hello, little man," Natalia's voice came over their comms. "You don't need that gun, do you. Sorry, if I hurt your hand, you should have let go of it."

They heard some gurgling sounds over the comm for a moment before Natalia's voice came back on.

"Oh sorry, I didn't realize you were so short. Would you like your feet back on the ground?"

They heard some more gurgling sounds. "Kal, I think I have number six here; short Chinese guy wearing all black. No insignia. Does that sound like him?"

"Matches the others," Kal said. "Is he under control?"

"He's having trouble talking," Natalia said. "His neck is kind of skinny, and I'm having trouble holding onto it without choking him a little. Liz, do you want to come out here and help me tie him up?"

"Belay that," Kal barked. "Liz, you stay with Marc and Cat. I'll be there in a few."

"Copy."

"Sorry, you're just going to have to keep gasping for a while," Natalia said. "Boss doesn't trust you guys."

Kal arrived shortly after, and zip tied the Chinese commando's hands behind his back. "Did he do anything after you grabbed him?"

"Nothing except hold my hand and try to lift himself up a little," Natalia said. "I think he was mainly focused on breathing."

"Bring him in here," Marc called out.

"Are you sure?" Kal asked.

"Hey, I've got three of the baddest asses around to keep me safe," Marc said. "I want to know what's going on."

Kal had Natalia drag the Chinese commando into the condo. Kal laid the backpack that the commando was carrying on the table and started unpacking it. He found a map and spread it out on the table; there were some zip ties, a camera, and a radio.

"So, kidnap mission or recon?" Marc asked while he looked at the map.

"Can't tell, the map's in Chinese."

"ADI."

"Captain, the translation should be coming up on your HUDs now."

"Got it," Kal said. After studying the map for a bit, he added, "It shows the dock, the battery manufacturing plant, the polysteel plant, and the one where we're making the Lynxes. And it also shows your condo."

"Do you want to explain yourself?" Marc said to their Chinese captive.

"No English," he said in a heavily accented voice.

"Come on, you don't expect me to believe you were coming here to infiltrate an English-speaking facility, and you don't speak enough English to read the signs?" Marc said.

"No English!"

"Damn. Well, we have four others, don't we?" Marc asked.

"Yes, sir. We captured four alive, one dead," Kal said.

"Good, maybe one of them speaks English. Natalia, you captured him, do you want to kill him?"

"Sure thing, Captain," Natalia said as she pulled her knife from her belt.

Marc watched the Chinese commando's eyes grow wide; he couldn't see the knife yet. "I'm guessing he does speak English," Marc said.

"Yes, I speak English. But I cannot tell you anything," the prisoner said.

"So, Natalia, I guess he is all yours."

"Wait. I was to capture you if we were detected before we reached our objective."

"How many are you?"

"Six, as you have already determined."

"What was your objective?"

"Data on your designs and production facilities. We were to take samples and any machinery we could get back with us."

"You must know we run around the clock; what were you going to do with the workers?"

"We hoped to find inactive facilities. If not, we were to subdue the workers and take the foreman back with us."

---

61

"How were you going to take all this back with you? And we know about your submarine. ADI, what kind of submarine is it?"

"Captain, it is a Yuan-class submarine, a diesel-electric."

"A Yuan-class diesel-electric," Marc repeated. "Well?" Marc said as he gave the commando a steely stare.

"We were going to take your yacht and rendezvous with our submarine."

"They were going to steal the Mea Huli," Catie shouted. "I think you should give him to Nattie!"

"Kal, have someone come pick him up. Blake, Sam, my quarters, please," Marc said.

Blake and Samantha came down the hall and joined Marc at the table. After someone from security came and took the prisoner away, Marc sat down at the table and looked at everyone.

"Okay, so now, what do we do?" Marc asked.

"With your captives?" Samantha asked.

"No, with the submarine."

Samantha grimaced. "What can you do?"

"We can blow it out of the water," Marc said angrily. He calmed himself down a little. "We could disable it or capture it instead."

"That sounds better. I think blowing it out of the water is definitely a bad idea," Samantha said.

"I figured you'd say that."

"What would you do if you captured it?" Samantha asked.

"Make them pay to get it back; keep it; melt it down," Marc said.

"I really don't think you want to piss the Chinese off that much," Blake said.

"Probably not, but I don't want them to walk away from this unscathed."

"You do have five of their commandos," Samantha said. "And you did kill one."

"Drop in the bucket."

"Give it to the Americans," Catie said.

"What?" Marc asked, shocked at the suggestion.

"Give the submarine to the Americans," Catie said again.

"How would we do that?"

"Tell them where it is and then disable it."

"Why not the Kiwis?"

"They're likely to just give it back," Samantha said. "Or just let the Chinese come get it while they keep it safe."

"Okay. So, what, we just wait for them to give up and head home?" Marc asked.

"Sure," Catie said. "They must have a minimum time before they expect them to come out on the Mea Huli."

"How do we tell the Americans?"

"Why not call Admiral Michaels?" Blake said. "You two hit it off so well, and he does seem to be expressing an interest in you."

Marc snorted. "Sure, why not. ADI, can you tap me into Admiral Michaels' cellphone?"

"You don't just want her to make a regular call?" Samantha asked.

"I'd rather it couldn't be traced back to us, or to him for that matter."

"Captain, I'm ready to establish a link," ADI said.

"Do it."

Admiral Michaels was surprised when his cell phone rang. Everybody knew he hated to be interrupted while he was reading through the nightly reports. He picked up his phone and looked at the caller ID. It read, unknown caller, so he pressed cancel and hung up on the call.

"He hung up," ADI said.

"Unknown caller," Catie said. "ADI, can you make the caller ID display his social security number?"

"Yes, Cer Catie."

"That will get his attention," Samantha chuckled.

"Do it," Marc said.

---

**63**

Admiral Michaels looked at his cell phone as it rang again. This time it displayed the caller's number. The number looked strange, then he recognized his social security number. He answered the call, "Who is this?" he demanded.

"Admiral, this is Dr. McCormack."

"How did you put . . ."

"Let's not worry about that now, Admiral. I was thinking I could do you a favor."

Admiral Michaels leaned back in his chair. "What kind of favor?"

"I happen to know that a Chinese submarine is going to be experiencing some serious problems in a few days," Marc said. "I wondered if the US Navy would like to help them out."

"And how would you happen to know that?"

"I can't tell you that, and I would prefer not to be connected with this in any way."

"I can't promise that, but I can promise not to bring up you or your organization myself. I'm not responsible for what the NSA uncovers or what the Chinese know or what the CIA gets out of them."

"That will work for me," Marc said.

"What kind of sub is it?"

"It's one of their Yuan-class submarines."

"We'd like to get a look at that," Admiral Michaels said.

"I would predict that it will be passing south of Guam in a few days when their temporary repairs will fail. Could you have a few ships around there to help them out?"

"I could, but that's a big area."

"I can give you more details on their location as they limp along back to China."

"That would be appreciated."

"I'll just text you their coordinates as I get updates," Marc said.

"That should work."

"Good day, Admiral."

---

"Good day."

"Okay, now we need them to have to go home," Marc said. "ADI, I understand we have a mine on the submarine now."

"Yes, Captain, we do."

"Can you put a second one on it?"

"Yes, Captain, I have the FX4 sitting just off of its stern."

"Okay, put the second mine where it will damage the comm tower but not disable the submarine."

"Yes, Captain. I am sending the mine over now."

"Isn't that going to point back to us?" Samantha asked.

"Maybe, but these aren't normal mines. They discharge an electric charge into the hull; I hope it will just look like metal fatigue."

"Coincidental to their trying to infiltrate us?"

"We'll wait until they're well on their way to wherever they're going next. We might only need one mine. They may be heading home."

"That would be best."

"ADI, let us know if the submarine sends anything else our way. Keep active sonar up."

"Yes, Captain."

"They're bound to get tired of the pinging and go home," Marc said. "Now everyone, go back to sleep. We'll get updates in the morning."

It was four hours before the submarine turned back toward China. Since they were going the right way, Marc just waited. Three days later, they were approaching Guam, and Marc had ADI text the admiral the coordinates. Two days later, they were just one hundred miles away from a small flotilla of the US Navy. Marc had ADI detach the second mine and set the first one to blow in two hours. He had her separate the drone from the mine to avoid losing it and their quantum relays. He had her pick up the two drones with a Fox that was shadowing the submarine. The first mine exploded and breached the hull of the submarine in its torpedo bay. The submarine was forced to surface, and the US Navy was quick to render assistance.

---

# 7    Prep for Space

"Okay, is everybody ready to get fitted for spacesuits?" Catie asked.

"Yes!" the twins yelled.

"Sounds like you ladies are ready," Fred said. "I've got the engines all warmed up."

"Where are we going?" Natalia asked.

"To the Sakira. It's the spaceship where we'll get our shipsuits fitted."

Natalia's eyes bugged out in shock. "A real spaceship?"

"Yeah, actually we have to use another spaceship to get there. That's the one we'll be taking when we go after the asteroids. But the Sakira is the mother ship, and that's where all the equipment we need is, as well as the tools to make our spacesuits."

"You people are really something," Natalia said. "A real spaceship."

Fred took them out three miles from Delphi City and set the Mea Huli to circling on autopilot. He walked to the back of the boat, followed by Catie and her crew. "This is our dock," he said as he wrestled the canvas bundle out of the hold and kicked it over the side. "Catie came up with this idea so they wouldn't have to get wet every time they wanted to get into the Lynx. I hear it really came in handy later." Fred pressed the release for the air tank, and everyone watched as the dock expanded.

"ADI, we're waiting," Catie said into her comm once the dock was fully expanded.

"Who's ADI?" Natalia asked.

"Our ship's computer," Catie said.

"Look!" the twins shouted as the Lynx came up out of the water and started to skim the surface. "That looks just like your plane," one of them said. Catie couldn't tell them apart, and they refused to wear different clothes so anyone could, so she never knew who was speaking.

"It is just like it. That's the original one, and we're going to use it to go into space," Catie said. "But right now, we're going to use it to go to the Sakira, she's underwater."

"Why?"

"Because she's a big secret," Catie said. "We hide her underwater so nobody can find her."

"Oh," the twins nodded in satisfaction.

"Now, you know you have to keep all these secrets," Catie added.

"Oh yes," the twins said together. "Mummy explained it to us. And explained it to us." The twins started giggling.

"Good," Catie said.

"Your chariot awaits," Fred announced, once the Lynx settled into the dock.

Catie led everyone over the dock and into the Lynx's main cabin.

"Wow, this is as nice as the G650," Samantha said.

"I think so. It's a little bigger and has a much bigger cargo hold," Catie said.

"And a shower," Liz added. "You're going to be real happy about that."

"Will the shower work in microgravity?"

"Sure, it sprays water on you. There's a drain with suction that pulls warm air from above and collects all the water," Catie explained.

"You guys know how to live," Natalia said. "I was figuring we'd be washing up in a bucket."

"Oh no girl, we're much too sophisticated for that," Samantha said. "We're going to be traveling in style. Gourmet meals, fine wine."

Liz laughed at Samantha. "You're going to have to figure out how to cook when the floor is really the wall."

"Oh no, she won't," Catie said. "The galley rotates so you can actually cook while we're accelerating."

"Now that shows some forethought," Samantha said. "I don't suppose the rest of the cabin does."

---

"Not actually, the shower and bathroom do; the couches will extend vertically instead of horizontally so it'll be easy to sleep. And a panel comes out of the deck to create a floor for that area, but you'll have to climb on the ladder to get around." Catie pointed to the ceiling and the ladder that was embedded in it.

"I never noticed that before," Liz said as she gazed up at the ceiling.

"We'll do some practice for a few days, so everyone gets used to gravity being ninety degrees out from normal."

"How?" Samantha asked.

Catie just extended her hand flat, with the fingertips pointing at Samantha. Then she rotated them up, so they were pointing at the ceiling.

"Oh, that makes sense. Pretty easy when we're in the water."

"Yep, it is."

"Shouldn't we get strapped in before we get underway?" Natalia asked.

"Oh, we've been underway since the hatch closed," Liz said.

"I didn't feel a thing."

"ADI is a good pilot," Catie said.

"Why thank you, Cer Catie," ADI said over the ship's intercom.

Liz showed Samantha and Natalia around the Lynx while Catie followed with the twins. The twins each had to use the toilet, they both wanted to take a shower also, but Catie was able to persuade them to wait until later to take a shower. The twins played with the couches, switching them from horizontal to vertical and back again multiple times. Catie was finally able to get them to settle down by bringing up their approach to the Sakira on the cabin's display. Finally, they were aboard the Sakira, and all the water was pumped out of the flight bay.

As they exited the Lynx and started toward the lock, Natalia stopped to admire the Foxes parked in the bay. She whistled, "Now these are some nice-looking babies."

"They're the Foxes. We have four of them. We'll be making some more soon, but we've got to make a few Lynxes and then the Oryxes first."

"What is an Oryx?"

"Think of a C17 on steroids," Liz explained. "Everything is the same except the engines and some mods to the wings so it can go supersonic."

"I assume it's going to be capable of reaching orbit," Natalia said.

"You got it in one," Liz said. "It's going to be our cargo hauler for space. We'll be using it to lift the materials we need for the space station."

"I should have guessed there'd be a space station with all the rest of this stuff going on."

"Smart girl," Liz said.

"My mamma didn't raise no dummy," Natalia said. "She couldn't afford to send me to college, but she made me work hard at my studies."

"This way," Catie said as she indicated the way to the airlock. "Were you going to go to college after the military?"

"I was taking classes," Natalia said, "but this offer from Kal was just too good. Good money, and I get my leg back."

"What were you going to study?"

"I was going to study environmental engineering. That is if I can figure the math out."

"Well, ADI can teach you all the material you need. We need an environmental scientist to maintain the systems in Delphi City as well as on Delphi Station when it comes online. I can help you with the math if you need it."

"Sure, but you don't have to bother, I know you're busy. Can't ADI teach math?"

"Yes, but she's not that good at helping you understand it."

"I heard that!" ADI announced over the ship's intercom.

"Well, it's true," Catie said.

"I know, but I'm working on it, Cer Catie."

"Good for you, ADI. Now here is the elevator, we'll take it up to the medical bay where we'll get fitted for our suits."

They all made it into the medical bay and looked around. "Nice digs," Natalia said.

"It is nice. Everybody, you need to tie your hair up on top of your head in a bun. You'll be able to keep it in a ponytail later, but right now, we have to get measured, and it'll interfere with the laser."

"I don't think I'll have a problem," Natalia said as she ran her hand over her buzz cut.

Catie laughed, "That's not a bad style for space, easy to clean, easy to get your helmet on and off. Anyone want to change hairstyles?"

"Not me," Samantha said.

"Me either," Liz added.

"We do!" the twins said.

"Oh, I didn't see that coming," Catie said. "We have to ask your mother first. Okay, so for now, let me tie it up for you."

"You can use the curtained-off area to undress and be measured," Catie explained. "We have to be totally nude to be measured."

"I don't care about privacy," Natalia said. "If you don't care, I'm good with stripping down right here."

The twins were already taking their clothes off. Samantha and Liz looked at each other, "Just us girls," they said and started stripping.

"Stand here, put your feet on the footprints and hold your arms out to like this," Catie demonstrated, standing on the footprints with her arms extended out to the side. "The laser just takes thirty seconds to measure you." The console beeped. "See, I'm done."

It took a few minutes to get the twins to stand still for the thirty seconds it took to get measured, but finally everyone was measured and dressed again.

"Okay, colors?" Catie asked.

"Huh," Samantha said.

"What color do you want your shipsuit to be? You'll have to wear it the whole time we're out there except when you're bathing. So, you might as well pick a color you like," Catie said.

"You don't want to establish a uniform?" Natalia asked. "It would be cool if we all were wearing the same colors."

"Oh, good idea," Samantha said. "What are the suits going to look like?"

"Just like a surfing suit, a snug fit all around."

"Oh, then we could have a soft blue with the dark blue highlights."

"We can be Spiderwoman!" the twins yelled.

"I was thinking something more subtle," Samantha said.

The twins booed and pouted for a bit.

"How about black with a blue chevron across the chest and blue stripes down the arm," Samantha suggested.

"Sounds good. ADI, can you draw that up?"

"Yes, Cer Catie."

"Hey, what's with this Cer business?" Natalia asked.

"Cer is like sir or mister, but it's gender-neutral," Catie explained. "We decided to go with first names since three of us were McCormacks. It worked out for our call signs too, except we shortened mine to Cat."

"That's the same reason I go by Nattie," Natalia said.

The women chatted while their shipsuits were being made. The twins wanted to know why Natalia had a buzz cut. They also worked around to asking about why her breasts were so big. They wondered if they would have big breasts like her. Natalia told them that big breasts were cool, but they were also a hassle. She explained that she wished hers were smaller so it would be easier to find clothes that fit and that her back wouldn't get so tired holding them up.

Finally, their suits were ready.

"Oh, I like them," Samantha said. "Of course, I'm not sure if I'm going to like them as much when I have it on."

Everyone slipped into their shipsuits.

"How do you zip these things up?"

"It's like a Ziploc bag," Catie explained. "Just press together from the bottom up."

Catie helped the twins zip their suits up while the others took care of their own.

"Hey, I thought these were pressure suits," Liz said. "They're kind of loose, aren't they?"

Catie walked over and rotated a small disk on Liz's suit. The suit shrank, tightening up until it was completely form-fitting.

"Um, that's snug," Liz said.

"Yeah, like wearing support hose for your whole body," Catie said. "The disk provides a small charge that makes the suit more stretchy and looser. It'll loosen up when you turn it back on so you can take your suit off. To turn it off, rotate it counterclockwise; on is clockwise. There's a separate one for the hood, so you don't have to wear it all the time. Just slip it over your head before you put your helmet on. The helmet automatically disengages the disk. You'll have to turn it on yourself to get the hood off."

"Well, don't you look all tight and sexy," Samantha said to Liz.

Liz walked over and turned Samantha's disk off. "Let's see how you look all skintight and compressed like a . . ."

"Hey, you didn't let me adjust things," Samantha complained. "A bit snug down there."

Liz laughed. "Well, Ms. Sexy, what do you think?"

Samantha looked at herself in the mirror. "Not as bad as I feared. This will definitely motivate me to skip dessert once in a while."

Natalia was working quickly to adjust her suit before someone came over and turned her disk off. When she thought she had everything arranged correctly, she twisted it herself. The suit shrank, compressing around her. "Hey, I think I can eat a few more desserts," she said as she admired herself in the mirror.

"Wow, it does look good on you," Samantha said. "I guess it's like a body girdle. So, we don't have to starve ourselves worrying about how the men will see us."

"I don't think so," Natalia said. "I'm thinking I'll start wearing this thing all the time."

Everyone laughed, and Catie twisted her disk. She rotated her shoulders to get the suit to settle in. "I don't have any problems," she said while pointing to her flat chest.

"Hey, count your blessings," Natalia said. "The only thing better than getting my leg back was getting Dr. Metra's nanites for my ovaries. I love not worrying about a period, and my friends love that I don't have mood swings."

"Yeah, but..."

"They'll come," Samantha said. "Just be patient and enjoy being young."

"Hey, what about us!" twins yelled.

Catie walked over and twisted their disks. They squealed as the suit tightened around their bodies. "This is neat," they said together.

"They definitely fit the suits," Liz said. "Better than I do. She did a few poses in the mirror to see how she looked from different angles."

"You look just fine from behind," Natalia said. "You're going to be drawing the men like flies to honey."

They all giggled at that. "Okay, what's next?"

"We need to try out our exosuits," Catie said.

"Exosuits?"

"When we go outside the ship, we want a bit of armor to protect us against any stray meteorites. The exosuit is just a thin set of armor to slip over the suit. Like what you'd wear to play football."

"Hey, what are these?" the twins asked, pointing to a small tube that was in a pocket on the inside of their legs.

"Those are drain tubes," Catie said.

"For what?"

"You know that soft part on the inside of your suit that was like panties," Catie explained.

"Yes."

"Well, if you can't hold it, then it absorbs your wee so you can keep working outside. Then your exosuit will pull it out and store it in a small bottle."

"You mean you wee in your panties?!"

"If you have to. You can't just run back inside the ship every time you have to go."

"Gross."

"That's what all the astronauts do. It won't be that bad, you won't even notice. The lining is designed to keep you dry, and it all gets pulled out and stored."

"Why do we save it? Why not just push it out into space? There's nothing out there, anyway," the twins said.

Catie was laughing so hard and trying not to show it that she couldn't answer. Natalia knelt down and looked the twins in the eye. "Because when I'm out there working, I don't want any wee bouncing off of my helmet."

The twins really giggled. "What happens if you have to do number two?"

"Well, that's not so nice, but the same thing happens," Catie said. "The suit pulls all the moisture out, and when you get back inside, you go and clean up. I suggest you try to hold it if you can."

"We will," the twins said.

Everyone's exosuits and helmets came up. "Okay, you just slip the exosuit on. Then pull your hood up and slip your helmet on. The helmet will grasp the collar on your suit and align and seal itself to the suit. Then it will turn the charge on your hood off, so it shrinks to fit; when all is nice and tight, it pressurizes. There is an oxygen canister on the back of your armor."

"Hey, this isn't very much air," Liz complained.

"The suit recirculates your air. It separates the oxygen from the $CO_2$ and stores the carbon, so you only need enough to supplement your requirement when you're working hard or to repressurize if you get a leak. The suits are self-repairing."

---

"This is way nicer than the armor we had to wear in Afghanistan," Natalia said as she was putting on the armor. "Way, way lighter, and no binding."

"Didn't Kal have you wearing armor?" Catie asked. She'd assumed Natalia would have been training in the same body armor that was the basis of the exosuit.

"Oh, I hadn't gotten to that part yet," Natalia said. "So, this is what the guys were yapping about. They kept trying to get me to bet on how much my rig would weigh."

"Good thing we snatched you away from those pirates," Liz laughed.

"Okay, pull your hoods up, then your helmet," Catie instructed as she helped the twins do theirs. She pulled her helmet on and felt it seal against her armor and shipsuit. "Everybody on comm?"

"Nattie copies."

"Liz copies."

"Sam copies."

"We copy," the twins said together, giggling the whole time.

"You two have to quit fooling around!" Catie scolded. "Space is dangerous, and if you want to go with us, you have to be serious. You have to follow orders, you have to identify yourself properly, so we know if anybody is in trouble, and you have to avoid doing anything that could get one of us hurt. Copy!"

"Aalia copies," she said meekly.

"Prisha copies."

"Better. Now everybody, check to make sure things fit; your HUD works; you've got good air; try running in place a bit to make sure you get more oxygen."

Everyone ran in place for about thirty seconds. The twins stopped first and sat down on the deck. Samantha and Liz were checking each other's suit after their short burst of exercise. Natalia kept running, and then she stopped and started doing punches, left, right, left, right. After a minute of that, she started rotating her arms, first back to front, then front to back. She hopped up and down a few times; did a few

75

squat jumps; dropped down and did a few pushups; then she stopped. She looked around to see everybody staring at her.

"What? I'm good. Just wanted to make sure I can work in it."

"You mean fight in it," Liz said.

"Well, that was the job Kal hired me for."

Everybody laughed at her a little, but they were also admiring how easily she was able to move in the exosuit.

"Okay, these are your kit bags," Catie said. She handed each of them a bag. "Take your exosuit off and put it in yours, your clothes as well. Here are another two shipsuits for each of you." She pulled a stack of suits out of the little cabinet where they had been made. "Shipboots should be coming up soon; they'll be a lot more comfortable than these armored boots. When they get here, we'll load up and take it all back to the Lynx."

The boots arrived by the time everyone had stripped their exosuit and stowed it in the bags. Catie was still explaining to the twins how to make everything fit, and why they shouldn't put things in the helmet, even if it did fit. "Put your boots on and follow me."

They all trooped back to the Lynx with their bags. The twins strained a bit to carry theirs, but they didn't complain. When they got to the Lynx, Catie had everyone go into the cargo hold. When everyone was inside, she motioned the twins to go through the airlock into the main cabin, telling them to take their kits with them.

"Sam, will you stay with the twins and keep them out of trouble? We need to go down to the Sakira's cargo hold and get some stuff. I think they've had enough excitement for the day."

"So have I," Samantha said. "I'd be happy to hang out here while you guys work." She laughed and gave a little wave as she cycled through the airlock after the twins.

"Cer Catie, I can have the cargo bots load everything for you," ADI said.

"I know ADI, but I think we need to get used to handling this stuff. We won't have cargo bots with us on the mission, and I'd rather we figure out how to maneuver the stuff now."

"Good thinking," Liz said as she slapped Catie on the butt.

It took them a little over thirty minutes to load the cart up and get back to the Lynx. Liz and Catie handed stuff to Natalia, who moved it into place in the cargo hold. Natalia easily maneuvered the boxes that had taken both Liz and Catie together to hand up to her. By the time everything was loaded, Liz and Catie were pretty tired, but Natalia looked like she'd just taken a brisk walk around the ship.

"Boy, I'm sure glad you're going with us," Liz said as she sat back on the cart and took a deep breath.

"Me too," Natalia said. "This was nothing; try loading a truck in one-hundred-twenty-degree heat in the desert. That'll toast your ass."

"I'll take your word for it."

Catie climbed into the Lynx's cargo hold and looked around. "I think we'll have to store our other supplies in the main cabin. There's not much room back here."

"Will that be a problem?"

"No, but we should probably pull out the back two rows of couches."

"Oh joy, more work," Liz moaned.

"I thought you were a Marine," Natalia teased.

"Operative word there is '*were*'. I've been getting used to the good life; besides, I was a pilot, didn't really have to lug that much equipment around," Liz said.

"Oh, quit whining," Catie said. "You should know you're not going to get any sympathy from me. Especially after that last training session we did. My butt still hurts from getting thrown on it so many times."

Liz laughed, "You'd better remember that there's always the next training session."

Natalia looked at them, trying to figure out what kind of training they were talking about, "Self-defense?"

"Yeah, Krav Maga," Catie said. "Whenever Liz is frustrated with me, she likes to work on throws and grappling."

"Oh, you've noticed that, have you?"

"My butt made the correlation," Catie said as she gave hers a rub.

"Would you be willing to teach me some moves?" Natalia asked.

Liz looked at Natalia and shook her head. "Sure, but don't you already know a bunch?"

"I learned a few in boot camp, but nothing that formal. I was a cargo specialist; we didn't get much training in hand-to-hand except for the basics."

"Okay, we'll have you join us for our next session," Liz said. "I just hope my back can handle throwing you around."

Natalia laughed and slapped Liz on the back.

Liz stumbled forward a couple of paces and looked back at Natalia. "Nattie, remember what Catie's butt told her," Liz threatened.

"I'll remember," Natalia chuckled.

It only took them twenty minutes to remove the six couches and put them on the cart. Catie had ADI drive it back to the hold and let the cargo bots deal with the couches.

"Okay, everyone, this is the suit cleaner," Catie explained when she got back to the main cabin. "You can change into your regular clothes and dump your suit in here. After an hour, they'll be all clean and fresh."

Catie stripped down and changed into her regular clothes then went to help the twins. Samantha had gotten one of the twins out of her suit. When Catie had the suit off of the second twin, she noticed a little whiff. She looked at the twin who just shrugged her shoulders.

"Okay, I guess I forgot an important element. If you need to go wee while you have your shipsuit on and don't have time to take it off, there is a little attachment in the head, that's what we call the bathroom. Anyway, you can hook your hose to it, and it will pull the fluid out just like your exosuit does." Catie carried the suit to the head and demonstrated. "You Do Not want to put it in the suit cleaner without doing this first, OKAY?"

Both twins nodded their heads. Samantha handed the other twin's suit to Catie and smiled at her. Catie looked at the other twin, who just shrugged her shoulders as well.

"Okay, let's go home. Take a shipsuit with you and wear it tomorrow. We start training at ten o'clock," Catie said.

"We'll get a lot of looks wearing these," Liz said. "Are you sure we shouldn't just wear our regular clothes and change on the Lynx?"

"We could, but all the Oryx pilots will be wearing these," Catie said. "ADI is making a suit fabricator that we can bring up. I think Uncle Blake and Fred will be handing them out to the pilots pretty soon. They'll start simulator training soon."

"Good," Samantha said. "I kind of liked the looks I was getting."

"I'm telling Daddy," Catie giggled.

"Oh, no you don't," Samantha said. "We're a team, and we have to keep our secrets."

"Right!" the twins echoed.

The next morning, they met at the Mea Huli. Catie and Liz had brought the twins, and Natalia had given Samantha a ride on one of the golf carts.

"Hey, Fred, you ready for us?"

"I sure am," Fred said. "And you ladies sure look nice. I think you'll be setting a new trend in women's casual wear."

Liz punched Fred on the shoulder, "Man the helm."

Once they were on the Lynx, Catie set everyone to work. "Okay, the first thing we're going to do is rotate the cabin. We'll do it a few times until we have it down pat. I want everyone to watch each step so you can do it if you have to."

She looked at everyone and got nods all around. "First we'll watch a short video to show us how to do it; ADI and I made these up last night. The first one is on rotating the galley."

They watched the video on the display in the main cabin. Catie pointed out the critical steps as they came up. "Okay, now, let's do this for real."

"Ouch!" Catie shook her hand after it was smacked by the oven door.

"Not as easy as it looked on the video," Natalia said.

"No, I guess we missed the step where you secure all the doors and cabinets," Catie said. "And we're supposed to be doing this in microgravity, but that's still a good idea." They went through and made sure all the doors were securely shut and fastened, then started over. After a few minor mishaps, they had the galley rotated.

"Whew, that was a lot of work," Samantha said.

"It'll be easier in microgravity," Catie said.

"It'll also be easier once you know how to do it," Natalia said. "You waste a lot of energy doing things that are confusing. You're tense, so you use the wrong muscles to move things."

"Well, we'll soon see," Catie said. "Time to rotate it back. Then we'll do it all over again."

After three tries, they were able to rotate the galley without any mishaps. "That's good, we'll try again tomorrow," Catie said. "Now, let's do the couches and bulkheads."

Those were easier, everything was automated, they just had to push the button and get out of the way. They did them a couple of times, then Catie suggested they all take a rest before they tried the shower and the head.

"Whew, I feel a little warm," Samantha said, "but these suits are keeping me dry and not letting me get too hot."

"We've got the cabin set to eighteen degrees C," Catie said. "Sixty-five for you Luddites."

"What's a Luddite?" the twins asked.

"A Luddite is someone who doesn't like technology," Catie said. "It comes from a society of textile workers who destroyed the automatic weaving machines because they were taking away people's jobs. It came to symbolize anyone who didn't like technology doing things that people used to do." Catie liked using answers to questions to sneak in a little teaching for the twins.

"So, why are we Luddites?"

"Because, some of us are still stuck using English measurements like feet, inches, miles, and degrees Fahrenheit."

"Ohhhh!"

"Well, sixty-five, or eighteen, both are a bit cool, aren't they?" Samantha said.

"It's easier for the suits to keep you warm than it is to keep you cool," Catie said. "By having the cabin just a bit on the cool side, the suit just has to regulate how fast it radiates your heat."

"Okay, makes sense. I might be packing a blanket," Samantha laughed.

"Okay, let's try the last two tasks," Catie said. "We'll watch the video on rotating the shower, then do that next."

The shower was easy to rotate. It was mostly automatic; they just needed to secure the soap and shower wand, then push the button.

"That was easy," Liz said. "But what do you want to bet the head isn't so easy?"

"I'm not betting," Natalia said. "Let's watch the video."

"That doesn't look too hard," Liz said after the video was finished. "Just make sure the cabinets are closed, and the lid is down. It's spring-loaded, so it'll stay that way."

They all proceeded to the back and watched as Catie and Liz rotated the head, then rotated it back.

"Hey, how does this toilet work?" Natalia asked. "There's no water."

"It maintains a mild vacuum," Catie said. "When you sit on it, you'll notice the air being sucked through it. That way, it collects everything right away. The flush is a power flush with the lid sealing it. You do not want to flush it while you're sitting on it."

Natalia laughed. "I guess not, so no courtesy flushes?"

"The vacuum takes care of that," Catie said. "I think it's actually a lot nicer than the ones in the condos. I'm thinking of having mine changed out."

"Can you do that?" Samantha asked.

"We're making them for the Oryxes and the Lynxes," Catie said. "I don't see why one of them can't make its way into my bathroom."

"After I've tried it a few times, I'll let you know if you need to send more than one on a walk," Samantha said.

"Me too," Liz added.

Natalia just laughed. "You people are so spoiled. When I was growing up, eight of us had to share one bathroom."

"Eww," Liz said. "That would be tough, but does that mean the rest of us should have to rough it?"

"I don't guess so, just as long as you realize how lucky you are."

"Oh, we realize it," Samantha said.

"Make sure everything is back to normal," Catie said. "Plan on spending the night tomorrow. We want to figure out how we like sleeping in this thing while we can still make changes."

"Didn't you guys sleep in it before?" Samantha asked.

"Yes, but then it was laid out flat. This time we'll see how we like it vertical. Plus, you have to sleep strapped in. So, you don't fall down to the back of the ship."

"Oh, good point. We should probably have someone keep watch so that nobody gets hurt," Samantha said as she gave the twins a pointed look.

"Good point. We'll set up a watch rotation," Catie said. Then she made her way into the cockpit.

"Everybody, strap in," Liz said. Liz made a point to sit next to Natalia. Once everyone was strapped in and focused on the display, Liz turned to Natalia. "Hey Nattie," Liz whispered.

"What's up?"

"I appreciate that you had a rough childhood, I think we all do, but I want to tell you something about Catie."

"I wasn't trying to make anyone feel bad," Natalia said.

"I know you weren't," Liz said. "But we all have hot buttons, and we want to make sure we don't accidentally push one. Now Catie has had a wonderful life, except for her parents getting divorced and her uncle almost dying in Iraq. Not much bad has happened to her, but . . ."

"What?"

"Well, she was kidnapped while we were raising the Chagas."

---

"What!"

"Yeah, scared the hell out of all of us, all of us except Catie. She still had her specs on, and when ADI was able to track her location, we were able to contact her. She was in the trunk of a car. When she woke up, she texted her father. Said she was gagged and in the trunk of a car. Then she told him to bring the Lynx out to Portugal so we could use it when we raised the Chagas."

"You can't be serious."

"I am. The girl is tied up, and she's making sure her plans for the Chagas are being taken care of. She was in the trunk of that car for almost four hours. Then they dumped her in the cabin of a fishing trawler. When we finally got there to rescue her, she had the gag off and had untied herself. We had her lock herself in the room until we could take care of the bad guys."

"That's amazing. She must have ice in her veins."

"You'd definitely agree with that if you ever had to fly against her."

"Yeah, I heard she's a pilot."

"Two kills," Liz said. She waved Natalia off, "I'll tell you about it another time. But the other thing I want you to know is this. When we were in Boston for Christmas, Catie saw a news report about working families who had lost their homes. She called one of the shelters that helps them and arranged for the families to have a shopping day at a local mall, then arranged with a bank to take care of their rent, utilities, and deposits for a year."

"Wow, that is generous."

"One would think so, but then she donated almost all the money she got for the Chagas to the shelter. So, I don't want someone making her feel like she's got it too good; who knows what she might decide she needs to do."

"Oh, my lord. She really is something," Natalia said.

"Yes, she is. Don't get me wrong, she's still rich, and I want to thump her once in a while, but she is pretty special."

"Thanks for telling me," Natalia said. "And I do want to hear about the two kills, but maybe we can get Catie to tell that story."

---

The next day they managed to rotate the Lynx cabin without any issues. They left it in the vertical configuration, everyone strapped in, and Catie had ADI rotate the Lynx so it was sitting on its tail in the water.

"Oh, that feels weird," Samantha said as the Lynx rotated.

The twins were giggling as they looked around.

"Okay, everyone, look around, get your head oriented to the position of things. You can stand on the bulkhead that is now under your feet, but it's a drop all the way to the back of the cabin if you step off and don't grab the ladder."

"You need to look both ways before you get on the ladder," Natalia said. "You don't want to step on someone's head, and you don't want someone stepping on your head."

"No way!" the twins yelled, putting their hands on their heads.

"ADI," Catie said, "can you put an alert on everybody's specs whenever somebody is on the ladder?"

"Yes, Cer Catie," ADI replied. "There will be a ladder in the corner of your HUDs, it will be red whenever someone is on the ladder."

"Thanks, ADI."

"You're welcome."

"Nattie, you seem to know ladder etiquette, can you give us some rules?"

"Sure. The person going up has the right of way. You should step off the ladder if you can, otherwise slide over to the left side until they pass. DO NOT try to pass while you're both moving. The person coming down stops and gets out of the way," Natalia said.

The twins both nodded solemnly to Natalia.

"Do not get on the ladder when someone is already on it, and they are going to pass you, wait for them to pass first. If they're going to get off below you, then you can start down, but it's still better if you can wait."

---

"Those rules make sense," Catie said. "Anyone think of something else?"

"One more thing," Natalia said. "If we're going to be in this mode long term, we should get a few backpacks so we can carry things up and down the ladder without using our hands. You need both hands free whenever you're on the ladder."

"Good idea, and we can have some lines in the cabin, so we can haul things up or lower them down. That will save a lot of time and hassle," Liz said.

"Okay," Catie said. "Sam, what's for lunch?"

"We're having Salade Nicoise," Sam said. "With French bread."

That night they decided to run three three-hour shifts. Catie would take the first since she usually stayed up that late anyway, Nattie would take the second shift since after her years as a Marine she could wake up, do a three-hour shift, and go back to sleep without a problem; Liz would do the third shift since she usually got up early anyway. They decided that Samantha needed her beauty sleep. She took the jab at her age with aplomb since it meant she got to sleep the whole night.

Natalia used part of one of the crates in the cargo hold to make a sideboard for the twin's cubicle. It created a one-foot barrier above the height of their couch that would keep them from rolling out or wandering out without thinking.

The twins figured out that they could lie next to each other on their own couches and hold hands and hug their stuffed animals. So, they quickly drifted off to sleep.

Catie started reviewing her Oryx plans while everyone else strapped in and slept.

"Wakey, wakey, time is flying by," Liz called out when it was 07:00, the agreed-to start time for their day. "Come on, Catie, you're our leader, you need to set a good example."

Catie groaned but rolled off her couch and headed back to the head. The twins just sobbed and covered their heads with their sheets.

Since there would be a line at the bathroom, Liz ignored them until the other three had at least gotten a chance to pee and brush their teeth.

When Samantha came out of the head, their time was up. "Okay, you two, up and at 'em. Time's a-wasting."

"Get up, you two," Catie hollered, "if I have to hear one more cheery wakeup saying, I'm going to barf."

"Okay," the twins sighed. They crawled off of their couches and headed down toward the head. They had figured that since they were going down, they could just hold the rails and use their boots to control their speed. The handrail made the entire span without any additional supports, so it was a smooth ride.

"Okay, showers?" Samantha asked.

"Why don't you go first since you're making breakfast," Catie said, "then Natalia, Liz, me, and we'll save the twins for last."

"No argument from me," Samantha said. She grabbed a fresh shipsuit and headed down to the shower.

"Any problems last night?" Catie asked Liz and Natalia.

"Not that I saw," Natalia said. "The twins slept like babies. Sam got up to pee and seemed to remember she needed to use the ladder. Other than that, nothing happened."

"All was quiet on my watch," Liz said.

"Mine too," Catie said. "I still want to keep watch for a bit longer until we're sure about the twins. After that, we might let ADI keep watch for us."

"I would be happy to Cers," ADI said.

Samantha came back up looking refreshed, her hair was still damp. "That is a nice shower," she said. "How long does the suit refresher run?" she asked.

"Fifteen minutes or so, it depends on how much cleaning the suit needs," Catie said.

"Then I would suggest you put your suit in the refresher, wear a towel while you use the toilet, then when you're done with your shower, your suit will be clean and you can bring it back with you, or just wear it again."

"Good logistics," Natalia said. "Saves having to strip out of this thing twice," she said as she headed for her turn through the facilities.

"Why the towel?" Liz asked.

"Some of us still have a sense of modesty," Samantha said as she slapped Liz on the butt. "Now, help me get breakfast started."

Catie had to physically drag the twins out of the shower. She scolded them sharply but really couldn't blame them. It was a nice shower.

After breakfast, they did a few exercises moving things around using one of their kit bags as a backpack. After an hour of it, Catie called a halt.

"Okay, I think we're good for now. We really can't practice working in microgravity until we can get into it. Dad doesn't want us to take the Lynx up just to practice, so we'll do that on our way out. So, everyone, get your stuff together and finish up whatever you need to do. We'll leave the first part of next week. I want to do one more overnight next Thursday, then we'll pick up the last gravity drives from the Sakira on Friday, and we'll be ready to go."

"I think we need to have another team-building dinner at the Flambé," Natalia said.

"I like the way you think," Samantha said. "I second the motion."

"I'm in as long as Catie's buying," Liz said.

"Yes!" the twins added.

"I guess I'm outvoted no matter what I think," Catie said. "I'll see if Fred will fly us over. We might have to invite him."

"Fred's okay," Samantha said. "We'll let him eat with us."

# 8 Board Meeting – May 27th

"This meeting is called to order," Marc said.

"You're getting more efficient," Blake joked.

"I try," Marc said. "Sam, any updates?"

"The Chinese want their submarine back," Samantha laughed. "The US Navy rendered assistance this morning. Seems it was about to sink, so they towed it to Guam to effect repairs. I suspect it will be a slow process." Samantha laughed again. "It seems the admiral kept his word, nothing in the press or on channels ADI is listening to mention Delphi City or MacKenzie Discoveries in connection to the accident."

"That's good."

"We're cleared to start building the airport," Samantha continued. "The Cook Islanders want access to it, I assured them we wouldn't have a problem with that."

"Can't see why we'd care or why they'd want access. It's kind of out of the way for them."

"Thinking of the future, probably. They've signed off on bringing in more refugees; we're good up to ten thousand. They're also asking us to help resettle any Cook Islanders who want to move back to the islands from New Zealand. I said we'd be happy to help. They are delighted with the economic stimulus we're generating. We've also got three doctors and four more nurses coming over during the next three weeks to augment Dr. Metra's staff. Johansson is producing cars as we speak."

"I hate to say this, but I think we need to accelerate our plans for the space station and the city," Marc said. "The commando raid just shows how vulnerable we are."

"How will the space station help?" Samantha asked.

"It gives us a completely secure location as well as the high ground," Marc said.

"High ground?" Liz asked.

"With a presence in orbit, it's more difficult for someone to force our hand; we wouldn't be completely dependent on Delphi City. I'm sure we could acquire landing rights in several other countries if necessary," Marc said.

"I see what you're thinking," Samantha said. "More options, less value in seizing Delphi City."

"Correct," Marc said. "Kal, how's our labor situation coming?"

"We've brought in three hundred refugees so far. Only seventy-five of those are adults. Dr. Sharmila has helped them to organize a day-care center for the children. We'll need to build a school and start staffing that."

Marc looked at Blake, "It's on my list," he said.

"Fifty of the workers are semi-skilled, and we're working them in to replace the islanders who want to stay ashore. Language gap is a hassle, but they're handling it. Catie and ADI have come up with a language training regimen that seems to be helping them pick up English pretty fast. Lono Marsters, one of the guys who's been on the crew since we started, has really stepped up and is handling the training of the new people. We'll see if we can keep him long term. He seems happy with the schedule."

"Where are we getting the refugees from?" Liz asked.

"We're pulling refugees from camps in Greece. They're mostly from Syria and Lebanon. We're also picking up a lot of people from the Caribbean who have been displaced by hurricanes and are happy to move."

"How are you deciding who to take?" Catie asked.

"We're prioritizing whole families and then mothers with children. It may sound cruel, but I'm avoiding single males. I don't know how to separate the trouble makers and criminals out of that lot."

Marc grimaced, "Yeah, it's too bad, they would give us a higher percentage of workers, but I'm good with focusing on families."

"Are you accepting children accompanying a family who they are related to, like aunts and uncles?" Liz asked.

"Yeah, as long as the family has at least one child of their own, we don't pay much attention to where the other children come from. But we are getting a higher ratio of children that way," Kal said.

"I don't care," Catie said.

"I'm okay with that. Let's really put some effort into getting the school started," Marc said.

"Oh, it's started. The mothers are teaching the children as much as they can. Most of the refugees don't have that high of an education, but we do have a few school teachers in the group. The trouble is, the ones with the highest education are the ones we want to work in the manufacturing plant."

"I understand," Marc said. "Just make it work. Let me know what you need. How's our security detail going?"

"We held a service for Katelyn yesterday, she's the one who was killed during the raid. Everyone is really upset about losing her. We're going through procedures and teaming people up from now on to avoid a repeat. I'm working with ADI to increase her ability to surveil the area. We're also expanding our passive sonar array, so we don't have anyone sneaking up on us again."

"Recruiting?"

"Going great, I'm bringing them in as fast as Dr. Metra can handle them. We're up to sixty-two, no sixty-one, since Catie poached one."

Catie stuck her tongue out at Kal, "Cry baby."

Kal laughed at Catie. "Next up, I've got a proposal to review with you and Blake: I want to set up a command structure. We're big enough now that I think we need another layer between the team leaders and me."

"Go over it with Blake," Marc said. "I'll sign off on whatever you propose."

"I'm happy to go over it with you if you want my input, but I'm with Marc. Whatever you want to do, I'll sign off," Blake said.

"If you don't mind, I'd at least like to talk it through with someone," Kal said.

"No problem, talk to my admin," Blake laughed.

"Cers, I've put it on his calendar," ADI announced.

---

"Okay, Blake, you're up, or should I just ask your admin for the update?" Marc asked.

"You wish," Blake said. "We've completed quad two's infrastructure and top deck. All it needs is some buildings and gardens. Quad three is in place up to the subdeck; we'll start adding infrastructure tomorrow. Quad four has pontoons and beams in place, we'll be adding subdecking soon. We'll put the first pontoons for the first quad of section two in this week. I'm going to focus on getting the strip on the south side complete, so we can actually land the G650 or a Lynx on it. I think that an Oryx might even be able to take off and land."

"Yep," Catie said. "Fourteen hundred meters."

"Hey, isn't that longer than a C17 needs," Liz asked.

"Yeah, but we have to have a smaller wingspan to handle the supersonic speeds, so we need a longer runway to get airborne."

"Anything else?"

"The school building is at the top of my priority list; we start construction tomorrow; it'll only take two weeks to finish. We're going to need teachers fast."

"I'll get right on it," Samantha said.

"We're continuing to crank out columns and pontoons for the airport. We'll be able to start construction on it in about one month. As soon as we have section four finished out to the subdeck, we'll be able to start making plates for the airport."

"Good to hear. Okay, Catie. How's our Oryx coming?"

"Design is ready, just waiting on production capacity. It's designed to reach an altitude of thirty thousand meters on just atmosphere and the fusion reactor. Then it goes ballistic and starts burning hydrogen and oxygen. She's at Mach ten at that altitude. Then she needs to double her speed and gain another three hundred thousand meters in altitude to reach orbit, which she does in about twenty minutes at two-G acceleration, and uses about seventy liters of water."

"How about reentry?" Marc asked.

"We have enough superconductor mesh to build three Oryxes. Since we didn't build them in space, they're not as efficient at absorbing the energy through the superconductor matrices. Since we have plenty of fuel, we'll actively slow the Oryx down before we hit the atmosphere so there won't be as much heat from reentry. That means they'll work okay. During reentry, an Oryx will hit her cruising altitude of thirty kilometers at just over Mach fourteen. Atmosphere has to slow her from there."

"Okay, what else?" Marc asked.

"Once we have manufacturing capacity in microgravity, we'll need to bring the equipment from the Sakira to build more superconductor matrices. We can build them on an Oryx while it's in orbit, but that's just logistics," Catie said.

"The Lynx has passed the first part of its certification with New Zealand, now they want to inspect the production facilities. They keep saying we're crazy to bring a functional jet to them instead of bringing them in at the design phase, but they haven't found any problems yet," Catie added.

"How long before we can legally fly one?" Blake asked.

"Probably another three to six months," Catie said. "They are really slow."

"Slow or cautious?" Marc asked.

"I think it's slow, they just take a long time to figure the engineering out. The Kiwis really want us to give them more on the sonic shockwave suppression, but I've said no. They say that means they'll have to certify each jet individually. I don't think that's a problem; it's not like we're going to be building hundreds of them, at least not for a while."

"When are you and your asteroid crew heading out?" Marc asked.

"Early next week," Catie said. "We're waiting on ADI to manufacture a couple of things we need. Apparently, some things are slow to make, even for her."

"Do you need anything?"

"We've finished the main part of the training I had planned. We'll keep that up until we have the parts, then we'll be ready to go."

"We're finished," Marc said. "Blake and Catie, can you stay behind, I have a couple of items I need to go over with you."

"What's up?" Blake asked after everyone else had left.

"Part of accelerating our timeline is getting more satellite coverage," Marc said.

"You mean with the Paraxean satellites?" Catie asked.

"Yes, there are only twenty-two of them up there now," Marc said. "ADI and I calculate that we need twenty-five hundred to give us full coverage of earth for communication and GPS."

"Why do we want to cover communication and GPS?" Blake asked.

"If we get into a big conflict with the major powers, I think we'll want to eliminate all satellites in orbit except ours," Marc said.

"Won't that just piss them off more?" Blake asked.

"Yes, but what are they going to do about it? We can take satellites out faster than they can replace them. If we replace the critical services, we can blind them by taking out the spy satellites, and if they're dependent on us for GPS, then we have a lot of leverage," Marc said.

"Okay," Blake said. "What do you need?"

"We're going to need to start printing mini-fusion reactors and gravity drives," Marc said, "plus, the computer circuits for the satellites."

"Those have to be printed in microgravity with the molecular printers," Catie said.

"Right, so we'll need to get those in orbit and running as soon as we can," Marc said.

"And you don't want to put the Sakira up there, right?" Blake asked.

"Right, so we'll need Oryxes to use as manufacturing platforms."

"Once we build enough," Catie said, "we can keep four in orbit with a printer on each of them. Then we just have to bring supplies up and rotate the crews."

"That will work," Blake said.

"Okay, I'd like to keep exactly what we're manufacturing on them between us," Marc said. "Blake, I'll have ADI forward you the work we've done on the satellites so you can create a manufacturing plan."

"Got it," Blake said. "You're really feeling the pressure, aren't you?"

"Yes, I thought we'd spend three years getting the city finished and the space station built, but every time I turn around, there seems to be something making it more urgent to finish sooner," Marc said as he gave a big sigh and rubbed his face.

"Captain," Catie said as she entered Marc's office.

"What happened to Daddy?" Marc asked.

"We're working. I want to talk about the mission."

"Okay, Cer Catie. Where are you?"

"We're ready to go."

"When do you want to leave?"

"Saturday night after dark. I'm assuming you want to minimize any chance we will be seen."

"You are correct."

"That gives you tonight to say goodbye to Sam," Catie grinned at her father.

"Thanks for the heads up," Marc chuckled.

"You know she could move in with us. It wouldn't bother me."

"Thanks for letting me know, but I think she likes having her own place."

"Just saying."

"I know. Now about your mission," Marc said. "A few things I want to add to the mission parameters."

"Yes, sir."

"I want you to bring the asteroids into Earth's orbit from the other side of the sun. That means you'll have to keep them next to the asteroid belt until the sun is hiding them from view. We don't want them to be seen by anyone here and start a scare about a killer asteroid. Once they're in the same orbit, we can slow them until they're at the proper leading position we want."

The tip of Catie's tongue poked out the corner of her mouth while she did some work in her HUD. "I can bring them into an outside orbit, having their velocity a little too slow, so they start decaying in toward the sun. Once they reach the right orbit, the Earth should have caught up quite a bit. We can goose them back to the right speed with the drives and adjust until they're where you want them. We can put the three of them in a tight orbital line if you want, so you can only see one from Earth."

"That should work."

"Okay, I'm staying with Liz and Natalia tonight, have fun."

Marc rolled his eyes and just waved Catie out of his office.

# 9   Spaceflight

## Day 1

"You guys ready?" Catie asked her crew. They were standing in the hangar looking at the Lynx that would be their home for the next three to four weeks. Each of them wore one of the shipsuits that they'd designed and had made onboard the Sakira.

"Girl, I was born ready," Natalia said.

Samantha and Liz nodded in agreement while the twins were figuring out that they could both stand behind Natalia and hide from Catie.

"Wait, group picture," Marc shouted. "Stand right there in front of the Lynx, and I'll get a shot for the archives. Natalia, stand in back, Liz and Sam, one of you on each side of her. Catie, you stand in front of Natalia with one of the twins on each side. Okay, say space."

"Space!"

"Take lots of pictures; someday we'll publish this, and you will all be famous."

"Sure, Daddy," Catie waved at her father as she shooed the twins into the Lynx.

Once everyone was aboard, Catie gave her father and Uncle Blake one more wave before she closed the hatch. "Everybody put on your helmet. And you'll have to put on the chest piece of your exosuit since that's where the air supply is."

"Are you telling us this flight isn't safe?" Samantha said, clutching her hands to her chest in mock horror.

"No, but better safe than sorry. This is the first time we've ever taken a Lynx into orbit, much less beyond that."

Samantha shuddered, "I didn't think of that. Is it too late to back out? . . . Just kidding."

"Once you're suited up, strap yourself to your couches. Liz and I will be in the cockpit, but I'll put the forward view up here on the display, with Liz and me in the corner here. We'll be on open comm the whole time so everybody can enjoy the experience."

"We're ready," the twins said as they finished strapping themselves in.

"ADI is preflight done?" Catie asked.

"Yes, Cer Catie. All systems are green."

Catie and Liz cycled into the cockpit and strapped in. Catie reviewed all the preflight data, then signaled Blake to open the hangar door. She started the engines up, letting them idle while she engaged the landing gear. The Lynx had motor-driven wheels that allowed it to move in any direction without relying on the engines.

"Okay, we're going to start taxiing now," Catie announced as she started the Lynx toward the hangar opening. She drove down to the end of the runway and turned the Lynx around. "Control, Lynx One requesting clearance for takeoff."

"Lynx One, you have clear skies," Blake responded, "you're cleared for takeoff. Have a safe journey."

"Bye, sweetie, bye, hon, bye, girls," Marc said. "Safe journey; stay in touch while you're out there."

"And we're off!" Catie pushed the throttle forward, opening up the engines. The Lynx rocketed down the fourteen-hundred-meter runway, lifting off well before the end and blasting into the night sky.

"Turning south and climbing to ten thousand meters," Catie announced to everyone. "Next stop, the South Pole."

"How long until we get there?" Samantha asked.

"A bit under an hour," Liz explained.

"Will we be able to see Antarctica?" Natalia asked.

"It's going to be dark," Liz answered.

"Oh, pooh," Samantha said.

"Can we get up?" the twins asked.

"No, you'll need to stay in your seats for about an hour. We're going to go vertical in a bit, and you're going to feel a lot heavier."

"Can you explain?" Samantha asked. "Inquiring minds want to know."

Catie laughed. "Sure. When we get close to the South Pole, I'm going to go ballistic, like a missile. We'll need to accelerate at 1.5Gs, one G to overcome gravity and 0.5Gs so we actually go somewhere. You will feel like you weigh over twice what you normally do. We'll do that for about forty minutes. After that, the force of gravity will be about one-quarter-G, so I will back off on the acceleration to conserve fuel, and everyone can move about. Of course, it will be just like in training, with the back of the jet being down, so you'll need to use the ladder."

Everyone soon noticed their weight moving to the back of their couch and slowly increase as Catie arced the Lynx into a vertical climb.

"Speaking of inquiring minds, how do we have the fuel to do this kind of burn?" Liz asked.

"Isn't it kind of late to ask if we have enough fuel to get there and back?" Catie asked with a laugh.

"Well, I was trusting you, girl, but now I'd like to understand," Liz said.

"So, would we," added Samantha.

"Okay," Catie said. "Although the Lynx mostly looks like a regular jet, its engines are really different. We have a small fusion reactor onboard that provides most of our power. We have these humongous capacitors that everything actually runs off of. All the energy absorbed by the hull is dumped into them, and whenever they drop below sixty percent, the fusion reactor kicks in and recharges them to ninety percent."

"Why capacitors instead of batteries?" Samantha asked. "And what are capacitors, anyway?"

"Capacitors are kind of like a battery. They store energy, but they can absorb and release it way faster than a battery can. That way we can change the power to the engines really fast. The reactor is kind of a big, slow engine. Lots of power, but it doesn't like to change how much power it generates very fast."

"Oh, okay," Samantha said.

"Anyway, when we're in atmosphere, instead of burning fuel, we use energy from the capacitors to superheat the air that passes through the engines and runs the turbines. So, it acts pretty much like a regular jet engine, hot air goes blasting out the back end, the change in the velocity of the air gives us the thrust. We can dump a little bit of hydrogen into the mix if we need some more boost, but we usually don't."

"Oh, that explains why you never have to refuel," Liz said.

"Yep. But once we get so high that the air is too thin to give us enough thrust, we have to either add a lot more hydrogen or switch to the space engines. The space engines run off of spent fuel from the reactors and the extra water we carry for reaction mass. Now our reactor takes in four deuterium atoms and fuses them into two helium-4 atoms, then it takes four helium-4 atoms and fuses them to make oxygen-sixteen; that's about the best we can do with fusion, so we store the oxygen-sixteen atoms in a tank in the hold when we're not using the space engines. But when we use the space engines, they take the oxygen-sixteen, accelerate it really, really fast, and eject it out the back of the engine. That's what gives us our thrust. But when we're spitting those oxygen atoms out the back, it's like a rail gun. They collide with the air in the atmosphere, and that slows them down, kind of like the cue ball colliding with another ball. They both go off in different directions, but the energy from the cue ball is split between itself and the ball it hits. I adjust our vector so that we don't keep hitting the same area, that way we don't create a zone of high-speed molecules. In space, the molecules we eject eventually collide with the hydrogen ions that make up the solar wind and get slowed down, but you wouldn't want one hitting you on the head."

"How fast are we ejecting them?" Liz asked.

"Right now, I've set it for one-tenth the speed of light. That's so the particles don't have too much energy when they hit the Earth's atmosphere," Catie said.

"Aren't they going to cause a problem anyway?" Liz asked.

"Not too bad. Like I said, their speed gets split between every molecule they collide with, but even with that, I'm sure we're leaving a bit of a light show behind us."

"Will they notice?" Samantha asked.

"You mean NASA?"

"Well, anybody."

"Maybe. We're on the light side of the Earth now so the show's happening in daylight, which should reduce the effect. They'll probably notice something but won't know what it is. Once we're a bit further away, I'll boost the exhaust speed to one-quarter-c, so we can conserve fuel, but I'll angle us, so the exhaust stream misses Earth."

"How much fuel does it take?"

"We're spitting out about twelve kilos an hour right now. Once I change the exhaust speed to one-quarter-c, we'll drop that to about three kilos an hour. The faster we spin them up, the less it takes to give us the push we want."

"So, we have plenty of fuel?"

"At three kilos per hour, we have almost a year's worth of fuel."

"Good to know."

"Any more questions?" Catie asked.

"Can you change the screen so we can see Earth?" Samantha asked.

"Yeah!" the twins echoed the request.

"Here you go."

It was an hour of quiet solitude as everyone watched the Earth recede in the view screen. Even the twins were mostly quiet, with just an occasional giggle between them.

"Okay everybody, grab a barf bag," Catie announced. "I'm going to ease up on the acceleration nice and slow and bring us to 0.2G. Then we can reconfigure the cabin for the rest of our flight."

"Barf, eww!" the twins squealed.

"I'm hoping by easing the acceleration slowly instead of cutting it off all at once, the transition won't make anyone sick, but we won't know until we do it," Catie said.

"And I don't want to be cleaning up any barf," Samantha said.

"Ready. Here we go." Catie eased the acceleration from one G down to 0.2G over ten minutes. "Everybody okay back there?"

"We're all good," Samantha said, obviously surprised how easy the transition went.

"Okay, Liz and I are coming back," Catie said. "We'll reconfigure the cabin, then I'll have ADI ease us back up to one G."

Catie and Liz made their way from the cockpit through the airlock. When they entered the main cabin, Natalia had already extended the partition bulkheads on the right side to act as a floor between the seats. Liz started down the left side extending those bulkheads, while Catie helped Samantha rotate the galley. Everyone was happy that the twins just stayed out of the way and watched. After she and Samantha finished rotating the galley, Catie went to the back and got Natalia to help her rotate the head and the shower.

"Okay, everyone, we're set. The head is working if anyone needs to use it. While we're underway, please be careful as you climb the ladder. We don't want anyone falling. We have an emergency medical kit, but I really don't want to have to use it."

The twins had already strapped back in and were watching a video on their HUDs. Catie and Liz took their seats in the front row, close to the cockpit, but they were going to let ADI fly the Lynx for now.

"Okay, ADI, we're ready, ease her back up to one G."

"Yes, Captain," ADI said.

"Ohh, it's Captain now," Liz said as she gave Catie a la-di-da wave of her hand.

Catie just grinned.

"How is ADI able to fly us when she's back on the Sakira?" Samantha asked.

"Oh, I guess you wouldn't know about that," Catie said. "Do you know what quantum entanglement is?"

"Not really."

"Well, if you take two atoms and get them to couple, they call it quantum entanglement, then when you separate them, one atom instantly reacts to whatever happens to the other. They maintain that entanglement no matter how far apart they are. We have a whole bunch of quantum sets in the Sakira. There's one half of one here on the Lynx, so ADI communicates with that. The Sakira acts like a switchboard, and ADI routes between one quantum pair and the others, or whatever form of communication that is available on the Sakira. So, you can talk between any of them with only the delay from the switching circuit. So, you'll be able to talk to Daddy anytime you want, and there won't be any lag."

"He said I could call him; I didn't realize it was going to be so easy."

"Yep, that's also one of the reasons ADI does so well in the stock market. We took some Internet switches and added a quantum relay to them; then generated some bogus work orders to have them installed next to all the key exchanges. She gets the market data sooner than anyone else."

"How does that help?"

"Milliseconds count in that game."

On the trip out, Catie had ADI ease the Lynx's acceleration to zero each day for three hours. This allowed them to practice working in a microgravity environment before they hit the asteroid belt. They organized games of catch; some acrobatic contests; moving around the Lynx; using the head. Samantha also made a point to cook one meal each day in microgravity. They would be in very low gravity or microgravity for up to a week as they searched for the right asteroids, mounted a fusion reactor and three gravity motors on each, and then sent each of them on their path to Earth.

Liz also took the opportunity to work on self-defense in the microgravity environment. It quickly became apparent that Natalia's extra bulk, while not particularly helpful in gravity, really gave her an advantage in microgravity. She could just hunker down and focus on blocking blows. Her inertia was so high that it was almost impossible to get her moving without gravity to help. Liz worked hard to come up with techniques where she could use a bulkhead to gain enough leverage to get Natalia moving. But getting Natalia moving didn't actually help all that much, because the same problem presented itself when Liz tried to change her direction. Natalia could just curl up a bit, and her momentum would break Liz's grip. Liz actually had to get her moving then switch to the side she was moving toward to be able to do anything remotely like a throw.

# Day 2

"Right!" Natalia barked.

Catie turned to Natalia's right, bumped into another crate, and dropped her end of the crate, spilling its contents all over the cargo bay. They were shifting the stores in the back of the cabin so they could get to some spices that Samantha wanted.

"Your right," Natalia said.

"How was I to know whose right you meant," Catie complained.

"My bad," Natalia said. "We need to work on terminology before we're standing on an asteroid getting our suits torn up because we don't understand each other."

"I agree," Liz said. She'd been watching as the disaster slowly unfolded. "Who knows the right vocabulary to use, or do we need to make it up?"

"I think we can just use the terms I learned in the Marines," Natalia explained as she bent down to gather some of the scattered supplies.

After they had finished restowing everything, they gathered everyone together for a lesson. "Okay, it's important that we communicate precisely what we mean, so we're going to learn some words that sailors and astronauts use to tell direction," Natalia explained.

The twins nodded seriously.

"First, we're going to learn about directions. When someone says *abaft*, they mean toward the rear of the ship," Natalia pointed to the back of the Lynx. "When they say *abow*, they mean to the front of the ship. *Aport* means to the left of the ship when you're standing on the deck and facing toward the front, think of it as the side with the hatch on it."

Natalia pointed to the front, "Which direction is that?"

"Abow," the twins said.

"That's correct. Now *astarboard* means to the right when facing the bow, the opposite of *aport*, so the side without a hatch. *Akeel* means toward the bottom of the ship, and *atop* means toward the top of the ship. Got it?"

The twins nodded their heads.

"You have to always know how you're positioned in the ship, so if someone tells you to move abaft, you know which way to go," Catie explained. She got more head bobs from the twins.

"Good thinking," Samantha said.

"Natalia is going to call out directions at different times during the day. When she says point abaft, everyone points in that direction, and then we can correct each other until we don't make any more mistakes," Catie said.

"Now the next set is easy," Natalia continued. "If I say right, left, up, down, forward or back, it is always your right, your left, etc. Does that make sense?"

"Yes," everyone agreed.

"Okay, we'll do those for today; tomorrow," Natalia said. "I'll teach you some more."

The next day Natalia added three commands, "*Avast*: stop doing what you're doing (typically with your hands) but you don't have to stop your body's motion; *Freeze*: stop doing anything and stop your motion; *Halt*: stop your motion, but not necessarily what you're doing with your hands." The twins turned out to be quick learners, Catie and Liz learned fast but not as fast as the twins, Samantha struggled a bit. She claimed it was because lawyers weren't used to taking orders from anyone.

# Day 3

Samantha was cleaning up after lunch, getting not very useful help from the twins. "Girls, why don't you two go to the bathroom before we start accelerating," she suggested.

"Sure," the twins headed aft.

"I saw that," Natalia said. "You're just getting rid of them."

"They are getting better, but they're so easily distracted. Unless Catie is ordering them around, they act like butterflies, going from one thing to the other."

Natalia laughed. "I think they're a kick. They are very clever, don't you think?"

"Nobody's disputing their intelligence, just their ability to focus," Samantha said.

Natalia helped Samantha continue to clean up.

"Hi Nattie," the twins said as they glided by, tagged the front of the cabin, and pushed off toward the rear again.

"They couldn't have gone to the bathroom yet," Samantha said.

"Why not?"

"They didn't have time. It takes me two minutes just to get my suit down and back up."

"I don't think they're taking their suits off," Natalia said.

Samantha's eyes went wide in recognition, "You mean after all that *'eww'* and *'how gross'* about having to go in their suits during EVA, they can't even bother to take them down when they're in the ship?"

"You have to admit, it's a lot more efficient that way."

"Not you too," Samantha said as she flicked her dishtowel at Natalia.

"Just saying, it's efficient," Natalia laughed as she pushed off and headed back to her seat.

"Everyone, strap in please," Catie commanded. She actually checked that the twins were strapped in before strapping herself in.

"Why do we have to strap in?" the twins asked.

"Because we're going to flip the ship," Catie explained.

"Why?"

"Because we're halfway now. We've been accelerating all this way, going faster and faster, but now that we're halfway, we need to start slowing down, so we don't just go blasting past all the asteroids."

"Why do you have to flip the ship?"

---

**105**

"Because we don't have any brakes. That means we have to use the engines, and they're on the back of the ship. When we flip the ship, they're pointed in the direction we're going, so when we run them, they slow us down."

"You're going to fly the ship backward," the twins giggled. "How can you do that?"

"We're in space, so there isn't any air. If there's no air, it doesn't matter how your ship is pointed, it just goes along the same line, vector, that you're already traveling in."

"Oh," the twins said as they thought deeply about what they'd heard.

# Day 5

"Okay, that's it for deceleration," Catie announced. "We're in microgravity or low-G until we find the asteroids we want. We'll be maneuvering around, so you'll want to make sure you're holding onto something, or you're strapped in. ADI will make an announcement just before she engages the thrusters. She'll say, 'maneuvering in five,' which means you have five seconds to grab onto something if you're not strapped in. Then she'll say, 'maneuver complete,' when she's done, and you can go on doing whatever you were doing before the maneuver."

"We're looking for an ice asteroid, but to find one this close to the sun, the ice has to be buried. ADI says they saw some like we want when the Paraxeans came through the belt on their way to Earth. We just have to find one like it."

"Why does the ice have to be buried?" Liz asked.

"This close to the sun, there is enough energy that it would have evaporated all the ice by now," Catie said. "Most of the ice asteroids are outside of Jupiter's orbit where the sun isn't strong enough to evaporate it, so the ice actually sublimates, going from solid directly to vapor."

"If the ice is buried, how will we know it's ice?" Natalia asked.

"It will have a low density," Catie said. "ADI can measure the density for us and tell us which ones fit."

"Okay, so what are we supposed to look for?" Samantha asked.

"We're looking for asteroids with diameters of between two thousand and five thousand meters," Catie pointed to the display in the main cabin that was showing the asteroid field they were coasting next to. Catie had brought them in above the asteroid belt, so they were looking down on the asteroids as they passed them. "ADI, please highlight ice asteroids within those parameters and with a density that indicates they have large amounts of ice."

The cabin display changed; it now had a few pulsing green spots. "The brighter the spot, the bigger the diameter," ADI informed them.

"Hey ADI, you're exceeding expectations, I like that," Catie said.

"I try, Captain," ADI said.

"Please add conformity to a sphere as a parameter, spherical being a positive attribute," Catie ordered.

The display changed with most of the bright green dots fading.

"There's one!" the twins yelled.

"Good," Catie said. "We'll keep track of that one. Now, let's see if we can find one on the edge close to us."

Everyone watched the display while the Lynx continued to coast along above the belt, traveling just a little bit faster than the asteroids in the belt. Every few minutes, ADI announced maneuvers as she adjusted their orbit to approach a promising group of asteroids.

Samantha excused herself to go to the restroom. When she came back in less than a minute, Natalia leaned over to her, "Being efficient are we?"

"When in Rome," Samantha said with a laugh.

"How about that one?" the twins asked. They'd quickly figured out to concentrate on the front of the display where new asteroids were coming into view.

"I like that one. ADI zoom in on this one," Catie said, pointing out the asteroid the twins had identified. "Put its parameters in the corner of the screen . . . forty-two hundred meters, pretty spherical, and no other asteroids around it. That gives us a clean way in and back out. ADI

107

put us next to it. Liz and Nattie, let's suit up, we've got an asteroid to wrangle."

"Can we come?" the twins asked.

"We're going to watch them from here," Samantha said. "That way, if they need something, we can get it for them."

"Okay," the twins moaned. They had quickly adjusted to not arguing, recognizing that they had to follow orders, even if they didn't like them.

Catie, Liz, and Natalia cycled through the airlock and into the cargo hold. They had their kit bags with them and quickly donned their exosuits and helmets. "Nattie, you're in charge," Catie announced. "You've got the most experience moving this kind of stuff around. I'll let you know where we want the engines and reactor, you tell us how to put them in place."

"Copy," Natalia said. "Everybody, check your air and thruster supply."

"I'm good."

"I think we should do a buddy check like when you dive," Catie suggested.

"I like that," Natalia said. "You check mine; Liz, you check Catie's; and I'll check yours when I'm clear."

Catie carefully checked Natalia's suit, verifying that the seam between her helmet and suit was completely sealed, and then checking that the thrusters and auxiliary $O_2$ tanks were full. She patted Natalia on her helmet, "You're good, except no tool belt yet."

"Oh, that would be embarrassing," Natalia said as she grabbed her tool belt and put it on before going behind Liz to check her suit out.

"We're ready," Liz said as Natalia patted her helmet.

"Okay, let's get this show on the road. As you'll remember, we have tools here at the front. Engines, reactors, cables, and anchors are staged from front to back. One full set for each asteroid together."

"I didn't realize we stacked them that way," Liz said.

"That's because we didn't stack them, Nattie did," Catie said. "We just lifted them into the hold for her."

"Oh well, that was smart of you, Nattie."

"Not my first rodeo," Natalia said. "Now we'll just take the plasma blaster for digging and leveling the sites. Four flags to identify which sites we want, and anchors for anchoring things well to keep them from floating off, and a driver to screw the anchors in. Liz, you grab the driver and anchors, I'll get the blaster, Catie, you grab the flags and some more anchors."

"Are we going to try to cycle all this stuff through the airlock?" Liz asked.

"Uh," Natalia looked at the gear they were carrying, "Can we open the cargo hatch?"

"Sure," Catie said. "ADI, please pull the air out of the cargo bay. When you're finished, open the cargo hatch."

"I guess it kind of is my first space rodeo," Natalia said.

"I wasn't going to say anything," Liz laughed.

"We'll all make a few mistakes," Catie said. "Let's just try not to kill each other."

A few minutes later, ADI announced that the cargo hold was evacuated, and she opened the cargo door.

"I think our captain should have the honors," Natalia said as she stepped back and motioned to Catie to be the first to exit the hold.

The Lynx was floating about two meters above the asteroid, with her wings parallel to the surface but upside down. Catie perched on the edge of the doorframe and looked up from the Lynx's perspective, down toward the asteroid.

"Remember slow and easy," Natalia said.

Catie nodded her head and stepped out of the hold. She used the cowling around the door to pull herself down below the Lynx's floor. Then she just let go, and her momentum carried her on down to the asteroid. As she contacted the asteroid, she bent her knees to absorb as much of her momentum as she could. She used her thrusters to counter the slight recoil, turned, and waved at Natalia and Liz. "Neil Armstrong, eat your heart out."

Catie moved out of the way as Liz made the same maneuver and landed much the same way. She moved over next to Catie, and they both watched Natalia float down. Natalia barely recoiled and only needed a short burst from her thruster to counter it.

"Any reason not to put the reactor here?" Natalia asked.

"Not that I can think of," Catie said. "ADI?"

"It is a good site, Captain. That's why I parked next to it."

"Of course," Catie laughed.

"Mark it," Natalia said.

Catie tried to push a flag into the surface and only succeeded in making herself bounce up about two feet. After she used her thruster to get herself back to the surface, she looked at Natalia, "Maybe a little blaster help?"

Natalia set the plasma blaster to its lowest setting and fired a short burst into the surface. Catie immediately stuck the flag into the spot jamming it down until its tapered edges grabbed onto the sides of the hole. It was a bit of a struggle moving around; as soon as one of them tried to move, they floated up and had to use the thruster to set themselves back down again.

"Let's face it. There's no gravity here, so trying to walk around on this thing is a waste of air," Natalia said. "So let's go full EVA and treat it like a spacewalk. We want this area level?"

"Yes," Catie said. "Once it's mostly level, we can set anchors for the reactor, then bolt it down."

"Okay, here goes nothing," Natalia said as she lay down just inches above the surface and started blasting. The blast immediately pushed her backward. She used her thruster to bring herself back and about one meter up. "I'll need an anchor right here," she pointed with the blaster, then dialing the setting back down, drilled a hole.

Catie glided over and set an anchor into the hole, then she used the wrench she had on her belt to twist it until it was tight. "Wow, it's hard to twist this thing when you can't set your feet," Catie said.

"Now that you have one anchor, you tie to it to give you some leverage," Natalia said. "I need another one here," she said as she pointed at the spot.

"Okay, give me a pilot hole first," Catie said.

Natalia fired her plasma cannon to make the pilot hole, while Liz ran a line from the last anchor to Catie.

They repeated the process until Natalia had three anchors set, then she anchored a line from her belt to two of the anchors and hooked her feet under the third. She lay back down and started blasting again. The force from the blast pushed her against the anchors, but the lines held her in position, forming a vee, with her body the point and the blast area between the two anchors connected to her belt. She just managed to keep her body level with the surface. It only took a couple of minutes, and she had a nice, flat-looking surface.

"Okay, next?"

"ADI, do you have the location picked out for the first engine?"

"Of course, Captain," ADI said. "I will need to guide you to it. I'll mark a point, and when you get there, I'll mark the next one, and then I'll need to do it one more time before you reach it."

"Will the others be able to see my flag when I get there?" Catie asked.

"Yes, Captain. It is just the laser reflection that is so minor and close to the surface that you cannot see it over fifty meters away."

"So, should I go first?" Catie asked Natalia.

"Yes, when you get there, wave the flag, then we'll follow," Natalia said. "No reason for more than one of us to zigzag around trying to keep track of that beam."

"Okay, ADI, I'm ready," Catie said.

"Captain, I'm lighting up your way-point with a laser now. It is at thirty degrees to your right."

Catie turned her head to the right and could just make out where the laser was reflecting off of the surface of the asteroid. "I'm off."

Catie used her thrusters to maneuver toward the spot that the beam was marking. She managed a pretty straight line, and when she got there, she waited for ADI to mark the next waypoint. When she

**111**

reached that one, she looked back at her friends. They were standing there watching her. She waved and turned to find the last waypoint. After reaching it, she raised her flag and waved it to Natalia and Liz, who made short work of reaching her since they didn't have to worry too much about which direction they were going.

"Okay, same process, but more efficient this time," Natalia said. "Flag here," she pointed the blaster and pulsed it. Catie drove the flag into place. "Anchor here, . . . here, . . . and here." With the anchors in place, Natalia made quick work of securing herself to them using the lines she'd kept from her previous effort. She lay down next to the surface and blasted another level spot. "We'll be able to use the anchors to secure the engines until we get everything lined up to embed them."

"I like that idea," Catie said. "So much better than letting them float around while we figure out how to install them."

"There's always one in every group," Natalia laughed at Catie's job-site humor. "Next location?"

"ADI?"

"It will be four marks this time," ADI said. "First one, directly to your right."

It took them two hours to level the last two engine locations. By then they were all tired and running low on thruster air. "Back to the Lynx," Natalia ordered. "We'll have lunch and decide if we're up to installing the reactor today."

"You're lead," Catie said as she gathered her tools. Ten minutes later, they were in the cargo hold, closing the door.

"Do we pressurize it or use the airlock?" Natalia asked.

"I think we leave it unpressurized for lunch, but pressurize it overnight," Catie said. "It won't hurt to have an extra layer of safety while we sleep."

"Good idea, Captain," Natalia said.

They cycled into the main cabin one at a time.

"That was so cool," the twins said. "Can't we go next time?"

"I'll tell you what," Catie said. "You behave yourself until we're finished setting the engines tomorrow, and we'll take you out and let you stand on the asteroid and play around in space a bit. But we're going to put safety lines on you."

"Yeah!"

After lunch, Natalia lugged the reactor to the cargo door. While she was doing that, Liz and Catie strung lines from the Lynx to the anchors they'd used to level the spot. After everything was ready, Natalia connected the lines to the reactor then gave it a gentle push out of the Lynx. Liz and Catie pulled the lines in as the reactor floated down. By the time it reached the surface, Natalia was there to slow its momentum and help it settle into place.

"That wasn't too hard," Natalia said.

"That was the easy one," Liz laughed. "The first gravity drive has to go about one hundred fifty meters away."

"But the same principle," Natalia said. "We'll hook long lines to it, I'll push, and you guys reel it in. There's nothing in the way, so it's a straight shot."

"Do you want to place the engines now, or set the reactor?"

"I like repeating steps," Natalia said. "That way, you don't forget what you did last time. So, let's place the engines today. We'll rest up tonight and think about what we need to do to set things tomorrow."

"You do the thinking; I'm going to sleep," Liz said.

"Right, we'll figure out how to set them tomorrow," Natalia said with a laugh.

It took them a little over three hours to move the engines, about an hour each. They left each of them anchored to the asteroid and made their way back inside the Lynx. They shed their exosuits in the cargo hold and made their way into the main cabin.

"Dinner will be ready in one hour," Samantha said. "Are you guys going to shower?"

"I think that was a hint," Natalia said as she sniffed her shipsuit.

"Nattie, you go first, you worked the hardest. If we run out of time, they'll be able to put up with one of us through dinner," Liz suggested.

"I'm not sure whether you're being nice or insulting me," Natalia said.

Liz sputtered a bit as she realized she'd essentially said Natalia stunk more than she or Catie did. Natalia laughed at her, "Gotcha. I'm glad to go first, I love the way those jets pulse on my muscles." She was already halfway out of her shipsuit by the time she reached the shower.

"Did you girls do your lessons?" Catie asked.

"We worked on geometry," Samantha said. "It seemed to be a good thing to do with the object lesson playing out in front of them."

"Yeah, we learned about arcs and circles. We already knew about lines," the twins said.

After dinner, the twins called their mother and showed her videos of the work on the asteroid. Catie called her father; after a brief chat and an update on their progress, she handed him off to Samantha while she stretched out on her couch and strapped herself down to sleep.

# Day 6

"Are we ready to go anchor those babies down?" Natalia asked as the three women were suiting up.

"I'm ready," Liz said. "Natalia, do I need to lug that driver around?"

"Yes, we'll just set the big anchors like we did the small ones, blast a pilot hole, and drive them in. But, I'm pretty sure you'll have to use the driver to set them," Natalia said.

"Darn it, I was hoping I didn't have to lug this thing around after not using it all day yesterday," Liz said.

"You and Catie grab the big anchors. We'll tie them down next to the reactor until we need them, but that'll save us having to open up the cargo hold every time we need more."

Catie and Liz each grabbed eight of the big corkscrew anchors, Natalia grabbed the blaster, and they made their way down to the asteroid again for the second day of work. After tying the extra anchors down, Liz went back for the dreaded driver.

After lashing down the anchors, Catie laid the template for the reactor over the pad they'd leveled yesterday. She marked the positions for ech of the three anchors with a shot of paint. She rolled the template back up, stuck it in the pouch on her tool belt, and signaled to Natalia that she was ready. Liz brought one of the big anchors over, and Natalia lined the blaster up with the first mark. She set the power down to the lowest level and started firing. She kept raising the power level up to make the hole deeper and wider, but after only a few seconds, she was floating up off the surface, pushed by the kickback of the blaster.

Catie pulled a small anchor out of her tool pouch, "I thought that might happen."

Natalia used her thrusters to bring her back down to the surface, drilled a small hole for the anchor, which Catie pressed the anchor into and then turned it with the wrench to secure it. Then using that anchor to hold her down, Natalia went back to drilling the hole. She gave Liz a nod when she calculated it was big enough, and Liz drove the anchor into the hole and attached the driver to it. She used the anchor Catie had secured to push against as the driver cranked the anchor down.

They repeated the process twice more, then Catie and Liz grabbed the lines from the reactor and secured themselves to the two farthest anchors. Natalia released the reactor and coaxed it along to the pad as Liz and Catie reeled their lines in. They had to adjust the anchor plates on two of the corners to get the reactor to fit down over them. Then they locked the reactor into place.

"Okay, we just have to do that three more times," Natalia said. "Any preference on which one we do first?"

"Let's do the left one," Liz said. "Just to be different."

"Sure," Natalia said.

Liz grabbed five anchors, and Catie grabbed another five.

"Why an extra?" Liz asked.

"A spare, in case we break one or something."

Liz nodded her head and continued to follow Catie, keying off the flag they had set yesterday.

They worked for an hour to set the first engine and moved onto the next. They completed the other two in forty-five minutes each and were heading back to the ship for lunch only three-and-one-half hours after they started their EVA.

"We're getting good at this," Natalia said as they were climbing back into the Lynx.

"The next two are going to be harder, especially the iron asteroid. We're going to have to really work to set the anchors on it," Catie said.

"That's why we have that driver," Natalia said. "I might have to run the driver when we get to those."

"Hey, I'm not that big a wimp!" Liz said as she slugged Natalia on the shoulder. She winced a little as her hand impacted Natalia's exosuit armor.

"Should have waited for me to get this suit off," Natalia laughed as she made her way to the airlock.

"I don't think it would have made much difference," Liz muttered.

Lunch was a simple affair of sandwiches and fries. The twins were very excited about getting to go out onto the asteroid afterward, so Samantha had kept things simple.

"Are you guys finished?" Samantha asked quietly, giving the twins a cautious glance.

"No, we still have to string the power cables," Catie said. "But Nattie and I can do that ourselves if you and Liz will watch the twins."

Samantha gave a sigh of relief. "Good, they are really excited."

"I can tell."

After lunch, everybody suited up. Natalia had everyone do a buddy check, with an adult checking each of the twins despite their protestations that they were buddies and could check themselves.

After getting ADI to take a suitable picture of everyone standing on the asteroid next to the reactor, Catie and Natalia went back up to the Lynx to grab the cables. Catie attached a line to an anchor and carried it back up with her.

"Geez, these things are big," Natalia said as she hefted one of the coils of wire. It was a twisted set of wires about three centimeters in diameter. The coil was a meter in diameter.

"And just think, they're superconductors. Imagine how big they'd be if they were copper," Catie said.

"Yeah, let's figure how we do this before we start."

"I'm assuming we'll take them all down, tie them to the reactor. Take one, attach it, and then anchor it right next to the reactor. We can use one of the plasma torches since we're only going to be setting the small anchors."

"How do we unroll this thing?" Natalia asked.

"I guess we don't want to try to roll it along the surface."

"How about we put some kind of stick through the center, then we each hold one end and fly over to the engine. It should just unroll itself."

"I agree, let's try it," Catie said as she looked around for a suitable stick. "You know, it doesn't have to be a stick, why don't we use a short piece of safety line. Then we can just attach it to our exosuit and have our hands free."

"Perfect," Natalia said as she grabbed a short piece of line. "I'll feed these three down to you if you'll tie them down when they get there. I don't think we have to worry about them bouncing a bit."

"Okay."

Soon they had the three coils of powerline down to the asteroid and were heading off toward the first engine, the first powerline spooling out behind them. It only took them two hours to wire up the three engines and secure the power lines with anchors.

When they got back from securing the last one, the twins were bouncing between the asteroid and the Lynx. They would push off of the asteroid; flip in midair, hitting the Lynx with their feet; and push back to the asteroid, repeating the process. They were going at a pretty fast clip by the time Catie and Natalia got back.

"Whoa, aren't they going a bit fast?" Catie asked.

"Not really," Samantha said. "If they miss, they land on their butts, and that's armored. They've only over-rotated twice."

"What else have they done?"

"They tried walking, got really frustrated with that. Then they played catch for a while. After that, they decided they could fly around in circles using their safety as a pivot. Liz had to move one of their anchors so they wouldn't hit each other. Anyway, that got boring. This takes more skill and is keeping them occupied."

One of the twins saw Catie and didn't push off when she hit the Lynx. She let her bounce carry her back to the asteroid while she reeled in her anchor line. "Hey, Catie, what do you think?"

"I think you two are naturals," Catie said. "Those astronauts on the space station don't have a thing over you two."

The twins giggled at Catie as one reeled the other back in.

"Are we done?" Liz asked.

"Just need to have ADI run the system check," Catie said.

"Running," ADI said.

## Day 9 – Board meeting – June 10th

"Our first interplanetary meeting," Marc said as they all sat down for the board meeting. "Catie, Samantha, and Liz are on the Lynx and will be attending remotely. First, I'd like to congratulate our astronauts on their progress, both in accomplishing their mission and making history. We'll get an update in a moment. Blake, where are we?"

"We've finished quad three, and quad four is ready to have infrastructure installed. We'll be putting the plumbing in tomorrow," Blake said. "Our airstrip on the east end is finished. I'll be finishing quad one of section two as soon as I can so we can make it longer."

"Manufacturing capacity here on Delphi City?" Marc asked.

"We have maxed out the space we set aside for manufacturing on section one, but that includes the facilities where we'll start manufacturing the Oryxes. The first one should be off the line next week," Blake announced. "It'll probably be done before you get back, Catie."

"That's good, but I would like to be there for the testing," Catie said.

"We'll have to see how the timing goes. Our wind tunnel is up," Blake said. "That's a huge amount of space, but it sure is nice to see those Lynxes fly in the tunnel before we have to send them out with a pilot."

"How is our school coming?" Marc asked.

"It will be ready this week, just need teachers," Blake said.

"They're coming," Samantha said. "You should have some already. They're actually the easiest to recruit. They love the idea of living in the tropics, a small community, and decent pay. Most are married, and fifty percent of the spouses are teachers, the rest are good candidates for Kal's labor force. But we're only talking about twenty teachers total for now."

"Hey, I'll take what I can get," Kal said. "Now if fifty percent are married to another teacher, then one-third of them are not married to another teacher. So, I get seven or so."

"Hey, who said he was stupid," Liz joked. "He can do math in his head."

Kal gave Liz a salute, or at least some people might think of it that way.

"Liz, since you're out, I've gotten Dr. Zelbar started on the design of the superconductor matrices we want," Marc said. "He's excited about it, said to say hello. He's also decided that he has to have a microgravity environment to make transparent polysteel. I've dissuaded him from asking NASA for time in ISS II, at least for now. Fred, how about a production update."

"Cars are selling as fast as we make them. Johansson is asking for permission to start building the bigger model," Fred said.

"Sam, do we have what we need from Honda?"

"Yes, I had ADI and Marcie take care of it yesterday. We're good," Sam replied.

"Then that's a green light, Fred," Marc said.

"Good," Fred said. "Battery production has seen a six-fold increase since our first month. We're now just managing to stay ahead of demand, but of course the new car model will change that, much less what's going to happen now that Tata has started manufacturing trucks."

"They've started building trucks already?" Samantha asked with surprise.

"Those guys are aggressive; they must have been working around the clock to get ready this fast. We're ramping up fuel cells as fast as we can. The trucks will really define the demand for them."

"Okay, Kal, anything on security?"

"We're doing good. Things are staying nice and quiet. The teams are gelling well. It's lots of fun; you're missing out, Liz."

"I think I'll live," Liz said. "But I'll jump right in when we get back."

"One last update before we have Catie give us her update on the mission," Marc said. "Dr. Metra has developed a process for manufacturing the Alzheimer's treatment. It produces the serum in a sealed tube that you insert into a syringe. If the nanites are exposed to air, or if they are not injected into a human body within thirty minutes, they fuse to the surface of the tube or to each other if they're not in the tube. I think we can create a dispenser that will manufacture them on-demand so we can have them at remote sites. The dispenser will have failsafes and booby traps, so if any tampering is detected, the whole thing fuses into a useless blob."

"That's great, Daddy. When do you think it will be ready?" Catie asked.

"We have all the parts, so two months," Marc answered.

"Thank you for working on this so hard," Samantha said. "I'll be ready to work out how to set the clinic up when I get back."

"I was happy to do it. We all have friends and family impacted by it, and coming up with a cure is going to make everybody feel better about life. Now, for the pièce de résistance, our mission update from Catie," Marc said, making a big show of handing off the meeting to her.

"We just sent the first asteroid toward Earth, it's the ice one," Catie said. "We're looking for a good iron one as we speak. We've learned a couple of lessons. One, vocabulary: You'll see the vocabulary we've included in the mission notes. It's critical; it's easy to make a mistake. Second, training: you want to do training in a safe environment. Nobody can explain how microgravity feels. It's nothing like swimming since you don't get the same inertial effect. Water training doesn't mean anything when you try to move about with nothing to slow you down once you start moving. The twins are adapting the fastest, they're actually putting the rest of us to shame. I'm not sure we'll be able to catch up to them no matter how much training and experience we get."

"That's a good point," Marc said. "We'll want to be sure and add some form of training before we expect our work crews to manage in space. We'll talk about that at the next meeting. Okay, we'll call it for the day."

"By the way, we hired your guy, Catie," Marc said.

"He's not my guy. Liz is handling the scientists," Catie said. "I just found him; I didn't adopt him."

Marc laughed. "Okay, I'll cancel the introductions. Have fun out there."

# Day 11

Music woke Catie up, "What's going on?" she asked as she looked about her.

"Good morning, Sweetie," Marc said.

As Catie synced her comm, she saw that everyone was in the boardroom, everyone on Earth that is. Everyone in the Lynx was stirring awake; apparently, the music had been blasted into everyone's comms.

"Why are you waking us up?" Catie asked.

"Yes, why?" demanded Samantha.

"ADI said you would be getting up from your nap about now," Marc said in his defense.

"Maybe, but we would have been waking up to our own rhythms, not to the theme of 'Close Encounters of a Third Kind'," Samantha said.

"Well, I guess the date would only resonate with Blake and me, but this is the one-year anniversary of our discovering the Sakira," Marc said. "In fact, according to ADI, it was one year ago at this exact moment in time that I was made the captain."

"And because of that, you wanted to surprise us," Samantha said.

"Surprise seemed to be appropriate for the occasion," Marc said.

"Okay, then I'm giving everyone the rest of the day off," Catie announced. "Especially after that exciting awakening."

"Yeah," the twins called out. "Can we play on the asteroid then?"

"Sure, we'll set up some playtime," Catie answered.

"Playtime?" Marc asked.

"They like to play in microgravity," Catie said. "We tie them on with a long lifeline, but they jet around and do stunts. They're really quite good."

"As long as they're safe," Marc said. "Dr. Sharmila sends me a message every day to remind me to tell you to be careful."

"We're being careful," Catie said. "We just have two more asteroids to finish up."

"So, what else do you have planned for this celebration?" Samantha asked.

"We were just going to have a toast," Blake said.

Liz rolled her eyes, "You woke us up from our nap to have a toast," she said. "We're not set up to have a toast up here."

"Just like men to do such a poor job planning a celebration," Samantha said. "Have your toast, and we'll see you when we get back. ADI turn those clowns off."

ADI cut the comm from Earth, "I assume you meant the captain and the others on Earth, Cer Sam," ADI said.

"You've got it right," Samantha said. "Now who wants to help me make a cake?"

# Day 13

The only new thing they encountered on the other two asteroids was that it was much harder to drive in the anchors, so Natalia had to take over that chore. It added a day to their efforts on each asteroid, but they were pleased with the results. ADI was flying all three asteroids toward their assigned orbits, and everyone was relaxing before they started back home.

"Hey, Daddy," Catie said as she finished her report.

Marc looked at her a bit askance, "What do you want?"

"Why do you think I want something?" Catie asked innocently.

"Well, the shift from Captain to Daddy was a hint."

"Okay; well, we're done here, and as we head back home, we go right by Mars," Catie said. "It would be a shame not to stop by. We could fix Spirit and Opportunity while we're there."

"Oh, give me a break," Blake groaned. "You're just a glory hound," he teased.

"Well, it is right next door," Catie said.

"How would you land the Lynx without an atmosphere?"

"We'll use the plasma cannon as the third engine," Catie said. "It just has to control the pitch."

"I assume you've run simulations with ADI," Marc said.

"Of course."

"How much time will this add to the mission?" Marc asked.

"Just a day and a half," Catie said. "And we have plenty of fuel, food, water, and air."

"Blake, what do you think?" Marc asked.

"I think she's going to be impossible to live with when she gets back," Blake said. "So delaying that by a day or two will be nice."

"You don't think letting her go to Mars will give her a swelled head?" Marc asked.

"I think it's already too late for that," Blake said.

"Come on you two," Catie said.

"Okay, don't be too obvious with the rovers," Marc said.

"I won't," Catie said. "I might just fix Opportunity. Spirit has been out for a long time."

"Okay," Marc said as he shook his head.

"You've created a monster," Blake moaned. Then he added. "Take plenty of pictures."

---

"We will, Uncle Blake."

Catie hung up and turned to the rest of the crew. They were all standing there waiting. Liz had one twin with her hand over her mouth, and Samantha had the other. They released them together and then immediately covered their ears as both twins started squealing with excitement. "We're going to Mars; we're going to Mars!"

"I knew he'd say yes," Samantha said as she gave Catie a hug.

"I did too, but I was still worried," Catie said. "You'll probably catch it from him tonight."

"Oh, I can handle your father," Samantha winked at Catie.

"Yeah, but you have to do it over a video link, with no privacy."

Samantha laughed, "Don't you worry, I have my ways."

"ADI set course for Mars."

"Yes, Captain."

# Day 15

Catie and Liz manned the cockpit while everyone else was glued to their couches as the Lynx approached the surface of Mars. Catie had them drop down vertically most of the way. Now that they were within fifty meters, she used the Lynx's thrusters to push it to an angle and the plasma cannon to keep the angle close to about forty-five degrees. This would let the Lynx settle down horizontally on her landing gear once Catie backed off the plasma cannon. She concentrated on the three-D image of the Lynx that ADI projected into her HUD as she guided the craft down.

"Touchdown in ten," she announced as she eased off the plasma cannon letting the nose drop down. The rear landing gear touched down, and she cut the engines and let the plasma cannon ease the nose down the rest of the way. She'd been burning hydrogen and oxygen for the last five kilometers to avoid causing too much disturbance to the Mars surface by the ejection of oxygen-sixteen atoms and water molecules at 0.1C. The nose settled down and Catie relaxed, "Touch down."

"We sure used a lot of water during the landing," Liz said.

"Yeah, but we won't need to use as much taking off," Catie said. "Once we get a little elevation, I'll be able to angle it so we're not hitting the surface, and really gun the engines."

"Good. So, let's head back and make our great step for womankind," Liz said.

"Is everybody ready?" Catie asked as she entered the main cabin behind Liz.

"Yes!" yelled the twins.

"Okay, into the cargo bay."

Everyone cycled through the cargo bay one by one. Once they were all in, Catie had ADI open the cargo door. ADI had already recovered all the air from the bay as soon as they had landed.

"After you, Captain," Natalia motioned for Catie to make the first step onto the Mars surface.

"No, I think this time, the twins should take the first step."

"Yeah!"

Everyone lined up at the edge of the door while the twins, hugging each other around the waist, stepped out onto the wing, then moved forward a few feet and stepped off. They dropped smoothly to the Mars surface. Their two inside feet touched together, then they took a big step to absorb their momentum, hopped a couple of times to turn themselves around, and waved.

"How did they pull that off?" Natalia asked. "Their feet touched at exactly the same time."

"They clipped their legs together," Samantha explained while pointing to the small clip holding the twins' two inside legs together. "They were always going to land together; they just didn't know they'd be going first."

"That is so cool," Natalia said. "Last one down is a rotten egg." She laughed as she jumped down.

Catie let Samantha beat her to the surface. "Now, what was that thing about rotten eggs?" she asked as she turned toward Natalia.

"Sorry, Captain," Natalia laughed. "It just slipped out."

---

"Okay, Liz and I are going over there to see if we can find the Opportunity and fix it," Catie said. "Nattie is going to collect some rock samples. You two and Samantha stay close to the Lynx until we get back. We have to get out of here in a little over an hour before the Mars Odyssey can see us."

"Okay," the twins giggled.

An hour later, Catie and Liz came back over the hill, "Is everybody ready to go home?"

"I sure am," Samantha said. "I want to take a long bubble bath, sleep in a huge bed all by myself, then go out and have a nice dinner."

"All by yourself?" Liz scoffed.

"Just the first night," Samantha said. "Or the first day, depending on when we land."

"I'm totally with you on that," Natalia said. "I wish I could manage the bubble bath."

"You can use mine," Catie said. "I'll use Daddy's."

"You're on."

"Did you get enough samples?"

"I got a bunch, whatever ADI told me to pick up," Natalia said. "Did you fix the rover?"

"Yeah. Solar panels were busted up. We set it up with a new battery pack and new solar panels. It should last a few years."

"When does it come back online?"

"It'll take a couple of hours to charge the battery pack, then it should be online."

"Won't NASA be surprised?"

"I can't wait to see what they say," Catie said. "Everybody, strap in. We're going to do about three Gs when we get this baby into the air, so, hang on."

Catie fired the plasma cannon so that it lifted the Lynx's nose up. When she had a forty-five-degree pitch, she fired off the main engines, and the Lynx leapt into the sky. After two minutes, she dialed the exhaust velocity up from five thousand meters-per-second to 0.5C. She pushed the throttle forward until the Lynx was accelerating at three Gs. In just another fifteen minutes, they had left Mars behind and were streaking for home. She backed off of the acceleration after another ten minutes and announced that she would be bringing their acceleration to zero in an hour so they could reconfigure the cabin again.

"Oh, so that's what they were doing," Samantha said as she watched the recording of their ascent.

"What?"

"They made a giant smiley face," Samantha laughed.

The twins giggled loudly.

"Will that be a problem?" Samantha asked.

"It's going to be hilarious if one of the satellites picks it up," Catie said. "I wonder what they'll say."

"Probably nothing," Liz said.

"You girls are very bad," Catie scolded, barely able to contain her own giggles.

"We were practicing our circles and arcs," the twins giggled.

"Very bad."

## Day 19

"Doesn't it look beautiful," Samantha said. Everyone was watching the Earth grow in the monitor as they approached.

"Yes, it does," Natalia said. "When will we land?"

"We've got another hour of descent before we hit thirty thousand kilometers and can start flying. Then we're just thirty minutes from home."

Catie and ADI had set up their descent so that the angle and velocity had them entering the atmosphere with their jet plume angled just above the horizon. They settled down to thirty thousand kilometers, and Catie switched the engines back to atmospheric as she flipped the Lynx so it was now heading in the direction of their descent. The wings bit into the atmosphere, creating lift, and Catie turned the nose of the Lynx toward Delphi City.

"Delphi City, Lynx One on approach," Catie announced.

"Lynx One, you have a clear sky, approach from the west, runway is clear."

"Lynx One, changing to heading . . . now at fifteen thousand meters."

"Roger, Lynx One. You are clear to land."

The Lynx approached the runway and set down one hundred meters past the edge, Catie cut the engines and braked the Lynx to a stop after eight hundred meters. She turned off the runway and headed to the hangar. As the Lynx entered the hangar, she could see a small welcoming committee, with her father at the front. She taxied to a stop, shut down the power, and exited the cockpit behind Liz. Natalia was already getting the hatch open when she entered the main cabin.

"Welcome home!" rang through the cabin as the hatch opened. Catie saw her father, Uncle Blake, Kal, Dr. Sharmila, and the ground crew, all waiting to greet them. She bounded down the ramp and ran into her father's arms.

"Welcome home, Sweetie," Marc said. "You did good!"

"Hey, Ms. fancy pants," Blake said, greeting his niece.

Catie kissed her father and then pushed him toward Samantha. She turned to her Uncle Blake and hugged him.

"I'm so glad to be back!" Catie really squeezed her uncle. She looked over to where the twins were hugging their mother; they were talking a mile a minute, and she was sure that Dr. Sharmila couldn't understand a word they were saying. Liz and Natalia were getting hugs from Kal, while the ground crew stood around looking embarrassed.

"Let's take this party inside and let these people get to work," Marc said as he turned, and holding Samantha's hand, led them all to the corner of the hangar and the office there.

As Catie and Blake followed, Blake leaned over to Catie and whispered, "A smiley face, really."

"I had nothing to do with that," Catie said.

"You were in charge," Blake said. "You'll forever be known as the mission commander who left a smiley face on Mars."

"I think it's funny," Catie said.

"It's hilarious," Blake said. "There's still no mention of it, although there is quite a buzz about Opportunity coming back online. Kids, the world over, are celebrating the fact that Opportunity is now communicating again. They're loving the new mission reports."

"Good. We accomplished that at least."

# 10    Growing Pains

Dr. Sharmila was doing clinic duty. With all the new workers and their families living in Delphi City, they needed to run a regular clinic to deal with the medical issues that come up in any community. She actually liked clinic duty; it gave her a chance to interact with other members of the community and to help out. Doing limb restorations was exciting, but she really spent most of her time in surgery and not so much with the patient.

She was leaving the treatment room, a simple cut that she was able to treat by cleaning it and applying a bandage with a discreet shot of nanites to heal the wound. She couldn't wait until they had cleared a few nurses to handle the nanites. That would allow them to increase their efficiency and provide the miracle cure to more patients. The nurse could have dealt with this case without needing a doctor if the nurse had been cleared to know about nanites.

Before she could enter the next treatment room, the head nurse pulled her aside. "Dr. Sharmila, I need you to see the patient in treatment room four now."

"What's the problem?"

"The woman has been beaten; she won't talk to anyone."

Dr. Sharmila hurried to the room, pausing at the outside to calm herself, and then entered the room quietly. "Hello, I'm Dr. Sharmila." The woman in the room had a black eye and was holding her left arm close to her body.

"I know, you did my exam when I came here," the woman said.

"I see that on your chart, Dareen. I'm sorry, but I don't remember you. Can you tell me what happened?"

"I didn't get pregnant," Dareen said.

"Dareen, you can't get pregnant, don't you remember? It says here that you opted for the birth control option. If you want to get pregnant, you have to come back for us to reset it."

"I don't want to get pregnant. I am studying to become a nurse."

"I'm happy to hear that. We really need more nurses," Dr. Sharmila said. "So, can you explain what happened again?"

"My husband beat me because I didn't get pregnant."

"Does he know about the birth control?"

"No, he wouldn't have allowed it."

"It's not his choice."

"He thinks everything is his choice."

"Let's get back to that," Dr. Sharmila said. "First, we need to get you fixed up. What are your injuries?"

"My eye, my arm hurts, and my ribs hurt."

"Anything else?"

"My pride."

"Let's fix the easy things first, then we'll get back to that one."

Dr. Sharmila first did a scan of the woman's head to make sure that there wasn't a fracture around the orbital socket or any brain swelling. Thankfully it looked like it was only a black eye, which could be easily treated.

Dr. Sharmila then had the woman remove her top so she could examine her ribs. She had severe bruises on the left side; it was obvious she had been kicked. Dr. Sharmila brought over the scanner and took a reading. She saw that Dareen had three cracked ribs. Dr. Sharmila then took a scan of her arm; Dareen had a dislocated elbow and tearing along the ligaments. Dr. Sharmila gave Dareen a shot near the elbow. It would isolate the pain receptors for the next twenty minutes. She also gave her a shot near her ribs to stanch that pain as well. She took swabs from each of the damaged areas and high-res photos of them as well.

"Okay, first, I'm going to fix your arm. You shouldn't feel any pain, but it's going to be uncomfortable."

Dareen just nodded.

Dr. Sharmila carefully manipulated Dareen's arm while watching the scan. She got the bones realigned, and after verifying that they were actually in the right place, she gave Dareen a shot that would bring the swelling down and eliminate the inflammation in the area.

The nurse had already gotten a blood sample and put it in the analyzer. Dr. Sharmila smiled, the nurse didn't know that the analyzer would not only analyze the blood for them, but it would extract stem cells, convert them to pluripotent stem cells so they would work on any tissue in Dareen's body and duplicate it.

She injected the arm with nanites that would dissolve the damaged cells in the ligaments. After they had a chance to do their job, she injected the arm with another set of nanites that would fill in the voids with neutral ligament tissue. This would allow the stem cells to come in later and convert the tissue to match Dareen's DNA.

Dr. Sharmila then moved to the ribs. She injected bone-grafting material that would heal the cracks. In two days, it would be impossible to tell that the ribs had ever been cracked. She added a booster shot that would ensure that all the swelling and any infection were taken care of.

A couple of injections took care of the eye. By tomorrow morning, Dareen would be back to her usual self, at least physically. Now she injected Dareen with a large supply of her pluripotent stem cells so that they would go in and finish up the repairs.

"Are there any other physical problems we need to deal with?"

"No," Dareen whispered.

"Okay, now let's talk about what we need to do next. You do know that what your husband did is a crime."

Dareen nodded her head.

"Has this happened before?"

"Not like this."

"What does that mean?" Dr. Sharmila asked.

"He's never beaten me before."

"But he has hit you."

Dareen nodded her head.

"Why?"

Dareen shrugged, "If I don't do something correctly, he slaps me."

"That is not acceptable."

"I know that is what your law says, but he says it is his duty to discipline me."

Dr. Sharmila shook her head and sighed. "He is your husband, not your owner. If he is not happy with you, he can talk to you about it, discuss it to help both of you reach an acceptable agreement on expectations. Maybe he expects too much, or maybe you don't understand how to do something. Hitting you is never an acceptable answer."

"What can I do?"

"You can leave him if you want," Dr. Sharmila said.

"But I can't afford to live, I don't make any money."

"That is not a problem. We can get you into a different apartment. As long as you're studying, you will be given an allowance; you'll be asked to help out here in the clinic, which will be good for your education."

"How can that be, who will pay for it?" Dareen was shocked at the thought that she would be taken care of until she finished her degree.

"You will."

"But how? I told you that I don't have any money," Dareen said, growing skeptical and confused. "Do you mean it's a loan?"

"No, I mean that once you finish your education, you'll work as a nurse. You'll pay taxes that will fund the government; you'll help the community, and that will pay back your education costs. If the government doesn't help you get an education, you won't be able to get a job and pay taxes. In the long run, the government comes out ahead."

Dareen nodded her head slowly. "I think I understand, but what about my husband?"

"Do you want to try to work things out with him, or are you ready to just leave him?"

"He has hit me for the last time," Dareen said. "I don't want to see him again."

"Okay," Dr. Sharmila said. "I'll have a woman come and take you to an apartment where you can rest. She'll ask you for a list of the things in your apartment that are yours and that you want. Can you do that?"

"Of course," Dareen said.

Dr. Sharmila pinged Marc and Kal and asked when they could come over and discuss a situation.

"Hello, Cers," Dr. Sharmila said as Kal and Marc joined her in her office.

"Good day. How can we help you?" Marc asked.

"I had a patient this morning who had been beaten by her husband."

"Crap," Kal said. "Well, we knew sooner or later we'd start having issues more serious than someone getting drunk and stumbling down the sidewalk."

"How did you handle it?" Marc asked.

"I took care of her injuries," Dr. Sharmila said. "Then I asked her if she wanted to try to work things out with her husband. She said she doesn't."

"Okay, where is she?" Kal asked.

"I had Alia, from Kal's team, take her to a new apartment to rest. She's bought her a change of clothes and given her a debit card so she can eat. She's a nursing student, so I've just put her in our training program."

"That's good," Kal said. "Do you think she'll change her mind?"

"I don't think so, but I would suggest we check back with her tomorrow," Dr. Sharmila said. "What should we do about the husband?"

"I'm going to arrest his ass," Kal said. "If she wants to try to work things out with him, we'll consider letting him stay. Otherwise, we'll have a hearing, and if it comes out that what she says is true, he can either be deported or serve his time. What's his name?"

"Her records show that her husband is Najib Maloof," Dr. Sharmila read from the file; she also gave Kal the address.

"I'll pick him up," Kal said as he looked to Marc for confirmation.

Marc nodded his head. "Let me know when you have him."

Marc entered the security office. "Where is he?"

"He's in interview room one," Kal said.

"What's he saying?"

"That it's his right," Kal said. "I just want to dump him off the edge of the city and see if he can swim fifteen miles to Rarotonga."

"That doesn't sound like standard police procedure," Marc quipped.

"I'm just saying what I feel like doing," Kal laughed. "How do you want to proceed?"

"Let's see how he wants to proceed."

Kal led Marc to interview room one, and they both entered. Najib Maloof was seated at the table. His left hand was handcuffed to the table. Despite that, he was leaning back in his seat, looking somewhat smug.

"Mr. Maloof, this is Marc McCormack, he's the CEO of MacKenzie Discoveries and the appointed Mayor of Manuae and Delphi City."

"What right do you have to hold me?" Mr. Maloof demanded.

"You've broken the law," Marc said.

"What law?"

"You are suspected of beating your wife," Marc said.

"What concern is it of yours what I do with my wife!"

"She is protected by our laws, and our laws prohibit the assault on any person; you were informed of this law and others when you came here."

"She's not a person, she's my wife," Maloof yelled. "I demand that you release me and return her to me. The Koran demands that I discipline her."

"She is your wife, not your property," Marc said. "That was also explained to you. I don't care how you interpret or misinterpret the Koran; you were told that individual rights superseded any religious custom or law. Did you not understand that when you came here?"

"I do not care about your laws . . ."

"Well, that is a problem," Marc interrupted. "You now need to decide if you wish to be prosecuted under our laws and if found guilty, punished under our laws, or if you would prefer to leave and go back to the refugee camp where you came from."

"You cannot do this to me. You cannot take the word of a woman over mine!"

"Yes, we can. We have quite a bit of evidence that you did, in fact, assault your wife. Your DNA was found in the injured area around her eye, and your fingerprints were found on the bruising on her arm where it was twisted until the elbow dislocated."

"Then I will take my wife and leave," Maloof said.

"You will leave," Marc said. "Your wife has decided to stay."

"She cannot stay!"

"She can. Under our law, she may divorce you by filing in the courts, and based on Islamic law, she can divorce you by Khul'. I believe she will be doing both. We have someone removing her things from your apartment now. In two hours, you'll be allowed to go and claim anything there that is yours. If you still wish to leave, you'll be flown back to Greece tomorrow."

"You cannot do this."

"Do you wish to stay and be subject to our laws?" Marc asked.

"No, I cannot live in a place where a woman is placed above a man."

"Then we'll send you back," Marc said with disgust. He stood up and walked out of the room with Kal.

"Let's make sure we add something in the school curriculum to clearly define the rights in a marriage," Marc said. "Also, let's beef up that part in the introduction training."

"Got it," Kal said.

# 11 Board Meeting – June 24th

"I call this meeting to order," Marc said. "Blake, you're up first."

"The first Oryx should be ready for a test flight on Friday. Since I was the acting administrator and had to deal with all the headaches, I think I should get to be the test pilot," Blake said. He gave Catie a look to see if she was going to object.

Catie gritted her teeth, she wanted to argue, but she didn't want to look like a baby in front of her friends. And she knew her Uncle Blake was right. "Okay," Catie sighed, "but I get to be your copilot."

"That was easy," Blake said under his breath. "If things go well, we'll start lifting material for your space station next week."

"It's our space station," Marc said. "What about the other two Oryxes?"

"The second will be ready in two weeks, the third, two weeks after that. We'll have to wait for superconductor matrices before we can build any more of them."

"Why can't you build them and put the matrices in later?" Samantha asked.

"The matrices have to be integrated into the polysteel, so we have to start with them," Blake explained. "Now for the city construction, quad four is mostly done, we'll start adding buildings now. I'm going to build quad one of section two first, so we can lengthen the runway. Then we'll add quad four, so we can expand along our northern edge. Catie has convinced me to add quad one of section three and quads one and two of section four to maximize our contiguous space so she can start her big park."

"I like the idea of a big park," Samantha said. "It will help attract higher-end talent."

"Yes, but getting the Lynx approved will be a much bigger attraction. Fast to Paris, remember?" Marc said.

"I'm working on it; I think we have them convinced to approve it with an inspection of each plane. They really like the idea of a regular shuttle service between major airports and Auckland."

"That requires that the other countries reciprocate."

"Of course, but they will have the same motivation. If we agree to provide a Lynx to carry passengers between the various major airports, then they'll see the potential to really boost their high-end tourism."

"Greed is such a great motivator," Blake said.

"Works for me," Marc said. "How about our airport?"

"Barring any unforeseen difficulties, we should be starting it next week."

"Great. Sam, how are you doing on the clinics?"

"Liz has figured out the dispenser design so nobody will be able to discover the nanites by stealing the serum. Now all we need to do is decide where to open the clinics," Samantha said. "My recommendation is Tijuana and the Bahamas for North and South America; Bosnia and Morocco for Europe and North Africa; Bangladesh for most of Asia; we'll handle clients from Southeast Asia and the South Pacific here or on Rarotonga."

"Where should we start?"

"Rarotonga and Tijuana," Samantha said. "Rarotonga since it's the easiest, Tijuana since it addresses the most lucrative market."

"Okay, what do you need?"

"We need a doctor to manage the clinic in Tijuana and a pricing plan."

"I assume you can find a doctor," Marc said. "As for the pricing plan, why don't we leave the 'discreet' price at one million dollars, no public record of the treatment, and the treatment here in Delphi City. Then five hundred thousand for the others. As demand falls off, bring the price down. Fifty percent of the patients pay based on their ability to pay. You'll have to figure out how to manage the list, but referrals from people who work for us should come first."

"I can work with that. What about the press conference?"

"Oh, I'm sure someone besides me can handle that," Marc said.

"I don't see how. We can't have Dr. Metra hold it; Dr. Sharmila really doesn't have much to do with the treatment," Samantha said. "Like it or not, you're the face of MacKenzie Discoveries."

"Okay, but we hold it here," Marc said.

"Oh, the press will love that."

"What have I done to deserve all this," Marc said, shaking his head. "Fred, manufacturing?"

"Tata is pumping out trucks as fast as we can get fuel cells and batteries to them," Fred said. "They have been adhering to our requirement that they produce the trucks in lower-income countries. We're getting lots of pressure to license the technology to other manufacturers, both from the manufacturers and from the governments."

"No surprise there. I think we sit tight on that for now," Marc said. "I want to see what concessions we can get if we license it more widely, so letting the pressure build up will be good."

"Okay, you're the boss," Fred said. "The car plant in Morocco is coming along nicely. I think they'll start producing cars in four weeks."

"Great. Kal, how's our labor situation coming?"

"We have a host of issues to deal with as we bring in more refugees. How many more do you think we'll need?"

"I think we should try to reach the ten thousand that Sam got the government to agree to. After that, we should focus on normal immigration and try to grow systemically."

"Okay, we're a little over halfway there. We do need to make changes. I'm sure everyone has heard about the problem Dr. Sharmila reported," Kal said. "We've deported the husband, but it brings up the fact that we need to have a regular police force. Our guys are good for security, but we need some people who are better trained to deal with the public and situations like this. One of my guys' first inclination would be to haul the jerk to the edge of the city and kick him off."

"As I recall, that was your first inclination," Marc said.

"Exactly my point. We should come up with a real police chief, and train people to handle things like that. We've got teenagers coming, so we'll have some petty theft, public nuisance things that usually come with them. Bar fights are happening now. My guys handle them okay, but sometimes it's hard to tell who started what after my guys go in and slap everyone around. Both sides of the fight generally team up and square off against them."

"I agree, but how do we find the right person or team, any thoughts?" Marc asked.

"It'd be great to get a small-town police chief, but they're not likely to want to move halfway across the world, or even the eighteen hundred miles from Auckland. We can use money, but then how long would they stay?" Liz said.

"We could train one of our guys, but I'm not sure they could dial it back enough," Kal said.

"What about a few of the women we have here already? The women are actually already running the place anyway," Liz said. "We could send them to New Zealand to be trained. The Kiwis use the British model of unarmed Bobbies, which would fit in nicely around here. We could select a few, send them to be trained, and then groom one of them to take the chief position. They would already be familiar with the problems in our refugee community."

"Kal, could you do that?" Marc asked.

"I can try. I'll ask Dr. Sharmila and Meg who the leaders in the community are; then I'll get recommendations from them on who we should train."

"Who's Meg?" Catie asked.

"Margaret Hannaford," Kal said. "She prefers Meg."

"Sounds like you have a plan," Marc said. "Liz, do you have anything?"

"Nothing of note. Our scientists are having a great time; they're driving me crazy, but I'm managing."

"Okay, then next up is our space station. Liz and I have finalized the design, and we're ready to start once we have the lift capacity to get our material up there."

"How are you going to go about building it?" Catie asked.

"We'll extrude the hub's shell, as suggested," Marc said. "We'll extrude the first shell, then when we do the second, we'll just let it travel into the first as it is extruded. Then we'll add the magnetic bearing between the inner shell and the cap on the outer shell. That will allow the outer shell to rotate independently of the hub's inner shell. Based on simulations, we'll need to add a couple of arms to the axis of the inner hub and attach thrusters to stop it when it picks up rotational energy from the outer hub. We'll extend the inner shell up through the magnetic bearing so we can attach the arms. Just the friction from the air in the space between the two shells eventually transmits energy to the inner hub. Also, as we move different masses around inside the hubs and anchor them to the shells, there can be changes where we'll need independent adjustments between the two shells. We'll have a big cargo door at the bottom so we will be able to take something the size of an Oryx through. As you know, we'll eventually be manufacturing all of our jets up there."

"We'll put crew quarters along the hull of the outer wall. If we spin the hub up to three revs per minute, it will give them about four tenths-G so they won't go completely nuts trying to live in microgravity," Marc continued. "We might have to adjust that down once we see what it feels like."

"What will you do with that space after the crew moves into the rings?" Blake asked.

"We'll convert it to low-G labs and manufacturing space once we have the first ring in place. The inner shell will support our microgravity labs and manufacturing facilities. We'll move the manufacturing of the superconductor matrices from the Oryxes right away. Then we'll add the manufacturing of polysteel panels for the interior walls. Once we've got all that going, we'll start on commercial products."

"Which ring are you going to build first, inner or outer?" Samantha asked.

"The reality of the elevator shafts means we have to do them from inside to outside," Marc said. "So, the inner one is first. We can spin it up to one-G until we get the last two rings finished. That'll provide an adequate environment to house people as soon as possible. It'll be a year before the outer ring is done."

"We'll need to start training people, and build the forms and plasma torches first," Marc said.

Catie looked confused. "Why?"

"We have to be ready to start using the material once we get it up there."

"We should just dump it out," Catie said. "One blob for the oil, another for the iron. If we grind the iron up and put it in oil, then it'll form a nice blob and freeze. Do two lifts a day; that gives you six hours of work each lift. Once we have a place to work, then you can change to three lifts per Oryx per day."

"How do we carry the oil and have a manufacturing space?" Liz asked.

"Use the lower cargo hold," Catie said. "You won't even be able to fill that given the weight of the oil."

"Okay," Liz said. "That maximizes our lift capacity and gives us plenty of time to get the sprayer and parts built. We can carry the iron up in palletized containers. I'm not sure we want to try to pump that slurry. There's no reason to since we really can't lift that much volume of iron anyway. That will give us plenty of room to make the larger parts. We can push the pallets and containers out while the team works, then just bring the empty ones back inside.

"We'll manufacture a couple of the apartment segments to leave in orbit. We can use them to house the crew full time. Once that's up, we can shift one of the Oryxes to three lifts per day," Liz continued.

"That will cut a few months off of our schedule," Marc said. "And hopefully, we can lift enough material to finish out the hub in a couple of months. We'll also need to start buying and manufacturing what we need to mine the asteroids. We want to be ready to start consuming them by the time they're in orbit."

"Marc, that should take care of your other worry," Liz said.

"What worry?" Blake asked. Catie swallowed the same question as Blake beat her to it.

"I want enough material in place before any of the major powers down here realize what we're doing," Marc said.

"Are you worried about an embargo?" Catie asked.

"That's exactly what I'm worried about. But this way we can really step up our order of petroleum. We have the two small tankers here;

they're both full, so we've got about twenty thousand metric tons we can lift now, then we can have another tanker here in a month. That will refill our tankers for Delphi City and give us another twenty thousand metric tons we can lift. If we order a third tanker for delivery in two months, probably nobody will notice the excess orders since we've been using about thirty thousand metric tons per month for the last six months," Marc said.

"That will give us sixty thousand metric tons to lift. We should be able to finish the hub with that and any ancillary production," Liz said. "We'll try to get a few superconductor matrices made ASAP so we can expand our lift capacity."

"Speaking of lift capacity," Marc said. "How's our airport coming?"

"I knew I wouldn't get away without having to do an airport update," Blake laughed. "We've got enough columns and pontoons to do about half of it. If we just turn the Oryxes around and send them back up, we can get by with half," Blake said. "We're ready to start running the beams and decking. I think we can start putting columns in this weekend, and start landing operations on a shoestring, two weeks later."

"Can you weld the columns to the pontoons ahead of time?" Marc asked.

"Already doing that. We were running out of space, so we started to weld them together and leave them floating nearby. They're all chained together out where we want to build the airport."

"Great! So that means we'll be doing four lifts a day off of the city airstrip," Marc said.

"If you want to start lifting right away," Blake said.

"Alright, that's the plan," Marc said. "Liz, are you ready to take over the logistics?"

"Sure thing. You go and do mayor-y type things, and we'll take care of getting Delphi Station built."

"What are you going to do when they notice the station?" Samantha asked.

"I don't know," Marc said. "It depends on what they do and where we are in our schedule."

Liz caught Blake after the meeting. "You could have let her be the test pilot," she chided.

"That's what I said, but her dad and Sam said no. Marc said she needs to learn that she can't have everything go her way."

"When was this?" Liz asked.

"Last night, I had drinks with them after dinner."

"So, he is paying attention to raising her," Liz said.

"More than you can imagine."

"Good, I was wondering who was in charge in that family."

"Oh, don't worry about that," Blake said. "Marc tries to make it look like things just happen, but he has every detail planned out. He reviews everything she does with ADI."

"Oh lord, when does the man sleep?" Liz asked.

"Not much, and with all the stuff Catie picks up, it's really getting hard on him."

"Anything I can do?" Liz asked.

"Just keep being her friend. Marc says that you've made a huge difference in her," Blake said. "He's a lot more comfortable with the decisions she's making and what she's doing since you two started rooming together."

"I'm glad to hear that," Liz said. "I really like her, kind of weird since she's only thirteen."

"Yeah, thirteen going on thirty," Blake said.

"Who approved this?!" the president yelled as he threw a newspaper on the table. The headline of the business section read, "Tata introduces all-electric trucks and electric fuel-cell trucks to U.S. market."

"Mr. President, it went through a standard approval process within the department of transportation," Secretary Blackburn, the current Secretary of Transportation, said. He looked around the Cabinet meeting room hoping to find some support, but none of his fellow cabinet secretaries seemed interested in speaking up for him.

"And why wasn't I informed?"

"I wasn't even informed," Secretary Blackburn said. "It was a standard submission."

"And how are our truck manufacturers going to compete against this?"

"I would expect them to adapt, license some of the technology, roll out their own improvements," Secretary Blackburn said.

"Like the car manufacturers are planning to do," the president yelled. "I get a call every day from one of them crying about how they're going to be ruined if we don't do something to curtail those cars coming in from Mexico."

"They'll have to compete on other factors," Secretary Blackburn said.

"Sure, what factors will they compete on? The cars from Fuerza Motores are based on one of the most popular selling cars in America, so they're already competitive based on features and style. Add those damn batteries, and they're impossible to compete with. Anyone can make a nice car, but how do you compete against one that runs four times as long on a charge, and recharges five to ten times faster."

"You're right," Secretary Blackburn said, impressed that the president actually understood those details.

"So, what are you going to do about it? And what about the trucks coming in now. What are American manufacturers going to do about them? They say these trucks will cut fuel costs by over thirty percent on long-haul routes, forty percent or more on local routes."

"That could potentially alter the climate change situation," said Director Carols, the head of the EPA.

"There is no such thing as climate change!" the president yelled.

Admiral Michaels stifled a chuckle. He had been asked to attend the cabinet meeting with the secretary of defense because of his historical knowledge of the activities of MacKenzie Discoveries.

"Admiral, what do you find so funny?" the president demanded.

"Sorry sir, just stifling a sneeze," Admiral Michaels said.

"Is this design from our friends at MacKenzie?" the president demanded.

"It has to be," Admiral Michaels said. "The design is almost exactly a scaled-up version of their car. They are not openly selling their battery technology to any vehicle manufacturers except for Honda and Tesla. It was obvious that they would be introducing a truck soon."

"Apparently not obvious enough! What do you have to say for yourself?" the president turned to Bill Lassiter, the Director of the CIA.

"We didn't have any indication other than conjecture that they were planning to extend their designs to major trucking, much less any indication that they could."

Admiral Michaels tried to hide his shock at the director's statement. But apparently, he didn't do a very good job of it as the president cornered him again. "Admiral, what now?" the president demanded.

"There was a publication about an induction brake that could be applied to semi-trailers. It was in the journal of mechanical engineering. The author was one of the scientists that MacKenzie Discoveries has collected. It makes sense that they would want to maximize the number of trailers in service that have brakes that could feed into the batteries to improve the value of a diesel fuel-cell, electric-truck combo."

"I am getting tired of hearing how MacKenzie Discoveries is introducing technology that we don't have and that they won't share with us!" the president fumed. "What's the latest on that new jet of theirs?"

"We have the design of the jet engine," Director Lassiter said. "They've contracted with Rolls Royce to produce the engines for them."

"Can we get them from Rolls Royce?" the president asked.

"Unfortunately, the deal is exclusively to provide engines to MacKenzie," Director Lassiter said.

"Can't we work with Rolls Royce to have them make a few extras?"

"Not really. There is a part that MacKenzie provides. It's the coils that the exhaust is forced through; the coils superheat the exhaust from eight hundred degrees Celsius to three thousand degrees. The coils are heated to over five thousand degrees Celsius. We don't have the ability to make that material or anything similar that can withstand the temperature and the pressure."

"Do we need the coils?" the president asked.

"They're what give them the increased efficiency to reach the higher Mach speeds without having to use so much fuel," Director Lassiter said.

"Get our guys on it. Have them figure out how the coils are made," the president ordered.

# 12    Maiden Flight

Catie sat in the copilot's seat while Blake taxied the Oryx to the end of the runway. "Delphi control this is Oryx One, requesting permission for takeoff."

"Oryx One, Delphi control, skies are clear, you're cleared for takeoff."

Blake pushed the throttle forward, and the Oryx shot down the runway. The Oryx accelerated hard and took off well short of the ski jump at the end of the runway.

"Nice takeoff, Uncle Blake."

"Yes, but she's empty, we'll have to see how she does when she's full."

"Okay, so you didn't notice any issues?" Catie switched to her business mode. They were, after all, on the Oryx's maiden flight.

"No problems," Blake said. "I'm going to take her up to thirty thousand meters and see how she handles in the thin air up there."

"What about handling down here?"

"We'll check that out on the way up." Blake banked the Oryx into a circle as he had it climb. He tightened the circle up with each revolution. "Nice handling while banking left."

Blake then let the Oryx straighten out. After a few miles, he started a slow right-hand bank as he continued the climb. Again, he tightened the circle up with each revolution. "Nice handling while banking right."

"Fifteen thousand meters," Catie read off. "Engines at fifty percent, speed Mach 1.2."

"Accelerating," Blake said as he pushed the throttle forward again.

"Speed, Mach 2.4," Catie read off, "altitude twenty thousand meters, engines sixty-five percent."

"So, we're dropping enough air resistance to allow for faster speed without cranking her up too much," Blake said.

"So far," Catie said. "We still have ten thousand meters to go, and we're only at Mach 2.4."

"Well, let's fix that," Blake said as he pushed the throttle all the way forward.

"Engines at seventy-five percent," Catie said. "Speed now Mach five; approaching twenty-eight thousand meters."

"Engines are at eighty percent; speed Mach 6.4; altitude twenty-nine thousand meters."

"Engines eighty-five percent; speed Mach 6.5; altitude thirty thousand meters."

"Why won't the throttle go forward anymore?" Blake asked.

"It's designed to limit engines to eighty-five percent," Catie said. "You're climbing without a load, so we've reached max V. You can probably go a bit higher since we're not loaded, but the air thins out real fast up here."

"Okay, so we've maxed out altitude and speed at Mach 6.5 and thirty thousand meters."

"That's the design."

"If the air thins out too fast to go much higher, how are we going to reach orbit?"

"The engines are in atmospheric mode," Catie said. "They're just using the air they scoop up and superheating it to generate the thrust. If we want to go higher, we have to start spending $O_2$ and hydrogen to power them. You shift to fuel mode on that switch, and the engines' capacity goes up thirty percent."

"Do you want to try that?"

"Next time, Uncle Blake; just take us back and land us. We'll do a loaded flight tomorrow; then you can become an astronaut on Monday."

"Oh, you just love to rub that in," Blake said. "You get into space a month before I do, and you're never going to let me live it down."

"Don't forget Mars," Catie laughed.

# Second Flight

"What did you load this thing with?" Blake asked as he was pushing the throttle of the Oryx farther forward.

"Saltwater," Catie said. "ninety thousand kilos. You're not going to put us in the drink, are you?"

"Don't worry your sweet head," Blake said. "We're going to make it," he groaned as he extended the flaps. The Oryx slowly lifted off, just clearing the ski jump.

"Can this baby take that jump?" Blake asked.

"I wouldn't recommend it," Catie said. "Maintenance crew will ream you if they have to go through and inspect everything after you do."

"I'll keep that in mind. I'll also see if we can get decking on section two, quad one, right away so we can extend the runway."

"I like that," Catie said. "How is she handling now?"

"She's doing nice, not as nice as she did unloaded," Blake said, "but nobody's going to complain."

"Okay straight ascent, eighty percent power," Blake suggested.

"That's the plan."

"Read it off," Blake adjusted the throttle and pulled the nose up.

"Mach 0.5; engines at eighty-five percent; altitude at five thousand meters."

"Mach one; engines at eighty-five percent; altitude at seven thousand meters."

"Mach 2.2; engines at eighty-five percent; altitude at twelve thousand meters."

"Mach three; engines holding at eighty-five percent; altitude at twenty thousand meters."

"Mach four; engines holding at eighty-five percent; altitude at twenty-five thousand meters."

"Mach 5.8; engines holding at eighty percent; altitude at twenty-seven thousand meters."

---

"Why did the engine efficiency drop?"

"Air's too thin, you have to add fuel if you want to push harder."

"So, we're maxed out," Blake said.

"Yes. We could do a little better if we were farther north, but that's not great for orbiting, so this is it."

"You want me to switch to fuel mode?"

"No, tomorrow. We should see how we land with this load," Catie said. Although Blake was the test pilot, Catie was still the program manager for the Oryxes. "Don't ding the runway."

"In your dreams," Blake laughed.

## Third Flight

"Today, you get to become an astronaut, or I get to become a failure," Catie said.

"Hey, a little redesign doesn't signify failure," Blake said, "so, don't worry about it."

"I'm not worried," Catie said.

Blake got clearance from the tower and started his takeoff run. "Why no load this time?"

"Don't want to change too many variables at the same time," Catie said. "Tomorrow, we'll take a load up."

"Okay, let's get up there," Blake said. It only took them an hour to get up to thirty thousand meters and Mach 6.5.

"Ready to switch on the fuel to the engines?"

"I'm ready," Blake replied. "Switching modes now."

Blake flipped the switch, and the engines started receiving a mixture of hydrogen and oxygen. When mixed and ignited, the gas burned at three thousand degrees C. When it went through the coils, it was compressed and heated to forty-five hundred degrees C before it was allowed to explode out of the rear of the engines. The Oryx accelerated slowly.

"Space engines at thirty percent," Catie read off. "Speed at Mach 6.6; altitude holding at thirty thousand meters."

"How high can I go before I have to use thrusters to adjust the pitch?" Blake asked.

"You did read the preflight and specs?"

"Of course, but it's nice to have it refreshed before I do it. That is why you're here."

"Okay," Catie laughed. "We can probably use the wings for another ten thousand meters, then you'll have to go ballistic."

"Can do. Read it off."

"Speed Mach eight; space engines at forty percent; altitude thirty-three thousand meters."

"Speed Mach ten; space engines at forty-five percent; altitude forty thousand meters."

"Using thrusters," Blake said. He fired the thrusters until the Oryx was at a thirty- percent incline, then he pushed the throttle farther forward.

"Speed Mach twelve; space engines at sixty percent; altitude forty-five thousand meters."

Catie continued to read off the speed, engine power, and altitude until they were at Mach twenty and four hundred thousand meters in altitude. The engines were at seventy percent when Blake cut the power, and they slipped into orbit.

"This is the same orbital height as ISS II," Catie said. "Dad is planning to put Delphi Station in a trailing orbit on the opposite side of Earth."

"Same speed?" Blake asked.

"Has to be, the speed is defined by the orbit," Catie said. "The higher the orbit, the lower the speed you need to maintain it. If you speed up, you'll climb higher and continue to climb since gravity's effect will drop as you climb. Soon you'll just be drifting off toward Mars unless you get caught by the moon."

"Right."

Blake spent twenty minutes checking out the thrusters, then he flipped the ship and started decelerating, firing the engines in the direction they were traveling. "Twenty minutes until we hit atmosphere."

"Okay. Are you going to ride her down on her tail until we start biting?"

"That's the plan. Once we start getting a bit of air drag, I'll drop her nose into the flight direction and start letting the drag slow us down. Keep an eye on the hull temperature. If it starts to heat up, I'll take us up to where the drag falls off enough that the matrix can keep it cool."

"Okay, shouldn't be a problem, but I'll keep an eye on it," Catie said. "Speed Mach eighteen; engines at twenty percent; altitude three hundred fifty thousand meters; hull temp three hundred degrees C."

"Speed Mach fifteen; engines at twenty percent; altitude two hundred eighty thousand meters; hull temp three hundred C."

Catie kept reading off the data every thirty seconds as the Oryx descended toward the atmosphere. "Speed Mach eighteen; engines at twenty percent; altitude one hundred thousand meters; hull temp three hundred fifty C. You should be feeling some atmospheric resistance."

"Just getting it now," Blake said. "Leveling off into atmospheric flight pattern. Nose forward, wings level."

"Speed Mach sixteen; engines at twenty percent; altitude seventy thousand meters; hull temp eight hundred C."

"Speed Mach fourteen; engines at twenty percent; altitude fifty thousand meters; hull temp twelve hundred C."

"Slowing our descent," Blake announced.

"Speed Mach twelve; engines at thirty-five percent; altitude forty thousand meters; hull temp holding at twelve hundred C."

"What's our fuel status?"

"We're at sixty percent reserves," Catie announced. "Speed Mach ten; engines thirty percent; altitude thirty thousand meters; hull temp one thousand C. We should switch to atmospheric engines anytime now."

"Speed Mach 9.5; engines at ten percent; altitude twenty-eight thousand meters; hull temp eight hundred C."

"Switching to atmospheric engines," Blake said as he toggled the engine switch to cut off fuel to the engines. Now they would only use the air being caught by the air scoop in front of the engines, pressurizing it and then forcing it through the coils which superheated it to four thousand C, causing it to expand and explode out the back of the engines.

"Alright, take us home," Catie said. "Next trip, we'll drop a load of oil off in Delphi Station's orbital position."

"Hey, we didn't find any problems," Blake said. "This was almost too easy."

"That's because we found all the problems on the ground," Catie said. "We have that huge wind tunnel that we used to check out all the aerodynamics. We found a problem with the flaps there. Then the engines were tested a month ago, we redesigned the coil twice during that."

"Then, I guess all that money we spent on the wind tunnel was worth it."

"I call it good program planning."

"Good thing you had someone managing that plan while you were off gallivanting around in space."

"I only work with the best," Catie laughed.

## Fourth Flight

"We're in orbit," Blake announced. "Now, what?"

"Give her a little boost," Catie said. "We're about one hundred kilometers off of Delphi Station's orbital position."

Blake eased the throttle forward and let the Oryx accelerate for two minutes, then cut the engines again. "Thirty minutes to get into position," he announced.

"Jerry, do you copy?" Catie called to their cargo man who was strapped in back in the cargo hold, waiting to dump the load of petroleum they'd brought up.

"I copy."

"We're thirty minutes from target, do you need any help?"

"Missy, I can't imagine what help I would need to turn on a valve," Jerry replied.

"Copy that, I'll let you know when we're in position."

"Did he have any problem with the transition to microgravity?" Blake asked.

"I'm afraid to ask," Catie said. "He sounded like he usually does."

"Oh, I recognized his sunny disposition right away," Blake chuckled.

"So how is this going to work?" Blake asked. "Just pretend I don't know."

"Okay," Catie sighed. "The nozzle will extend from the belly of the Oryx, and the oil will be ejected at about one-meter-per-second. Its surface tension will coalesce it into a ball. Eventually, it will freeze as it radiates its heat out into space. When they want to use it, they'll just push the ball into place and put a pump on it. The pump will heat the oil up so it can be extracted. They'll have to move the pump around every so often as most of the ball will remain frozen."

"And you came up with all this on your own?"

"Well, ADI helped some. But this part was pretty easy."

"Approaching position," Blake said. "Flipping in ten."

Blake flipped the Oryx so that the engines were pointing in their direction of travel, then he engaged them for two minutes to bring their speed back down to the orbital speed for Delphi Station.

"Jerry, we're in position," Catie announced after checking all the instruments. "You're free to unload."

"Unloading in thirty," Jerry replied.

It took an hour to pump all the oil out of the Oryx. They sealed the ship back up and headed home. The return flight was uneventful.

"Alright, landing in five minutes," Blake announced. "First load delivered, only six hundred forty-nine more to go."

"Let's hope we can manage them without drawing too much attention," Catie said. "Who are you taking up next time for training?"

"I'm taking Fred up," Blake said. "If you take him up on your flight, he'll be qualified and ready to train the rest of the pilots, and we can go back to our day jobs."

◆ ◆ ◆

"Well, Jerry, how did you like space?" Blake asked as they deplaned. The ground crew already had a pump hooked up to the Oryx to fill it up with petroleum again.

"It wasn't too bad. That microgravity thing was nothing," Jerry said. "Just like swimming. Of course, I needed those lines to move myself around. I'm not so sure about these shipsuits we have to wear."

Jerry was a rather portly man, and the shipsuit wrapped his body tightly, causing him to look pretty much like the Pillsbury Doughboy.

"I'm sure there are others who would agree with you," Blake laughed. "But, it sure beats those heavy and bulky suits the astronauts wear."

"But then you'd look a proper astronaut, not like some cartoon character."

"There is that. You can put it in the suggestion box."

"I'll do that while I go to the bathroom," Jerry laughed.

# 13   Board Meeting – July 8th

"I call this meeting to order," Marc said.  "Catie, why don't you tell us how the test flights for the new Oryx have gone."

"As everyone knows, we completed the test flights of the first Oryx last week.  Uncle Blake and I took it through its test flights without any issues.  The second Oryx came out of ground testing on Friday.  It has completed the first three test flights and passed with flying colors.  Tomorrow, it will do an orbital delivery as its last test flight.  I don't anticipate any issues, and if all goes as expected, it will rotate into the lift schedule.  I believe Uncle Blake intends to start the twelve-hour schedule with the two of them so we can start microgravity production of the critical components we need here as well as those on Delphi Station."

"Way to steal my thunder," Blake said.

"Oh, I'm sorry, were you expecting to surprise someone with that announcement?" Catie said, completely deadpanned.

Blake laughed at her.  "No, I wasn't.  But you took care of half my update.  Now everyone will think I'm goofing off."

"We already know that," Liz said.

"Okay, back on track," Marc said.  Although he liked the banter, he needed to keep it under control, otherwise, the meetings would last for hours.  "How about the other aircraft?"

"We have produced six Lynxes," Catie continued.  "We're going to stop there until we decide how many we want for standard aviation.  I've started working with ADI on the design of the Foxes.  They're a direct adaptation of our existing Foxes but without the orbital capability.  Currently, we are planning a limited run of eight, unless the board decides the situation demands more.  I'll let Uncle Blake explain the tradeoffs."

"Thanks," Blake whispered loudly.

"We also desperately need to add to the runway length or get the airport up," Catie said.

"Why?" Marc asked.

"It's pretty short for taking off in an Oryx with a full load. Most of our new pilots are electing to use fuel to get more boost to provide extra margin. You don't want to hit the ski jump with a full load," Catie said. "They're completing their missions with less than twenty percent fuel reserves. I really would prefer that they fit the model Uncle Blake set of completing the mission with forty percent reserves."

"I'm on it," Blake said. "I'll explain in my update."

"Okay, Catie, anything else?"

"That's it for now."

"Dr. Metra," Marc nodded at her.

"Nothing major to report. But I have asked Kal to start some basic testing of the refugees before we transport them here. We had several cases of tuberculosis in the last group, and I would prefer to isolate them before they share a plane with other refugees. We'll be testing for tuberculosis, cholera, measles, hepatitis, and malaria. I'll add to the list as we come across more diseases, and as I am able to create a quick test for them."

"Are you going to reject them if they're sick?" Catie asked.

"No, but we'll treat them before we fly them here," Kal said. "We want to minimize any spread of the disease."

"I agree with that," Marc said. "Blake, you're up."

"As Catie mentioned, we have the second Oryx into test flights. The third one has just started the ground-based testing. It should be ready for its test flight this weekend.

"As she also mentioned, we'll start doing some basic production during the lift missions. Each Oryx will stay in orbit for an additional eight hours on one of their runs so we can do some basic production while we're up there. The schedules will be set so we can essentially have an eighteen-hour production window if we need one by skipping a lift with one of them. We've been doing some crew training on the flights so far, getting everyone used to operating in microgravity while the payload is being unloaded.

"Also, as Catie *mentioned*, we have to decide how much production to allocate to the Foxes since any material we put into them will not be available for the space station. But we all recognize we need to be able to defend our little area of the world.

"As for Delphi City, we've started the second section. We have quads one and four in place. Quad one will allow us to extend the runway, and we should be putting decking on it by midweek. Also, as I said before, we're completing the quads around the center of our city plan so Catie can complete her park design. We'll work on them starting this weekend. Kal tells me it will really help the community, plus we'll be able to put a small luxury hotel there and bring in some tourists and potential immigration candidates."

"It will definitely help with recruiting," Samantha said.

"I've already been convinced to sign off on it during private negotiations," Marc said, giving Catie a smile.

"Our airport is now officially under construction. We laid the pontoons for the first section last week and will be adding decking this week. We're purposely not putting any major infrastructure under the runway to both expedite getting it laid, as well as to avoid exposing it to the jarring it would receive from aircraft landing and taking off. I'm hoping we have it ready for flights in four weeks. We'll need to load them while they're on the runway since there won't be any other space available for a few more weeks. Planes will have to land in the city when they need maintenance, but we should really cut down on the traffic over here."

"That sounds great," Marc said. "I'm sure all of the pilots will love to hear both pieces of news regarding runways."

"Everything else is on schedule per the weekly reports," Blake said as he finished up his report.

"Okay, Kal, you're up."

"I met with the leaders in the community and have selected eight women to go to the police academy in Wellington: Four Arab women, three from the refugee group from Antigua, and the wife of one of our teachers. The training is sixteen weeks, they seem like a smart bunch, so I'm hopeful that there's a chief of police there."

"So, we have to wait sixteen weeks?" Samantha asked.

"The instructors at the academy have agreed to have half of them do eight weeks, then they'll come back here and work until the next class starts. They'll have to repeat the material, but it shouldn't hurt them, and the experience they pick up here will help them learn more from the material when they review it. The other four will come back after the class finishes," Kal reported.

"I like that," Marc said. "How about the rest of security?"

"Security training is going well. I've instituted the command structure I mentioned earlier, and it's really helping with performance and consistency. I've got more time for my other duties. Speaking of which, we're doing well in the resettlement efforts, our refugees are fitting in very well. All of our agriculture and maintenance positions are filled. We've got a good daycare center up. The school is ramping up; we still need another five or six teachers, but the computerized coursework is filling the gap. We need to improve our recruiting."

"Lynxes and a park," Samantha said.

"Speaking of Lynxes," Marc said, giving Samantha a look.

"Yes, I've gotten the New Zealand Aviation Ministry to certify the Lynxes; it's contingent on an inspection of each plane. I am working with them and the governments of several countries to get reciprocal certifications."

"That's great. So, we can hop over to Auckland or Wellington anytime we want now," Marc said, giving Samantha a smile.

"It will definitely improve our dining choices, as long as we have a pilot."

"Are you suggesting I need to get certified?" Marc asked.

"Daddy, I've been telling you for months that you should."

"Okay, I guess now I'm really motivated," Marc said. "Anything else, Kal?"

"We do have one issue, food. Many of our refugees are importing their food because they don't know if what we grow and produce here is halal or kosher," Kal said.

"That's right," Catie said. "I have on my list to ask Sam if she would help me meet with the rabbi and the imam about the food. Everything

I've been able to research says they should be okay with it, but it's a delicate subject. We need to explain to them our processes and give them a tour. We will need to set up a process for them to do their thing."

"We can coordinate schedules after the meeting," Samantha said. "Oh, I see you've already found a slot. That works for me."

"Catie, that's something I would like to hear in your update," Marc said.

"Why?" Catie asked. "It won't be a problem unless they say no, and we won't know that until we talk to them."

"It's important enough that you should give the board a heads up," Marc said. "Someone else might have an idea or some special knowledge that might help."

"Okay," Catie said as she processed the new expectation.

"Liz, how are our scientists doing?" Marc asked to get the focus off of Catie.

"For those of you who didn't hear the cheering or loud party in the lab building, the nuclear physicists managed to create a sustained fusion reaction last Saturday," Liz said. "They've been insufferable since. They are so happy and drunk with power that they want to start the design of an actual reactor. That new guy Catie suggested seems to have them hopping."

"That is excellent news," Marc said. "We'd really like to be able to introduce that to the world soon. Not only would it dramatically reduce carbon emissions, but it will change a lot of the economics as well. Low-cost power will help a lot of developing countries."

"It might help to reduce the tensions with the major powers as well, or at least distract them while they figure out how to handle it," Samantha said.

"I agree," Marc said. "Fred?"

"Pilot training is going well," Fred said. "We're scheduled to build the matrices we need for more Oryxes at the end of next week. We should have new Oryxes coming off the line two weeks later."

"That's really great," Marc said. "If we hold to that schedule, I think we'll be able to start station construction the first week of August."

# 14   A Favor for Fred

Fred knocked on Marc's door, "Got a minute?" he asked.

"Sure, come on in. What's up?"

"I have a favor to ask."

"Shoot."

"I have a friend, just got out of the Air Force, a good pilot."

Marc nodded, waiting for Fred to continue.

"His son was slated to go to the academy but was blinded in some high school prank. The kid was, no, is one hell of a pilot. He's qualified to fly quite a few airplanes, including the Albatross, a Czech supersonic trainer."

"And you'd like to bring them here?" Marc asked.

"Yeah, it's just the kid and his old man, wife left years ago. He retired right after the accident to be able to take care of his son."

"I'm sure we can help the son, but the father's just out of the military, you don't think that poses a risk?"

"Not if you fix his son's eyes," Fred said. "He lives and breathes for that boy. He was never a rah-rah patriot. I don't think he'll be a problem; besides, we're no threat to the US, just to some rich idiots and people currently in power there."

"I like your sentiment," Marc said. "Go get them."

"You mean, like now?"

"Now, tomorrow, whenever they're ready," Marc said. "I trust you, Fred, and we need pilots."

"Thank you."

"Not a problem," Marc said. "Happy to be able to help."

◆ ◆ ◆

Fred called his friend up that night. "Hey, Kevin, I heard about the kid, how's he doing?"

"Hi, Fred," Kevin replied. "He's doing about as well as could be expected. He's depressed, but working through it. He's seeing a counselor and we're trying to figure out his next steps."

"That's why I called. I'm down here in the Cook Islands working for MacKenzie Discoveries. We're doing some neat stuff with technology and aircraft. We could use a couple of good pilots."

"I'm afraid Jason's flying days are over. He barely sees well enough to get around. He even has trouble reading. That idiot prank really messed him up."

"That's what I heard, but we have a medical clinic down here that does some amazing things."

"Fred, I've taken him to the best doctors in America, they all say there's no hope."

"I hear you, but I want you to trust me. They can fix your son's eyes."

"Fred, I can't take a chance, getting his hopes up. If it doesn't work, it'll kill him."

"Kevin, if they can't fix his eyes, I promise I'll never fly again."

"You're that sure?"

"Positive. A friend of mine was blind in one eye and had terrible burns on the left side of his body. Now he looks better than he did before the accident, and sees better too."

"Okay, what do we have to do?"

"Commit to three years down here working for us. Then just pack a bag, and I'll come get you."

"Hey, we can fly down there ourselves," Kevin said.

"Sure you can, but I'm flying a G650 right now; I'll pick you up at Salem airport whenever you're ready and have you back here the same night."

"They'll let you take that jet just to pick us up?"

"That's what my boss said. We might wind up picking up some other passengers, but you're the priority."

"We can be ready whenever you get here," Kevin said.

---

"You good to fly us back?" Fred asked. "I'll head out now, but after seven hours, I'd need someone to fly us back."

"I'm not qualified on a G650," Kevin said.

"That's okay, I'll see if I can find a pilot around here who owes me a favor. I'll see you at McNary Field in about eight hours," Fred said as he hung up.

"Catie," Fred said after he called her up on his comm.

"What's up, Fred?"

"What are you doing for the next sixteen hours?"

"Lots of stuff," Catie replied. "What do you want me to do?"

"I've got to make a flight to Salem, Oregon, and back. Can't do that without an eight-hour break unless I have a copilot."

"Where's Susan?"

"Vacationing in Sydney," Fred said.

"But I can't fly alone," Catie said.

"Strictly saying, that's true. But over international waters, we can get away with a lot. I'll certify you flew the big leg in the middle. Unless someone gets real nosy, it will work."

"What do I get out of this?"

"A bunch of flying hours and the joy of helping out a friend."

"Too bad we can't take the Lynx," Catie said as she texted her father.

"I definitely agree with you there."

"Daddy says I can go," Catie said as she read her father's reply. "When do we leave?"

"When can you be ready?"

"Meet you at the strip in thirty minutes," Catie said.

"Catie, this is my friend, Kevin Clark, and his son, Jason," Fred said as Kevin and Jason boarded the plane.

"Hi, happy to meet you," Catie said with a yawn.

"I'm happy to meet you too. By the yawn, I'm guessing you flew most of the way here," Kevin said.

"Yeah, that way, Fred can fly back. He got six hours of sleep, or so he says."

"Well, I'll sit in the cockpit with him and make sure he stays awake," Kevin said.

"Welcome aboard, we'll get you settled in," Jennie said.

"This is our flight steward, Jennie," Fred said. "She insisted on coming along."

"Someone has to take care of these two," Jennie said. "Now come on back and sit down or we'll miss our takeoff slot."

"Bags are loaded," Natalia said as she boarded behind Kevin and Jason. "I'm going to get some sleep."

"Okay, Nattie," Catie said. "We'll try not to wake you."

"She's not very friendly," Jason said as Catie led him back to their seats. She sat them next to each other so they could talk. "Nice jet," he added as he settled into the leather seats.

"Oh, she's okay," Catie defended Natalia. "She just got off of a two-day training session, so she's really exhausted. She slept most of the way here, but she's making up for forty-eight hours without sleep."

After they took off and Jennie had served drinks, Catie turned to Jason. "Fred told me you're a pilot."

"I was a pilot," Jason said with unmistakable bitterness in his voice.

"You don't think our doctor can fix your eyes?"

"Every doctor we've seen has said there's no hope," Jason replied.

"Well, I'll tell you what, she fixed my uncle's eye, and it was glass," Catie whispered.

"Don't joke about it."

"I'm not--God's honest truth. He lost his eye in Iraq; got burned on his left side, way worse than you look. He's our second-best pilot, and the women think he's gorgeous."

"Who's your best pilot? Fred?"

"No," Catie said. "I am."

"No way."

"I beat Fred every time on the simulator," Catie said. "I even beat my Uncle Blake. Of course, he's an ace, but I still outfly him whenever we go against each other."

"I bet that pisses him off."

"Half and half," Catie said. "Half, he's proud of me, half he hates that a thirteen-year-old girl just smoked his ass."

"You're just thirteen?"

"Last November," Catie said. "How old are you?"

"I turned seventeen last month," Jason said.

"Huh," Catie said with surprise. "Fred said you were going to the Air Force Academy this year."

"You just have to be seventeen by July first of your class year."

"So, you finished high-school a year early."

"Yeah, skipped the first grade."

"Nice," Catie said. "Hey, let me set you up with your new phone and stuff. Then I'm going to need some sleep."

Catie set Jason up with a comm, had ADI duplicate his phone onto it, and then had him put the earwig in his ear.

"ADI, say hello to Jason," Catie said.

"Hello, Cer Jason," ADI said.

"Hi," Jason said. "Who's Adi?"

"She's our tech person," Catie said. "I'm going to have her show you how to use the comm and stuff while I sleep. I'm not sure how well these specs will work for you, but until you get your new eyes, they might make getting around easier. It takes about two weeks to make new eyes, so this will help you until then. Just put them on and let ADI show you how they work. ADI, Jason is blind in one eye and has lost most of his sight in the other. Can you help him adjust the specs so he can use them?"

"Of course, Cer Catie. Cer Jason, let me know when you have them on."

"Okay guys, I'm going to get some sleep."

"They're on," Jason said.

When they landed, Catie jumped out of her seat, pulling Jason behind her. "Come on, I'll take you to Dr. Metra so she can get started on your new eyes. You're staying in the same building where I am, so I'll stay and take you back when she's done."

"What about my bags?"

"Your dad or one of the crew will take your bags to your new place."

They were out of the hatch and on the tarmac, with Natalia rushing to catch up before Fred and Kevin got out of the cockpit.

Kevin watched as Jason hurried after Catie. "How did they get off the plane so fast?"

"He and Catie just rushed to the front and down the stairs as soon as I got it open," Jennie said.

"Did she help him down the stairs?"

"He didn't look like he needed help," Jennie said. "Now Natalia could have used some help. She barely woke up before she was having to rush after them."

"Would you two slow down?" Natalia hollered.

"Oh, sorry, Nattie."

"Where are we going?"

"The clinic," Catie said. "Dr. Metra needs to get a blood sample so she can make him some new eyes."

"New eyes, we should hurry then," Natalia said as she picked up her pace. "She can even fix up that face a bit. You're cute, but you'll be cuter after she fixes up those burns. Of course, you might want to think about it, I hear the women down here like a man with scars."

"That is true," Catie said. "Uncle Blake got way more action on Rarotonga than he ever did in Hawaii."

"I'm not looking for action, I just want to fly," Jason blurted out, trying to hide his embarrassment.

"Hey, an Oryx is coming in for a landing," Catie said, pulling up to a stop.

"Where?" Jason asked

"ADI, highlight the Oryx for Jason."

"Yes, Cer Catie."

"Oh, there it is.  It looks like a C17," Jason said.

"It's based on that design," Catie said.  "We just added bigger engines and supersonic speed."

"No way that thing can go supersonic."

"Yep, when you get your eyes, you'll probably be flying it," Catie said.  "The third one finishes ground testing on Friday.  You want to go up in her for the test flight?"

"Could I?"

"Sure, I'm the test pilot for it, so I can bring anyone I want.  You can sit in the copilot's seat if you want.  I'll have the copilot sit in the navigator's chair."

"Doesn't the copilot need to sit in the copilot's seat?"

"No, they're just along to read off the instruments and record results.  They can do that from the backseat," Catie said.  "I'll even let you fly her."

"I don't think that's a good idea," Jason said.

"Oh, sure it is.  I'll just have you make a few sweeps, we'll be over the middle of the ocean, nobody around for miles.  But let's get you to the doctor now."

◆ ◆ ◆

Jason sat in the copilot's seat while Catie taxied the Oryx to the end of the runway.  Liz was sitting at the navigation station.  "Delphi control this is Oryx three, requesting permission for takeoff."

"Oryx three, Delphi control, skies are clear, you're cleared for takeoff."

Catie pushed the throttle forward, and they were airborne moments later.

"Smooth takeoff," Jason said.

"Thanks, these are nice jets," Catie said. "You're going to love flying them."

Catie did some easy maneuvers as she continued to gain altitude.

"Engines running at thirty percent," Liz announced. "Your speed is Mach 0.9

"Jason, take the controls and do a few slaloms while we're gaining altitude."

"Are you sure?"

"Absolutely. Do you have your HUD providing instrumentation?"

"Yes."

"Jason, take over."

"I have the controls," Jason said, the excitement in his voice was palpable.

"You have the controls," Catie echoed back.

Jason's HUD amplified the view of the flight path and marked the targeted path for him. He just had to adjust the controls to keep the Oryx inside the green path. "This is nice."

"I'm glad you like it. Do you feel anything in the yoke that shouldn't be there?"

"No, it's rock solid."

"Okay, take her on up to twenty thousand meters."

"Climbing to twenty thousand meters," Jason called off.

"Speed Mach 1.2; engines at fifty percent; altitude fifteen thousand meters," Liz read off

"Speed, Mach 2.4," Liz continued to mark their climb, "engines sixty-five percent, altitude twenty thousand meters."

"Go ahead and crank her up," Catie said, "we want to get to thirty thousand meters."

"Are you kidding, how can this plane fly that high?"

"Special design," Catie said. "We'll give you a detailed briefing later. Now push her."

Jason pushed the throttle all the way forward.

"Speed now Mach five; engines at seventy-five percent," Liz read off. "approaching twenty-eight thousand meters."

"Speed Mach 6.4; engines at eighty percent; altitude twenty-nine thousand meters.

"Speed Mach 6.5; engines at eighty-five percent; altitude thirty thousand meters."

"We're here," Catie announced.

"Where?" Jason asked.

"The edge of space. To go any higher, we have to add fuel and go into orbit."

"You're not telling me this thing can reach space!"

"Sure, it can. Wait until your next flight, we'll make sure that one goes all the way up."

"Now I know you're pulling my leg," Jason said.

"If you don't believe me, ask your father," Catie said. "I think he's scheduled for a full flight this afternoon."

"How's our hull temperature?" Catie asked.

"We're holding steady at five C," Liz read off.

"Why is it so cold?" Jason asked.

"Reentry," Catie said. "The hull is designed to bleed off the temperature and feed the power back into the engines. We're not fighting any air resistance, so it's stabilized at five C. Just warm enough to avoid any ice buildup. When you're slowing down from Mach ten, the hull is really absorbing a lot of friction energy even up here."

"I'll talk to my dad," Jason said skeptically.

"I have control," Catie announced.

"You have control," Jason said as he released the yoke and sat back in his seat.

"Let's go home."

That night Jason texted Catie, *"Wow, you were telling the truth. Dad said he loved flying in space."*

# 15　Board Meeting – July 22nd

"The meeting will come to order," Marc said. "What's our food situation?"

"We met with the rabbi and the imam," Samantha said. "Catie explained how we grow the meat. They only asked that we move any pork products to a separate building, and have them come in once a week to inspect."

"They didn't have a problem with our growing meat?"

"Surprisingly no," Sam said. "They were very impressed with the process and said they would need to think about how that impacted their prohibitions on certain meat products."

"Very progressive," Marc said. "Good job, you two." Catie smiled at the compliment. "Anything else?"

"Yes, Australia reciprocated on the certification of the Lynx. So, Sydney is now on the dinner destination list."

"Great," Marc said. "Still working on my certification. Fred says two months."

"Nice," Samantha said.

"Blake, construction update."

"Sure. The runway here on Delphi City has been extended, we have the extra eight hundred meters, which makes all of our pilots happy. The new airport will be ready to start handling flights next week."

"Yeah!"

"About time, I'm tired of those night takeoffs and landings," Samantha said.

"Well, at least you're not having to make them," Liz said. "But I will be happy that on my nights off, I won't get awakened by an Oryx landing eight hundred meters from my bedroom."

"Kal, security?"

"Our candidates started training last week," Kal said. "Early reports are good."

"Anything else?"

"No, just the standard training stuff."

"Fred, how's production going?"

"We're finally on top of the curve for batteries and fuel cells," Fred said with obvious pride. "The first batch of matrices is done, so we started up the Oryx production again. We'll have the fourth one out by the end of the week. We're set up to deliver them one per week. Once we get to our goal of eight, we can start making orbit-capable Lynxes."

"Excellent. When are we going to start making Foxes?"

"Three weeks," Liz said. "By then we'll have finished the space station's hub, and we can afford to divert capacity."

"Okay," Marc nodded his head. "So where are we with the hub?"

"We will finish extruding the exterior shell of the hub by Monday. We'll immediately start on the inner shell, so it should be done before the end of next week," Liz said. "I've been reviewing the way we're planning to handle cargo, and based on that, ADI, Catie, and I have designed a docking ring we'd like to propose."

"Go ahead," Marc said.

"The main goal is to allow unloading of multiple Oryxes without blocking the main access to the hub. We don't want cargo handling to get in the way of taking a new ship out of the manufacturing plant," Liz said.

"That was bothering me," Marc said. "I'm glad you've come up with a way around it."

"The ring is designed so the Oryx can back into position. Then we can attach a docking clamp and extend a cargo jetway to it. It will seal against the Oryx so you can lower the rear door and unload cargo without losing pressure. It also has a tube that will extend to the crew access door so you can deplane without having to crawl through the cargo bay. We'll have plumbing for pumping fluids from the Oryx into the station or vice versa. It requires a short EVA to attach, but it's quick. The ring can accommodate eight Oryxes at a time, while still allowing full access to the center door into the hub." Liz finished flipping through the slides, ending on the one showing eight Oryxes docked to the station while a Fox could be seen exiting via the main hub door.

"I like it," Marc said. "How long to make it?"

"We'll start manufacturing as soon as we have approval. I estimate three weeks before it's ready to attach. We're essentially extruding a thirty-meter internal hub and then adding all the docking equipment. After that, we'll add the magnetic coupling between the ring and the main hub. Passengers and crew will have to deplane through microgravity."

"You have approval unless someone sees a problem."

"And what is this?" the president yelled, throwing photos of an Oryx on the table, followed by photos of the new floating airport.

"The plane looks like a C17," Secretary Blackburn said.

"Unfortunately, it's not," Director Lassiter said. "It is similar, but we've tracked one doing Mach six. It's possible that it can go faster, but it got out of range of our radar."

"Why the hell would you need a supersonic cargo jet?"

"We don't know."

"And that?" the president asked, pointing to the floating airport.

"It's what it looks like," Director Lassiter said. "It's a floating airport. They've been building it for a while. They just launched one of those cargo jets from it last night."

"Why wasn't I informed?" yelled the president.

"It has been in the briefings," Director Lassiter said.

"I don't remember anything about an airport!"

"We didn't know it was going to be an airport at first," Director Lassiter said. "It looked like they were making parts to expand the city. It wasn't until last week that they started to attach them together. I suspect they were trying to hide the fact that they were building an airport."

Admiral Michaels caught himself shaking his head. It was too late; the president saw him. "What Admiral?"

"Sorry, sir. I was wondering, wouldn't they have needed permission from the government on Rarotonga to build the airport?" Admiral Michaels asked. He knew they'd asked for permission since he'd kept his asset in place despite the CIA taking over the surveillance operation.

"Well!" the president turned to the CIA Director.

The Director gaped at the president, "Sir I'm not aware of it, there may have been something about an airport, but they have one on Manuae. I would naturally have assumed it was about that."

"I am surrounded by idiots," the president thundered. "And you knew!" The president scowled at Admiral Michaels, his face red with anger.

"Sir, I'm just here to provide background. I've been told to leave the investigation work to the CIA."

"And what do you think of this jet?" the president demanded.

"The only thing I can imagine is that they want to move perishable cargo," Admiral Michaels said. "Maybe they want to go into the seafood export business."

"You're fired!" the president yelled.

"Fired?"

"Yes, as in you don't work for the US government anymore. Now get out of here," the president yelled. "I will not have people working for me who find it amusing when we are being stymied by some two-bit company. Or who don't tell me everything they know when I ask a question."

# 16    Exodus

Admiral Michaels left the White House and made his way to his office. He knew he'd made a mistake with the comment about the jet, but he was just tired of the CIA being so incompetent. He had misjudged the president's loyalty to Lassiter. The two of them went back a long way, but he'd thought the president was ready to hang his old friend; apparently not. He had only been trying to get the president riled up enough that he would light a fire under the CIA director. Well, he'd lit a fire alright, just under the wrong person. The president's obsession with MacKenzie Discoveries and Marc McCormack was becoming a problem. Instead of finding ways to pull them into the US sphere of influence, his reactions were guaranteed to push them away. Eventually, that would hurt the US. He wasn't a fan of the president, but he was dedicated to the US constitution and what it meant for the people and the country. Now he had to do the hardest thing he had ever done in his life, walk away in order to find a way to save his country from the current administration.

He picked up his car keys and a few personal items he still kept in his office; he left his office keys and White House pass on the desk, let his assistant know that he wouldn't be back, and then walked out. He got into his car and drove toward his home in Alexandria, Virginia. He got off of the I-95 early and drove to Fort Ward Park. He parked at the visitor center, opened the trunk to the car, and pulled out the burner phone he kept in the wheel well beneath the spare tire. He then walked up Seminary Hill. During the walk, he took the opportunity to verify that he was not being followed. At the top of Seminary Hill, there were a few park benches, nobody was about at this time, so he settled down on one and dialed the number he'd memorized just two weeks before; he pressed star-six-seven to block the caller ID.

"Sloan Associates," the woman answering the phone announced.

"Yes, may I speak with Ms. Sloan?" Admiral Michaels asked.

"May I say who's calling?"

"Please tell her it's an old friend of Marc's, her boss."

"Just a moment, please."

"Marcie Sloan here," Marcie said as she came on the line.

"Ms. Sloan, I'm an old acquaintance of Marc's. I wonder if you could get a message to him."

"I'd be happy to give you his number. It's nine o'clock his time, so he's probably in his office right now."

"Thank you for telling me, but I really need you to send the message if you don't mind."

"Depending on the message, I can probably do that for you." Marcie's voice clearly showed her skepticism at the unusual request.

"Please tell him that the toy set he sent me was missing some Chinese soldiers, and I need to speak to him about it," Admiral Michaels said. "If he can call me the same way he did when he arranged for the delivery of the set, I would appreciate it."

"I guess I can deliver that message," Marcie said. "Toy set is missing some Chinese soldiers, to call you the same way he did when he arranged delivery."

"Correct," Admiral Michaels said. He set the phone down on the bench and leaned back to wait. It was only five minutes before the burner phone rang. He hadn't been sure which phone Marc McCormack would use, but he wasn't surprised that he used the burner phone.

"Hello," he said as he answered the phone.

"Admiral Michaels," Marc said. "Don't worry, this call cannot be traced or listened in on. I see you're in Fort Ward Park by your home."

"I am."

"How can I help you?"

"I was hoping I could do you a favor and maybe have you do one for me in return."

"I would certainly consider it, sir."

"I find myself unemployed and looking for a safe and quiet place for my family and me to spend a few months while I figure out what I want to do next," Admiral Michaels said. "I understand you own some real-estate in just such an area."

"I do, and I'd be happy to have you and your family come visit," Marc said.

"I would really like that, but I'm a bit worried about transportation."

"I can see that being a problem; we're flying back and forth all the time. Just let me know a convenient location where we can have you picked up."

"I would really appreciate that," Admiral Michaels said. "Now if I were you, I'd be thinking the same thing about my friends and family. A few months in the sunshine with ocean breezes would do wonders for their health and safety."

"I appreciate the sentiment," Marc said. "Let me consider it, and I'll get back to you about transportation."

"I'll be looking forward to your call."

Marc hung up the phone, "Blake, Kal, we need to talk now!" Marc cut into their comms.

"On my way," Kal replied.

"What's up, bro?" Blake asked, sticking his head into Marc's office.

"We've got a problem," Marc said. "Come in and sit down."

Blake sat down and looked at Marc expectantly. Marc smiled back but didn't say anything.

"Talk to me," Blake said.

"Let's wait for Kal." Marc closed his eyes and thought while he waited.

Two minutes later, Kal came running into the office. "What's the problem?"

"I just got a call from Admiral Michaels," Marc said. "Well, actually he asked Marcie to ask me to call him. He very carefully worded the request so it wouldn't give anyone a hint who he was."

"So, he's worried about something," Kal said.

"He's looking for a safe place for his family, and he has suggested we do the same," Marc said.

"Oh, he's *really* worried about something," Blake said.

"So, who do we need to pull in for a while?" Marc asked.

"I'd start with Linda," Blake said, "add Marcie, and we should check with Sam."

"You think we need to go that far?" Marc asked

"They've had spies looking at us, so they're bound to have picked up on your relationship," Blake said.

"Kal, how about you?"

"I think I'm okay," Kal said. "My family would never leave Hawaii, and I'm not really high profile like you guys."

"What about our parents?" Blake asked.

"Why don't you call Mom and offer her a vacation down here," Marc said. "I'll talk to Linda and see if she wants to bring her parents."

"And you'll talk to Sam?" Blake asked.

"Yes, I'll talk with Sam. Kal, talk to Liz, and see if she has someone she would like to bring out, tell everyone not to make any calls without talking to me first," Marc said.

"Got it," Blake said. "I wonder what has the admiral spooked."

"He said he was unemployed," Marc said.

"He didn't say retired?" Blake asked.

"No, unemployed."

"That doesn't sound good," Kal said.

By evening they'd made all the necessary arrangements. Samantha wanted to bring her sister out. She had just finished law school and was now studying for the bar. She had jumped at the offer of a few months' all expenses paid, vacation on the beach while studying. She would drive to Canada and fly out of Toronto for Jamaica, where she would have a week to have fun before meeting up with Marc's parents for a flight to Delphi City.

Linda wanted to bring her brother, her parents, and her boyfriend, Zane. Her brother and parents would visit her in San Diego in one week. While there, they would simply cross the border into Mexico and meet the plane at the airport in Tijuana. Her grandparents refused to leave Boston. They actually thought it might be exciting to have the FBI pull them in for questioning.

Admiral Michaels would also travel to San Diego with his family for a long-deserved vacation. They'd visit Mexico and meet the plane in Tijuana.

Marc's and Blake's parents would book a flight to Jamaica for a vacation at a resort there. They would be picked up right after they landed and continue on to Delphi City with Samantha's sister.

Liz's younger brother was visiting her parents in Hawaii. He would take a flight to Auckland the next day. Once there, he would spend some time deciding whether he wanted to stay there or come to Delphi City.

Marcie already had a flight scheduled for the end of the week. She was heading to a trade show in Germany. It was decided she would go ahead and attend the show, but then come to Delphi City afterward. She would take her two children with her to the show, which wasn't unusual since school was out.

# 17  Board Meeting – Aug 5th

"This meeting will come to order," Marc said. "First, I'll update everyone on the status of our families. We have a plan that gets everyone out of the US within the next week. We'll bring most here to Delphi City, while others are considering whether they would rather stay in New Zealand or Australia. Our analysis and discussion with Admiral Michaels indicate that these locations should be safe. Of course, ADI can give you an update on the status of your relatives at any time.

"Sam, do you have anything to share?"

"Of important note, Mexico has authorized a Lynx landing in Tijuana and wants us to bring one for them to evaluate before they fully certify it," Samantha said. "This is great news for those of you picking up your families and friends in Tijuana since you'll be able to make the trip quickly. It is also great news for future certification efforts; it will put tremendous pressure on the US to certify the Lynx since if they don't, most of their high-end tourist travel will be exiting and entering the US via the Rodriguez international airport in Mexico. You can access that airport without having to technically leave the US."

"I like hearing that," Blake said. "It would be nice to be able to just hop over to New England for some lobster or a clam bake."

Samantha laughed, "And on a more serious note, we are on target to open the clinic in Tijuana. It should open on the twelfth."

"That's good timing; it'll make our trip out there look like a business trip," Marc said. "Blake, construction?"

"We have the condos ready and furnished for our relatives. So hopefully that all goes smoothly, or I'll be hearing about it from Mom," Blake said. Then he signaled Masina, Marc's admin, and she came into the room, rolling a cart with a couple of bottles of Champagne and glasses.

"The airport is now officially open, and all Oryx traffic has been moved to it. I'm sure all of you whiners will want to toast its opening and the start of quiet nights in Delphi City."

"Okay," Marc said. "We'll take a fifteen-minute break while everyone grabs a glass and toasts Blake for *finally* getting that airport open."

"Killjoy," Blake retorted.

"I try, I try," Marc laughed.

After everyone had a chance to make a few toasts about the airport, Marc brought the meeting back to order. "Fred, how are we doing with our lift brigade?"

"I'm sure everyone will be happy to hear that Jason's vision has been restored and he has rotated into the Oryx flying brigade. We have the fifth Oryx ready for test flights, and it should be in the rotation before the end of the week. When it joins the rotation, we will be lifting approximately eighteen hundred metric tons of material per day into orbit. And in three weeks, we will be lifting almost three thousand metric tons per day."

"Liz, is that going to keep you on schedule?" Marc asked.

"Definitely," Liz said. "We've been consuming raw material faster than the deliveries up to now, eating into our reserves to keep everything moving. But if Fred's schedule holds, we'll start building a reserve again. And we'll need it once we start to make the rings."

"Great planning, Liz. Our reserve here is holding out. Our latest shipment arrived last week so we should have enough to last until we can start accessing the asteroids. Anything else, Liz?" Marc asked.

"Dr. Zelbar has scheduled time on one of the Oryxes to run a test on his clear polysteel process," Liz added.

"That is great! If it works, we can start exporting that material," Fred said. "A glass that is as strong as steel and lighter than glass is pretty unique. It'd be nice to be sending the Oryxes down with cargo instead of empty."

"That's Catie's and your problem," Liz said, referring to the fact that Catie had taken responsibility for balancing the Oryxes' load between the station and Delphi City. "We finished extruding the outer shell of the hub, and the inner shell should be finished by the end of the week. We're waiting for those monstrous magnetic bearings so we can slide the inner can into place and add the docking ring."

"Kal, security?"

"Word back from Wellington is that our police cadets are doing well, I'm keeping my fingers crossed," Kal said. "I just had our sonar net recalibrated to make sure we'll catch anything trying to sneak by. We'll be running drills all week to test the perimeter defenses. We identified a few issues last week, so we're rerunning them."

"Excellent," Marc said. "Now I'd like to discuss some priorities for licensing our technology, which is especially acute, giving the current tensions. The first candidate would be the polysteel process. Liz, you were looking into that, what did you find?"

"The coal miners would love you," Liz said. "The polysteel process readily adapts to using coal instead of petroleum. And, let me bring up my notes; Dr. Zelbar and Dr. McGenty both have agreed that the process would do an excellent job of siphoning off all the bad stuff you find in coal in useful, environmentally sound ways.

"Basically, you make a slurry out of the coal so you can feed it into the plasma field. The nitrogen would be extracted and either stored as liquid nitrogen for sale or simply released, no nitrous oxides. Of course, we've already dealt with the $CO_2$ question; all the carbon goes into the polysteel, so just oxygen is released. Same with sulfur, sulfuric acid is recovered for sale. Mercury will be collected; it can be sold or sequestered. I guess there's a good market for the stuff, but this process might saturate the market."

"We really need to address the energy problem before that, don't we?" Samantha asked.

"It would drive up the price of coal, but is that a problem?" Blake asked.

"It is for developing countries; they'll be burning more coal and having to pay more for it," Samantha said.

"On that note, how are your nuclear boys doing?" Marc asked.

"It's only been a month," Liz said. "They've got a basic design. I've been steering them toward ADI's designers to take care of the details, so she's been able to move them along quickly. But they still need to finalize it and then actually build the thing." ADI's designers is how they covered up the fact that ADI did much of the design under Catie's direction, everyone assumed they were contracting out the work. Only a select few knew the full truth about ADI.

"How long?"

"ADI says three months."

"Licensing the polysteel process is pretty straightforward," Marc said. "We'd probably have a lot of license violations since once the process is out, it can be reverse-engineered. But I'm okay with that. How would we go about licensing the fusion reactor?"

"The secret to the sustained reaction seems to be in how well you can feed the fuel in and balance the plasma field. They've only managed it when ADI was controlling it. Maybe that's our lever."

"Yeah, we could release the design, but keep the plasma field and fuel-feed controller proprietary," Catie said. "Make it like your dispensary. Any tampering, and it shuts the reactor down and fuses into a block."

"But can we make a controller that doesn't require ADI to manage it?"

"Sure, the problem is speed. When we can make the computer chips in space, we can get the speed and density we need, then it's just programming. You could almost do it with about twenty comm units," Catie said.

"Okay, do you want to work on that?" Marc looked at Catie.

"I can help with it," Catie said. "A lot of it will be ordering manufacturing equipment for integrated circuits. We have to lift them to the station and set up the lab. Are we going to be able to hire experienced technicians?"

"Fred, do you want to take care of setting up the IC factory?" Marc asked.

"Sounds more interesting than the schedule and order management," Fred said.

"Good, it's yours with Catie as support," Marc said. "So what about hiring skilled technicians?"

"I would bet we can recruit pretty well," Samantha said. "A three-month rotation into space and big dollars sounds like a pretty good deal. Especially for technologists."

"We might even be able to shorten the rotation time," Blake said. "Add some passenger seats to the Oryx like we did when we all went up to watch the hub being extruded. Then just carry them up and down with all the cargo."

"What about licensing the jet engines?" Fred asked, bringing the discussion back to the original thread.

"I'd like to be more comfortable with our situation before we give up that edge," Marc said.

"I agree," Kal seconded.

"Maybe we can use the nuclear fusion reactor as a lever to reduce tensions," Liz said.

"Just removing the competition for oil will help a lot. Countries are desperate to guarantee their energy sources, which causes a lot of the tension," Samantha said.

"Okay, keep thinking about it. I'd like us prepared to have the conversation with Admiral Michaels once he's here," Marc said. "Back to work people."

# 18    Family Reunion

"Hey, Mommy," Catie said as she hugged her mother.

"Hello, Sweetie," Linda said as she hugged Catie back and kissed her forehead. "Fancy meeting you here."

"No way was I letting someone else pick you up."

Catie turned to her grandparents and gave them a hug, too. "Hi, Grandma, Grandpa."

"Hello, Love," her grandmother whispered in her ear as she hugged her and gave her a kiss.

"Hey, Uncle Conner," Catie gave her uncle a quick wave. He waved back then put his hand back into his pocket and leaned back against the wall. He looked totally bored.

Marc gave Linda a quick peck on the cheek and hugged her parents.

"This is Zane," Linda introduced her boyfriend.

"Hello," Marc said as he shook Zane's hand.

"Our other guest should be here, momentarily," Marc said as he looked around for the admiral and his family. He was looking right at Admiral Michaels for several seconds before he realized the man in the Hawaiian shirt, shorts, sandals, sunglasses, and a ball cap was the admiral. His wife was dressed in a flowing Hawaiian dress, and the two kids matched their parents in style.

Marc gave his head a shake at the absurdity of the picture. "Here they are now. Hello, Paul, it's been a while," Marc said as he and the admiral shook hands.

"Marc, I'd like you to meet my wife, Pam; my son, David; and my daughter, Sophia."

"I'm pleased to meet all of you. Why don't we head to the plane, we can finish introductions there?" Marc said. He signaled to Natalia, who had the baggage cart; she grabbed their luggage and piled it onto the cart.

The admiral gave a quick nod of agreement and steered his family behind Marc and his group.

As they made their way across the terminal, Catie fell in step with the admiral's daughter, Sophia. "Hi."

"Hi," Sophia said. Her tone indicated that she was not pleased with her current situation.

"How was San Diego?"

"We just landed, Dad changed clothes into that ridiculous outfit, and we took a taxi down here. Now we're getting onto another long flight."

"It won't be that long," Catie said. "Only one-and-a-half hours, and there'll be plenty of room on the plane."

Sophia looked at Catie like she had two heads. "It's farther than Hawaii."

"Yeah, Hawaii would only be forty-five minutes, you'll see."

"Sure," Sophia said with disdain.

They entered the general aviation area of Rodriguez International. Marc led them to gate five, where they exited the door and onto the tarmac.

"Oh joy," Sophia said. "A small jet."

Catie shook her head and grinned. "Just wait."

"Which seats do we have?" Sophia asked.

"Open seating."

"Double joy."

Marc led the group up the ramp and onto the plane. As Catie and Sophia made their way up the ramp, Jennie greeted Catie with a hug. "So, you're not flying us back?"

"No," Catie said. "Daddy says I'm supposed to play hostess. This is Sophia."

"Sophia, I'm Jennie. Let me know if there's anything you need to make your flight more comfortable."

"You know the flight attendant?" Sophia asked Catie in a whisper, she was clearly surprised by the personal greeting.

"Sure, she works for us," Catie said as she steered Sophia around the corner into the aisle of the plane.

Sophia gasped, "What is this?" She was shocked to see the luxurious leather seats and spacious spacing.

"This is a Lynx," Catie said. "I like to sit in the back."

"Really?"

"Well, I really prefer to sit in the very front, but Dad said I couldn't fly on the way back."

"You mean that wasn't a joke," Sophia said. "You can really fly this thing?"

"Yeah, I had to let Liz land it, but I flew us here," Catie said. "It's a new plane, and we had to get special permission from the Mexican government to fly it. But they thought it would be cool to be the first North American country to have the Lynx land in one of their airports."

"Why would they care?"

"Because it's the first passenger jet to be able to go Mach four," Catie said.

"Mach four? That means four times the speed of sound, right?"

"Yep. We'll be at Delphi City in less than two hours."

"Wow," Sophia said as she sat in her seat. "With these seats, I wouldn't care if it took longer."

"Aren't you excited about going to Delphi City?"

"I don't know. A floating city seems kind of weird. What can you do there?"

"We have three restaurants, a few nice stores for shopping, a few public parks, the condos all have a swimming pool, and soon we'll have our own beach, but don't tell anyone that, it's a secret."

"Wow, that sounds kind of insane," Sophia said. "Cool insane," she quickly added when she saw Catie's face fall. "How could you fit all that in a floating city?"

"It's over one mile by one mile," Catie said. "Uncle Blake is going to add the three quadrants around the center so we can add the beach.

He's mainly working on the second section now. We had to hurry so we would have a long enough runway for the Oryxes to take off."

"You have an airport?"

"Just a runway in the city," Catie said. "We have a big airport that we keep away from the city so we don't get the noise from it. We use it for the big jets and cargo flights."

"This might be more exciting than I thought," Sophia said. "What's the internet like there?"

"We have the best," Catie said. "We have one-gigabyte speed at the condos, and we get all the Netflix material and Hulu, plus all the US channels."

"How do you get all the US channels, are you using a proxy?"

"No, MacKenzie Discoveries pays for all the content access," Catie said. "It keeps everybody happy."

Natalia came through the door from the cargo bay; she patted Catie on the shoulder as she sat down in the seat across the aisle from Catie and Sophia.

"What's up with her?"

"Oh, that's Nattie, she's my bodyguard. Actually, she's acting as the bodyguard for both me and Dad."

"You need a bodyguard?" Sophia gasped.

"Some people think I do," Catie said. "But Nattie's cool."

"Everybody, please buckle in," Jennie said. "We'll be taxiing for takeoff in one minute. We should be airborne right after that. Our flight time to Delphi City will be one hour and twenty-five minutes."

After they took off, Jennie came back and started taking orders from everybody.

"Do you want anything to eat?" Catie asked.

"I'm starving," Sophia said. "We didn't get anything on the flight out except a sandwich that was so horrible I couldn't eat it."

"Well I hope our sandwiches are better, we have a chicken breast sandwich and a tuna melt. We also have salads."

"Oh, a chicken breast sandwich sounds great."

Natalia got up, "Do you want anything, Cat?"

"No, I'm good," Catie said. "I'll just wait for dinner tonight."

Natalia turned to the back of the plane and the galley. She pulled out a sandwich from the heated bag, added a bag of chips and a bottle of water, and brought it to Sophia. "Here you go, Miss, Jennie will be by to ask about drinks."

"Thank you," Sophia said. "Your bodyguard plays flight attendant too?" she whispered to Catie.

"Not usually, she must have been worried you'd start nibbling on me," Catie said.

Natalia looked up at Jennie, who then messaged to her what she needed up front. The McGinnis crew was fine since they were on West coast time, but it was 8:00 P.M. for the admiral's family, and they hadn't gotten much to eat on the way out. Natalia went back to the galley and got two tuna melts and salad and carried them forward for Jennie. Jennie finished getting the drink orders, and everyone settled down.

"Where do you go to school?" Sophia asked.

"I homeschool," Catie said. "We have a small school in the city. It's growing, so you can choose that or homeschooling; what grade are you in?"

"I'm going to start the ninth grade when school starts."

Catie used her specs and looked up how big the ninth-grade class was. "We have six students in the ninth grade," she said. "Two boys and four girls."

"How did you know that?"

"I looked it up," Catie said, pointing to her specs. "They're like Google Glasses but better."

"Oh, can I get a pair?"

"Sure, I'll set you up tomorrow," Catie said. "Will your brother want a pair?"

"Oh yeah, but let me get mine first.  He always gets the new tech first because he's *older*."

"Sure, we won't say anything," Catie flicked her eyes up and looked up some additional info.  "You're scheduled to go through the orientation on Monday.  They'll talk about the specs then.  So, I'll come by tomorrow around noon and set you up.  Then you'll be able to lord it over him all weekend."

"What, you don't get up until noon?" Sophia said, teasing Catie.

"Actually, I'm getting up at seven o'clock tomorrow.  I have a test flight to do."

Marc had been listening in on Catie's conversation with half an ear, but when he heard her mention the test flight, he turned around, "Catie!"

"What!  It was scheduled weeks ago, before we knew about this," Catie said.

"You have guests," Marc said.

"Daddy!"

"Well."

"What if I move the flight up to 06:00, I'll be back by 08:30 then."

Marc just nodded his head and sighed.

"What's a test flight?" Sophia asked.

"We have a new Oryx that's just finishing up its preflight," Catie said. "Tomorrow is its first actual flight.  We'll take it up and make sure it handles correctly, that everything works."

"Isn't that dangerous?"

"Not really, we've already run through almost all the tests in the wind tunnel and on the runway.  This is just to verify things at actual altitude and at higher speeds than the wind tunnel can produce."

"How fast does it go?"

"Really fast," Catie said.  "Faster than a Lynx."

"That's so cool.  When did you learn to fly?"

"I learned last summer, but my friend, Fred, and my Uncle Blake ran me through all the formal stuff this winter, so I'm actually certified.

But I have to have a certified pilot with me whenever I fly anywhere except Delphi City, the Cook Islands, and New Zealand since I'm only thirteen. You have to be sixteen to have a real license."

"You can't be just thirteen," Sophia said.

"Well, I'll be fourteen in November."

"This is amazing, I can't believe you do all this stuff. When do you have time for school?"

"That's what's nice about homeschooling. I can fit my studies in between my other stuff. I don't watch very much TV or stuff, so I manage it."

Catie knocked on the Michaels' door at 09:00 the next morning. Mrs. Michaels answered the door, "Good morning, Catie, what can I do for you?"

"How are you feeling this morning?" Catie asked.

"I'm doing just fine; those pills they gave us last night worked wonders. I slept like a baby and woke up this morning, just like normal. No jet lag or anything. The admiral's down at the gym doing his usual workout. Now, what can I do for you?"

"I came by to see Sophia. I've got her specs for her."

"Sophia's not feeling too well this morning," Mrs. Michaels said. "And please call me Pam."

"Is it Catie?" Sophia called from the kitchen.

"Yes, honey, it is."

Sophia came out of the kitchen, wearing a bathrobe. "Hi Catie, come on in."

Mrs. Michaels opened the door wider and invited Catie in. Catie walked over to Sophia and gave her a small hug. "Are you okay?"

"Yeah, just cramps," Sophia said.

"You should eat bananas," Catie said.

Sophia looked at Catie with a grimace. "Not those kinds of cramps, dummy, *cramps*."

"Oh," Catie exclaimed, feeling embarrassed. "Sorry."

Mrs. Michaels patted Catie, "It's okay; you probably don't get them yet."

"Oh, most of the women here decide not to," Catie said.

"What do you mean decide not to?" Sophia asked. "It's not like you have a choice."

"Oh, but we do. The doctor can give you a shot, and you don't ever get them," Catie said.

"What if you want to get pregnant?" Mrs. Michaels asked.

"You go to the doctor, and she gives you another shot, and you have two weeks to get pregnant," Catie said. "They'll explain all about this at the orientation on Monday."

Sophia groaned, "Do I have to wait for the orientation?"

"Not really. You just have to go to the clinic," Catie said.

"But it's too late, Honey," Mrs. Michaels said. "You're already having your period. Hormones can't change that."

"Oh, but Dr. Metra can take care of that too. I heard her explain it to another woman once. She just does some kind of localized blood thinning, and it's all over in an hour."

"Get dressed, Honey," Mrs. Michaels said. "This is going to make this ridiculous trip worthwhile. How do we get to the clinic?"

"I'll take you," Catie said. "Do you want me to make an appointment for Sophia? It'll save time."

"Please make two appointments," Mrs. Michaels said.

After the clinic, they went back to Catie's condo, and she set both Sophia and Mrs. Michaels up with specs. She had to have ADI clone their phones from their Internet accounts since the admiral had made them leave their phones behind.

"You use your eyes just like a mouse," Catie said as she explained how to use the specs. "The specs follow your eyes and highlight where you are when you're looking in the menu area. If you blink, it selects that option, blink twice and so on."

"How do you press and hold?" Sophia asked. "Close one eye?"

---

Catie laughed, "No, you do a short pause between two blinks to hold and just blink again to release."

"Okay, so if I want to look up services, I just go to the directory and scroll down; how do I scroll?" Mrs. Michaels asked.

"You just look at the end of the list, and it will keep scrolling, it will scroll faster if you look a little farther down."

"That's cool," Sophia said.

"Ah, I see," said Mrs. Michaels. "I'm seeing medical, dental, hairdresser, masseur; I can't find a chiropractor."

"What's a chiropractor?" Catie asked.

"Someone who adjusts your spine," Mrs. Michaels said.

"Why would you have someone do that?"

"Oh, I hurt my back years ago playing tennis, and now I have to have it adjusted to keep it from hurting. It's been bothering me after all that flying yesterday. Not that your lovely plane caused any problems, but the flight before was horrible, and we were in coach."

"If your back bothers you, you should just go to the clinic. I wish you'd said something before; I probably could have gotten you an appointment with Dr. Sharmila while we were there."

"Oh, doctors either want to operate or give you pain medication," Mrs. Michaels said. "I don't want any of that."

"She could probably fix your back in just one visit," Catie said.

"It's more complicated than that, dear."

"Mom! Remember what we just had done," Sophia said.

"Oh right, well it can't hurt to try," Mrs. Michaels said. "What did you say her name was?"

Catie walked Mrs. Michaels through how to make an appointment with Dr. Sharmila, then left her and Sophia practicing with their specs, while she continued down to her father's office. The office was just two blocks down from their condo; Natalia, her shadow followed quietly behind.

"Hi, Daddy," Catie knocked on his doorjamb. "Are you finally going to tell me what this is all about?"

**195**

"Yes, how about that?" Blake asked as he followed Catie into the office.

"Admiral Michaels says that the president and his staff are taking an unhealthy interest in MacKenzie Discoveries. He felt that based on the level of the president's obsession and the intensity of his demands to discover our secrets, either he would order, or one of his staff would take it upon themselves to do something drastic. The president fired him from the Navy because he was frustrated that his people weren't keeping up with us. He told me the president even suggested that they steal the design for the Lynx engines."

"Let them try," Catie said, her eyes flashing with challenge. "You can't make them without the heater coils, and we're the only ones who can make them."

"That's the point. How would they be able to extract that information? We saw what the Chinese were willing to do. What would these guys do, especially with so many of our family and friends conveniently located on US soil?"

"What about Grandma and Grandpa McCormack?" Catie gasped.

"They're on their way to Jamaica," Marc said. "Fred will fly there to get them and Sam's sister."

"Oh good, what about the grans?"

"They weren't interested in moving, and I don't think anyone will try to leverage them," Marc said. "And now that Mack McGinnis is back to his old self, he says he'd love for them to try."

Catie and Blake laughed at that. "Sounds like him, but if they try something, it's Agnes they'd better watch out for," Blake said.

"Welcome Admiral Michaels. This is our board. First, my brother, Blake McCormack; he coordinates all of our building activity; he is also one of our top pilots and does pilot training. He is also one of the major shareholders in MacKenzie Discoveries."

"It's an honor to meet you, Commander McCormack," Admiral Michaels said as he extended his hand to Blake.

"I'm just Blake, or Cer Blake if you want to be formal," Blake said. "Welcome aboard, sir."

"Next," Marc continued around the table, "Fred Linton, another of our pilots; he manages the pilot training and coordinates our production schedules and a few other things you'll pick up as we go.

"And another pilot, Elizabeth Farmer. As you know, we've managed to collect some of the world's preeminent scientists. Elizabeth, Liz, as she likes to be called, provides support for them by beating on Blake to add to their lab space or me to procure more equipment for them. But more importantly, she coordinates between them, bringing the different fields together when she discovers an overlap in their activity."

"I'm pleased to meet you," the admiral said.

"This is Samantha Newman, our lawyer slash diplomat. She's the one we call up when we need both brains and tact on the problem. She's our main liaison with the governments of the Cook Islands and of New Zealand. She is also the person we turn to when we need to recruit special talents, like Marcie Sloan, whom you've recently dealt with."

"I'm very pleased to meet you," the admiral said. "Ms. Sloan was very helpful."

"Our pleasure," Samantha said.

"Kalani Kealoha, known more familiarly as Kal, is our head of security, our de facto chief of police, and our labor coordinator," Marc said as he continued the introductions. "As labor coordinator, he's guiding the development of our new refugee community, making sure we have the schools they need for themselves as well as their children."

"A former Marine as I recall," Admiral Michaels said as he shook Kal's hand. "Nice to meet you."

"Likewise."

"Dr. Metra here heads up our clinic as well as our medical research. She's responsible for the cure we've developed for Alzheimer's and a few other diseases. And before you ask, we are starting to create satellite clinics where we can provide those benefits to other parts of the world."

"A pleasure," Admiral Michaels said.

"And last but not least, my daughter, Catie. She is another of our pilots; she coordinates the design of our aircraft and does quite a bit of the design herself. She is also our agriculture coordinator; she has a horticulturist on her staff as well as a couple of agriculture scientists. They're working to make Delphi City as close to self-sustaining as possible. She is also the self-appointed champion of greenery within the city. She's designed our parks and coordinated the installation of trees and flowers along the walkways that you see as you move about the city. And besides myself and Blake, she is the other major shareholder in MacKenzie Discoveries."

"That is most impressive," the admiral said. "And Catie, I would personally like to thank you for being so helpful with my wife and daughter. They are both much more enthusiastic about being here after meeting you than they were when I first proposed this change."

"You're welcome," Catie said.

"The admiral has agreed to join us and provide insights to the world military and diplomatic situation as well as what prompted him to bring his family here and recommended we do the same for our families," Marc said. "Admiral."

"What tipped the balance for me is that the president fired me," the admiral said. "And he didn't just dismiss me from the job I was in at the time, but from the service. That is an unusual move, even for him. That leads me to believe that someone else is feeding him information and pushing his buttons; prompting him to make decisions that are not necessarily in the best interest of the country."

"Who would do something like that?" Samantha asked.

"The recent technology introductions from MacKenzie Discoveries threaten a lot of US interests," the admiral said. "But if I were going to put money on it, I would say someone in the energy industry. They were big contributors to his campaign, and they have enormous influence. The predictions from key White House advisers are that the changes in the trucking and auto industry will cut the price of oil by twenty percent."

"So, it's about money," Blake said.

"It's always about money," the admiral replied. "Now don't get me wrong, the president is convinced that he's doing the right thing for America, he's just getting some bad advice or bad information. And if they're willing to go to the lengths they have to sway the president's opinion on this, I'm not sure to what lengths they will go to ensure that something doesn't get in the way of their agenda."

"Do you know who it is?" Marc asked.

"No, I don't," the admiral replied.

"Did you try to figure out who it was?"

"Spying on the president of the United States is not something I was willing to do, especially with my family at risk," the admiral said. "I do think that it has to be more than one person. Possibly a group of key leaders in the energy industry is collaborating on a response to the huge changes they see coming."

"So, any predictions on what he'll do next?" Blake asked.

"I wouldn't want to guess," the admiral said. "But I predict that the president will not be willing for the US just sit on the sidelines while you change the world."

The board and the admiral spent another hour discussing what the admiral knew and suspected before Marc called an end to the meeting.

"We have a board meeting in one and a half weeks. At that time, we will revisit the discussion," Marc said. "In the meantime, I want everyone to think about what we've discussed here and be prepared to offer their opinion and insight into what we will be facing."

# 19    Space Station Tourist

"How is everybody doing back there?" Catie asked over the Lynx intercom.

"We're just fine," Linda answered. "I don't think anybody threw up."

"Good, I was going to wait until someone cleaned it up before I came back."

"Oh, come back here so I can swat you one," Linda said.

"I'm on my way." Catie and Liz made their way into the main cabin of the Lynx.

They were in microgravity, in orbit next to Delphi Station's new hub. The board had decided that they would come and watch as the inner shell of the hub was extruded. Catie had argued successfully to have her mother and Jason included on the trip. Jason had seen the hub during his many Oryx flights ferrying up cargo, but this would be the first time he would actually be able to examine it up close, and his first time to actually walk in space. He'd done a lot of microgravity work, but had never been outside the Oryx. They were upside down, looking down on the hub and the extrusion form for the inner hull.

"Liz will explain what's going to happen," Marc said. "Those of us who have heard this can stand in the back so the new people can be up front."

Linda and Jason floated up to the front and sat on the two forward couches and strapped themselves down. Natalia took the one across the aisle from them. She was ostensibly there to provide security, but she was really there because she thought it would be fun.

"Feel free to interrupt with questions," Liz said. "If you look on the display, you can see the large ring that's floating above the hub. It is the form that we'll be using to make the inner hull. It's actually two rings. The inner ring is one hundred eighty meters in diameter on its outside; the outer one just a few centimeters bigger on the inside. The shell will be formed between them. They're made of polysteel and then coated with a material, so they're non-conductive and non-stick. They are thirty centimeters tall, and there are wheels in the bottom that will start pushing the hull out of the form once we start the process.

They're temporarily held together at the bottom by a layer of foam. That will get pushed down by the hull once we start the extrusion."

"How did you make them?" Jason asked.

"I'll let Catie explain since it was her idea."

"It was done with a similar process," Catie said. "But the form was rotated with the plasma gun. Once it reached a stable rotation speed, the gun was turned on, and the material started to extrude. The construction crew latched onto the first part of the extrusion and anchored it to another big blob of material, so it was stable. The extrusion continued until it circled back on itself. The form just slides over the beginning piece allowing them to be fused together, then the plasma guns and the foam guns shut down."

"Cool," Jason said.

"You can see the four plasma guns that will be used to deposit the polysteel to make the shell, they're each ninety degrees apart around the form," Liz continued. "There are two big blobs of material, one of petroleum and the other a slurry of oil and iron. They're inside the hub and have been carefully placed so that the new inner hull will slide around them with plenty of clearance. They're the anchor for the whole process as well as the material supply. Each has a pump with a heating system that will melt the material and pump it up to the plasma guns."

"Why do you have to melt it?" Linda asked. "Isn't oil liquid?"

"Normally, it is," Catie said. "But in space, everything radiates its heat away. So, unless it's being heated by the sun and even then, only half of it gets heated, it radiates most of its heat and reaches an equilibrium between what it's absorbing from the sun and what it's radiating. Which means it freezes."

Linda nodded her head and smiled at Catie. "Thank you."

"Now we're about to start. The guns will start rotating, and when they're up to speed and are stable, they'll start depositing the material. They're raised up a few millimeters per rotation until they've filled the form. Then the wheels will engage and start extruding the hull a few millimeters per rotation."

"Here they go!" Catie said as the guns started to rotate. "Now those of you who want to go out and see them up close need to put on your exosuits and helmets."

"I'm fine right here," Linda said.

Jason immediately started to put on his exosuit, as did Marc, Kal, and Fred. They hadn't had a chance to walk in space. Blake had made a few walks while setting up the process and was happy to stay in the cabin and keep Linda company. Liz, Catie, and Natalia suited up to do the tour and help the first-time spacewalkers out.

They went out the airlock to the cargo bay, where the cargo door was open. Liz had each of them attach a safety line and assigned each an experienced spacewalker. Catie took her dad, Liz took Fred, and Natalia took Kal. Jason had enough microgravity experience that he was able to take care of himself. Kal was not particularly happy when he was assigned Natalia; he was trying to remember if he'd been too hard on her during one of the training sessions recently, given that this would be the perfect opportunity for her to get even. At least with Liz, he knew she wouldn't really hurt him.

They all practiced moving around using their thrusters to maneuver, learning how to stop. When Liz felt they were skilled enough that it was unlikely they would get tangled up in the plasma guns, she led them over to the rotating guns where they could watch the shell coming out of the form.

"Wow, those guns are really slow," Jason said.

"They only lay two millimeters of material down per pass, the guns are rotating at 2.5 revolutions per minute, so the hull is being extruded at twenty millimeters per minute."

"How long does it take to do the whole thing?"

"Three-and-a-half days," Liz answered.

"We're not staying up here the whole time, are we?" Jason asked.

"No, just long enough to say we were here," Liz said. "We can go back inside anytime you're ready."

When they got back to the main cabin, Blake and Linda were sipping something from a plastic bag.

---

"What have you guys got there?" Marc asked.

"Champagne," Blake said.

Marc rolled his eyes. "Oh, brother."

"That's right, I am your brother, and we're toasting to the success of your project."

"Did you bring enough for everybody?"

"Of course, I'm always well prepared," Blake pointed to the galley, "in the refrigerator."

"I'm so glad I ended up with you guys," Jason said. "Just think I could be at the Air Force Academy being yelled at by an upperclassman, probably doing pushups while singing the academy fight song."

"And you get to fly way cooler jets than they have," Catie added.

"That's for sure. When are you going to let me fly the Lynx?" he asked.

"Tell you what. I'll give you your first chance at the controls when we hit the atmosphere," Catie said.

"Thanks."

# 20    Board Meeting – Aug 19th

"I call this meeting to order," Marc announced. "Admiral Michaels will be joining us soon, and I'd like to review his position and set some ground rules. He knows we're trying to create a better Earth by developing and sharing technologies in such a way as to equalize the income levels across nations. He does not, nor do I want him to know about the Sakira. He clearly suspects we have some access to technology or information that has helped us get where we are, but he does not know what it is. I have told him that I do not intend to share everything with him. Any questions?"

"Do you trust him?" Samantha asked.

"Mostly," Marc said. "But only so much. He could be a spy placed here by the president to exploit our past relationship, but I don't think so."

"What about the capabilities of the Foxes, or some of our other weapons technology?" Catie asked.

"I suspect he knows more than we think he does," Marc said. "At this point, I don't see why we should hide those kinds of facts from him. If I or anyone feels there is a specific technology or fact that we should withhold from him, send a message to the board member and we'll hold a private meeting to discuss it."

"What if you ask something here that we don't think he should know?" Liz asked.

"Just say you're not ready with the answer and will get back to the board later," Marc said. He gave the group time to think up more questions, when none was forthcoming with any questions, he asked Masina to show Admiral Michaels in.

"Hello, Admiral Michaels, how was your orientation meeting this morning?" Marc greeted the admiral.

"Most enlightening," Admiral Michaels said. "My wife has been telling me all weekend to go get my knees looked at, but apparently, that's part of your standard process here."

"Yes, Admiral, we will give your entire family a complete workup. You should each have your appointments scheduled," Dr. Metra said.

"We do," Admiral Michaels said. "But my wife is so delighted with the improvements to her back after Dr. Sharmila treated her that she wanted me to go get my knees fixed right away. Apparently, I complain about them quite a bit."

His comment elicited a good laugh from everyone.

"You met everyone at the last meeting, but feel free to ask for one of us to fill in the gaps of your knowledge," Marc said.

"Sam, can you spend some time with the admiral going over our contract slash treaty situation?"

"Of course, will two o'clock be okay?" Samantha asked.

"That will be fine," Admiral Michaels said.

Samantha wrote a note to herself. "I've added it to my calendar," she said.

"Samantha, I notice you're writing with that stylus, but you're writing on the desktop. Can you explain that?" the admiral asked.

"First, call me Sam," Samantha said. "As to the writing, it's a function built into our specs. I'm sure they introduced them to you at the orientation."

"Yes, they did."

"Well those of us who are not so technologically adept as others initially resorted to the tried and true method of handwritten notes, which we later scanned in or had transcribed. Eventually, we realized our comm units were very adept at interpreting our handwriting, so we didn't have to have the notes transcribed later. Then Catie, our resident 'Duh' person, suggested we just write the notes with a stylus. The comm displays what we are writing via our HUD display, and it looks like we've written on the desktop. It's quick and easy to tell if your comm is transcribing it right or not."

"That's very interesting," the admiral said.

"Now others, like Catie, hold their comm under the table where you can't see them type on it. The underside of the table is reflective, so the comm can see your hands and displays the keyboard on your HUD display. So Catie sits there looking like she's not doing anything, but is passing notes to everybody the whole time. Of course, she has an eidetic memory, so she doesn't need to take notes for herself, but she likes to help the rest of us out. Kal, over there, emulates Catie because he thinks it's cool. Liz just types on the desktop using the keyboard displayed by her specs; nobody knows what Dr. Metra does, but she usually just tells us what she's going to do, so she doesn't get very many action items. Marc just pauses the meeting, states what he wants in the record, and lets his comm record and transcribe."

Catie looked at Samantha, surprised that she had figured out what she was doing. She had always thought everyone assumed she was typing by using her eyes in her HUD. Her appreciation for Samantha's powers of observation went up immensely.

"You'll have to pick the best method that works for both your ego and your technical prowess."

"I appreciate the quick lesson and introduction to the board personalities," the admiral said.

"Okay, Sam, now that you've provided a quick summary of the note-taking habits of the board," Marc said with a laugh, "do you have anything else to add?" He was also surprised at Samantha's powers of observation, especially since he had thought Catie was typing with her eyes.

"We opened our Alzheimer's Clinic in Tijuana on the twelfth as scheduled," Samantha said, "but given the situation, we've delayed holding a press conference."

"Smart move," Marc said, very happy to avoid the press conference. "Anything else?"

"No," Samantha said. "I'll yield my time to the admiral. I'd like to know how long we might be in this hunker-down mode."

"Kal, anything?"

"It's in the weekly reports," Kal said.

"Okay, Liz?"

"We finished extruding the second shell for the space station on Friday. We're building the cap for the top end and getting ready to build the docking ring."

"What space station?" the admiral gasped.

"I told you to be prepared to be amazed," Marc said. "We're building this." Marc put the view of the station's hub up on the display. "This is the hub of the first section with the docking bay attached." The display showed the image of what appeared to be a big can.

"How big is this thing?"

"The hub is one hundred meters tall, with a diameter of two hundred meters."

"My god, that is enormous," Admiral Michaels gasped. "And dare I ask what you mean by hub?"

"Let me show you," Marc smiled. Here it is with an Oryx docked. He changed the slide, and an Oryx appeared at the bottom of the hub attached to a docking arm extended from the hub docking ring.

The admiral's eyes grew wide. "Okay, I can deal with that."

"The docking ring adds an additional thirty meters to the overall height of the hub. There are fifteen more major components to add."

"Fifteen more?"

"Yes," Marc said. He flashed through the next three slides which showed the station after each ring was added until he was showing a completed section with three rings.

"Oh my god," The admiral said as he sagged back into his chair.

Marc showed three more slides displaying how the station would grow as each new three-ringed section set was added.

The admiral's face was ashen as he asked, "How are you going to lift all that material?"

"We're not prepared to share that information at this time," Marc said. "Suffice it to say we have a plan. Lifting the material for the first section is the most critical, and we have most of that in orbit now."

The admiral shook his head. "And how long before someone actually notices that thing?"

"That's a complicated question to answer. Its orbit is opposite the ISS; the station itself is made of energy absorbing material so it will not be easy to spot by telescope or radar. The odds are good that nobody has noticed it yet."

"I can assure you that was true as of one week ago," Admiral Michaels said. "But that convoy of Oryxes lifting material?"

"That will be observable, at least by the various spies located on Rarotonga," Marc said. "But they won't know where they're going. Nothing specifically indicates that they're going into orbit. The people who know have been sequestered here in the city while we get the first section up. I assume you're concerned about the US reaction once they become aware of it."

"Specifically, the president's reaction. He will go ballistic," the admiral said.

"Can you help us understand that?" Samantha asked.

"The president has convinced himself that all this technology you have is the rightful property of the United States. He bases that on his belief that you possessed most of it, if not all of it, while you were a US citizen, therefore it should belong to the US."

"Fascinating logic," Samantha said. "What do you think he will do?"

"I'm afraid," the admiral said, "that he's going to want to take control of it."

"The US doesn't have the kind of assets to mount any space operation," Marc said.

"I know," the admiral whispered. "But Delphi City is not in space."

Marc gave everybody a thirty-minute break before he asked them to return to discuss what the president might do and what they should do to protect Delphi City. When Marc walked back into the room, he saw Blake holding a bottle of scotch.

"Blake, as much as I need a drink right now, I think it would be better if we waited until after the discussion," Marc said. Blake groaned but acquiesced and put the bottle back in the cabinet.

Once everybody was back in the room, Marc started the discussion. "Admiral, please feel free to make suggestions or corrections as we go. You're probably more familiar with what we're about to discuss than any of us."

Admiral Michaels nodded his head to acknowledge the point but stayed quiet.

"First, I think we should list what options the US might take to, as Admiral Michaels said, *take control*. The first thing I can think of is the one we've already experienced, that is to launch a commando raid to try to seize control of Delphi City," Marc said.

The admiral nodded his head in agreement, but Marc thought he should be getting a little more out of him than just simple agreement. "Admiral, can you help us to understand what such a raid might comprise?"

"I gather from your comments that the Chinese tried a raid," Admiral Michaels said. "Can you tell me a bit more about that?"

"They sent six commandos via submarine. We managed to detect the sub, which alerted us to the raid. Our internal forces intercepted the commandos, and we eventually deposited them in Singapore. I think three of them defected, but we lost track after that." Marc replied.

"That's what I had surmised," Admiral Michaels said. "I didn't share my assumptions with anyone. I'm not sure that US intelligence has been able to get that information from the submarine crew since I suspect that only the captain and first officer would have known about the mission. I didn't hear any comments about the sub and MacKenzie Discoveries while I was at the White House."

"That was our hope," Marc said.

"So, the US doesn't know that you,
A) were able to detect the submarine,
B) that you actually intercepted and defeated the commandos, and
C) that you were able to disable the submarine.
Can you tell me what you have done since then to augment your defenses?"

"Yes," Marc said and nodded to Kal.

"Sir, we have

1) expanded our sonar detection array out to fifty miles.

2) We've increased the size of our security force.

3) We've switched to two-man patrols to avoid having one guard taken out without our knowing about it; the comms did warn us pretty quickly that a guard was killed, but having that intel earlier certainly would have helped.

4) We've added torpedoes to the weapons array on the Foxes, but unfortunately, we have a very limited number of them.

5) We've added more sensors and cameras around the perimeter of the city to detect unauthorized access."

Kal looked at Marc to question if there was more he should add.

"Foxes?" Admiral Michaels asked.

"The Foxes are the jets that the Chinese carrier pilots encountered back in March," Blake said. "I'm sure you're familiar with the incident."

"One point you should be aware of," Marc added, "is that the Foxes are capable of acting as a submarine. That is how we placed the mine that disabled the Chinese submarine for you."

"What can't you people do?" the admiral asked, shaking his head in amazement. "I would say you're set up to handle a commando raid, but you should be prepared for a force of up to twenty commandos. If they choose that option, they'll be looking for a low profile so I wouldn't expect more, but they're going to come in big and hard if they come in."

"Other methods?" Marc asked the board members around the table.

"They could just threaten us," Liz said. "That or enact an embargo."

"I would agree on the threats," Admiral Michaels said. "But an embargo would be too slow and too public. It would quickly involve the Kiwis, and then the United Nations. I could see them trying to interdict your tankers, but that would require that they know about them. You've done a good job of hiding which oil tankers are yours, and they don't really know why you're bringing them in. Also, they know you have two small tankers here, so any effect would be delayed."

Marc looked at Samantha, asking if she had anything to add.

"I think he's right about the embargo," Samantha said. "Seems an unlikely choice."

"So, if they threaten us, what would they threaten us with?" Marc asked.

"For the same reasons that the embargo is unlikely, the threats would have to be about taking us by force; otherwise it takes too long and involves too many players," Samantha said.

"What kind of force?"

"A missile strike," Admiral Michaels said. "One or two cruise missiles hitting this city would certainly get your attention."

"It would," Marc said, "but I'm confident we could shoot down any missiles."

"I didn't notice any antimissile defenses."

"We have four Foxes that would probably be able to take out any missiles fired at us. We also have local laser weapons that could take them out at about one thousand meters. The plasma cannons could hit any that get within five hundred meters."

"Shit!"

"Admiral, there are children present," Samantha said, barely containing her laugh as she saw Catie's face turn red at being called a child.

"Sorry about the language."

"I was just trying to lighten the moment a bit," Samantha said. "Catie, will you forgive me?"

"Right after I get even," Catie said as she stuck her tongue out at Samantha.

"Well, it will be an interesting discussion when they threaten you, should threats be the strategy they employ," Admiral Michaels said.

"What else?" Marc asked.

Catie was staring at the admiral with her 'Duh' face, urging him to say something. The admiral finally noticed her stare and shifted in his seat. "Um," he hesitated, "I think their most likely move would be to put a carrier strike force twelve miles off your coast."

Catie sat back in her chair; everyone could tell she was saying '*finally*' in her head.

"What would that mean?" Samantha asked as she looked at the shocked faces of everyone in the room besides the admiral's and Catie's.

"If they include an amphibious assault ship in the strike force, and I would, it would mean over sixteen hundred marines within minutes of the city."

"How would they enter the city?" Samantha asked.

"Helicopters," Liz said.

"We could shoot those down," Kal said.

"But it would be an act of war," Blake said.

"Wouldn't it be an act of war to launch military helicopters at the city?" Liz asked.

"Yes, but once American lives are lost, the public opinion will swing in favor of the president taking even more aggressive action. They will spin the story in a way that makes us look like the aggressors," Samantha said. "Oh, we do have a problem."

"Yes, we do," Admiral Michaels said. "I never imagined this."

"Why not?" Samantha said.

"The space station; who could have known that you intended to, much less were capable of putting something like that in orbit. Without that, I assumed that the worst thing the president would do is send in commandos. But that changes everything. He will not even bat an eye at launching a strike force; even risking an act of war against New Zealand will pale against losing the strategic high ground that a space station like that would give you."

"We have to win this in the public minds," Samantha said. "Not on the battlefield."

"I would agree," Marc said.

"Now I know why I never wanted to be an officer," Kal said. "They shoot at you, you shoot back. That's so much easier."

"Think of it more like a recon mission," Admiral Michaels said. "They shoot, but you don't shoot back so they don't know where you are, or if you're really out there."

Kal just made a little circling motion with his head, as if he were nodding yes then shaking his head no. "Can we have some scotch now?"

Blake looked at Marc, who just shrugged his shoulders. That was all it took. Blake hurried to the cabinet and brought his bottle of Glenlivet out. "Admiral, this is really good, fifteen-year-old scotch," Blake said as he poured the admiral a glass. He poured all around and got an eye from the admiral when he poured a splash in Catie's glass.

"Okay," Marc said, "How do we change the game?"

"We need to get the public on our side," Samantha said. "To do that, we need to show everybody that the president is overreaching, that he is ignoring the rule of law."

"How would you propose to do that?" Admiral Michaels asked.

"If we could get audio of him ordering a strike on Delphi City," Samantha said, "that would help."

"How could you do that? He won't give that kind of order where it could be intercepted. And if you somehow got one, he could claim it was fake."

"Not if the audio and the subsequent action matched up, especially if we could release the audio before the action took place."

"We won't know before the strike force moves, which one he'll use. I would expect him to communicate directly with the admiral in charge of the strike force and just tell the fleet commander that he's operating under his orders."

"We'll know as soon as we see a strike force moving toward us," Liz said.

"Yes, but that's not as easy as it sounds. If the president wants to be cautious, they'll schedule several fleet training maneuvers and simply have the ships pull out and gather at sea. There won't be anything that signals which ships and when; at least not that your agents would be able to pick up. I assume you have agents."

"Sort of," Marc said, "but we won't have trouble seeing an aircraft carrier form up with other ships and head this way." Marc was glad that they had managed to expand their satellite coverage. They had managed to add over one hundred satellites since the first Oryx had begun operation.

"Of course, you won't," Admiral Michaels shook his head and took a long sip of scotch. "But there's still the problem of intercepting the message. I hope you can't break into our military-encrypted transmissions."

"ADI?"

"Who's ADI?" the admiral asked.

Marc held his hand up to signal the admiral to wait.

"Captain, I would not be able to break the encryption in time to be useful," ADI replied. "And the US 3$^{rd}$ Fleet currently has two carrier groups out on maneuvers. There are sufficient numbers to form the strike force Admiral Michaels has suggested."

"ADI is our tech specialist; she listens in remotely." Marc said, "She says she can't break the encryption, but she has informed me that there are two different carrier groups from the 3$^{rd}$ fleet out on maneuvers."

Admiral Michaels' eyes rolled up as if he were reading off a HUD, "Those have been scheduled for months. But it would give the president a chance to commandeer one for this purpose. You can't intercept the message; you don't know which ships yet; how do we get the information you need?" he asked.

"We're going to need to think about it," Marc said. "Okay, we'll meet again next Monday to discuss options and other ideas. Keep doing what you're doing, we cannot slow down, but we need some ideas."

"You have some time, it will take a strike force at least five days to get here," Admiral Michaels said.

"Captain, it will take 6.5 days for the closest group, 8.2 days for the other," ADI told Marc.

"Okay, see everybody on Monday."

"Daddy," Catie called out to hold Marc back.

"What's up?" Marc asked.

"I got a text last night. It was from my friend Alyssa in Boston."

Marc nodded.

"She lives across the street from Grandma and Grandpa McGinnis' house."

Marc suddenly became very interested. "What did she have to say?"

"Three black SUVs drove up to the house yesterday morning. A bunch of men got out and checked around the house. Then they left," Catie said.

"Did they go into the house?"

"I asked, but she didn't know," Catie said. "Who do you think they were?"

"Probably FBI," Marc said. "I guess we made the move just in time."

"What about Grandma Ma and Grandpa Pa?"

"Cer Catie, your great grandparents are currently in their backyard," ADI announced.

"Oh thanks," Catie said.

"Why don't you call them," Marc suggested, "Have ADI route the call."

"ADI?"

"Calling."

"Hello, Grandpa Pa," Catie said.

# 21   Meltdown

"What is that thing?" The president asked. Nancy Blaylock, the Director of NASA, had just displayed an image of Delphi Station on the screen.

"Mr. President, I believe that is a space station," Director Blaylock said.

"What, it's just a big can."

"You can see here on the zoomed-in portion, that one of their jumbo shuttles is docked. There's room for eight of those shuttles to be docked at once."

"That's bigger than the International Space Station," General Wilson said.

"It's bigger than a football stadium," Director Blaylock said.

"How did they get that thing up there?" General Wilson asked.

"It seems they built it up there. They've been sending a jumbo shuttle up at least every hour for weeks."

"Why didn't we know what they were doing before now?" demanded the president.

"Sir, we knew they were sending the shuttles somewhere, but we never managed to find out where they were going. We never thought that they were even capable of making orbit. Even after seeing one docked at that station, it's hard to believe it. The shuttles are hard to see, and their exhaust plume is nonexistent once they're in orbit. We don't understand how they're getting thrust, much less how they have enough fuel to make it into orbit. The space station is difficult to see; it seems to absorb light, so it just looks like empty space."

"Then how did we get this image?"

"We got it from the last SpaceX flight to ISS II," Director Blaylock said. "Once we realized those shuttles were going into orbit, we started to collect data. We estimated where they must be going, and we had SpaceX extend their reentry orbit so they would make a pass close to where we thought this would be."

"Still, how could they have hauled all that material up there?"

"It still doesn't make sense. Calculating the cargo area of those shuttles, they must have filled every square meter of the holds with material. And even then, our scientists say that wouldn't have been enough material."

"Unless they shipped the material up in bulk and manufactured the parts up there," General Wilson said.

"That's absurd," Director Lassiter said. "And how could they possibly assemble that thing in just a few weeks?"

"Unknown."

"Where are the solar arrays?" Secretary Mathews asked.

"There are none," Director Blaylock said.

"Then how are they powering the thing?" the president asked.

"We don't know," Director Blaylock said. "One would have to assume some form of nuclear energy."

"So, the nuclear physicists finally made something," Director Lassiter said.

"What!" the president demanded.

"As you probably remember from Admiral Michaels' briefing, MacKenzie Discoveries hired two very prominent nuclear physicists. We don't know what they have been working on, but this suggests it was designing a reactor to power this space station," Director Lassiter explained.

"Get Admiral Michaels in here. I want to know more about this."

Everyone around the table looked at each other nervously. After a brief pause, Director Lassiter continued, "We can't, Mr. President. You fired him."

The president looked confused for a moment. "Oh, right. Well, get someone in here who can explain this!"

# 22    Teenagers

"Do I have to go?" Catie whined.

"I thought you liked Sophia," Linda said. "And Jason will be there."

Catie blushed when her mother mentioned Jason. "But for a whole four hours," Catie continued to whine.

"Mrs. Michaels has set this up so her children can meet some of the other teenagers here in Delphi City. You're on the board of MacKenzie Discoveries, so besides being Jason and Sophia's friend, you're representing the board to the community. We can't have people thinking that you don't want to associate with the other teenagers here in the city. Besides, you need to learn how to socialize with other people. Going to parties is one of the ways people socialize."

"Gawd," Catie groaned. "And we're watching some long movie. How do we socialize while we're watching a movie?"

Linda sighed. "It's about having a shared experience that you can talk about later."

"Then why can't I just watch it myself. I can run it at 2.5 times speed and save two hours."

Linda smacked Catie on the shoulder. "You just go and have a good time. And I've instructed ADI to disable your comm except for emergencies."

"Oh, you're mean," Catie said.

"I just know you, and I know what my daughter needs. Besides, you like Star Wars."

"When I was six!"

"Oh, come on, you'll have fun. The Last Jedi is supposed to be very good, and stars a young woman," Linda said. "Now you're just wasting your breath, you're going, and that's it."

"Oh, jeez," Catie wheezed. "Okay, but I'm not wearing a dress."

"Jeans will be just fine. Why don't you wear that outfit you wore when I met you at the Prudential Center? I can do your hair up."

Catie flounced herself down on the couch in her mother's condo. She wondered how she was going to deal with having both parents trying to do what's best for her. *"I had it so good when Daddy was busy, and Mommy was in San Diego,"* she thought.

Catie rang the Michaels' doorbell. She could hear the noise of the party coming from inside the condo, *'Gawd! How am I going to survive this?'* she thought.

"Hi Catie," Sophia said as she opened the door. "I like your outfit. You did something to your hair too."

"Yeah, my mom curled it a little," Catie mumbled.

"It looks good. Come on in and meet the rest of the group."

Catie followed Sophia into the condo, "Hey everybody," Sophia shouted over the music, "This is Catie, Catie this is everybody," Sophia laughed. "I'll take you around in a bit, but let me tell you who everybody is.

"You already know Jason, and my brother, David. That short guy over there with the glasses is Artie Gillespie, he's a nice guy but a bit of a nerd, his parents are both teachers. The cute guy with the black hair is Chaz Murillo, he's mine. His mom's a doctor, and his dad is working as a foreman in one of your factories. The brunette over there is Annie Halloway, her dad is one of your pilots, and her mom is working as a lab assistant for the Zelbars. The blond girl is Barbara Kerr, her mom and dad are both nurses."

"How old is everybody?" Catie asked.

"Except for Jason and my brother, they're all fourteen."

"Oh, and when are you showing the movie?"

"It's seven o'clock now," Sophia said. "Mom's starting the movie at eight."

"What are we supposed to do until then?" Catie asked. She was aghast at the thought of an hour doing nothing.

"Mingle, talk to everyone. Come, let's get you something to drink. What do you want, we have coke, ginger ale, root beer?"

"Just water," Catie said.

"Boring."

"I try," Catie laughed nervously.

"Here, take this and go say hello to Jason. He's been talking to Annie since he got here."

"But . . ."

"Go."

Catie took a drink of her water and walked to where Jason and Annie were talking. "Hey Jason," she said as she caught his eye.

"Oh, hello, Catie," Jason said. "This is Annie Halloway; Annie, this is Catie McCormack."

"Hi," Annie said with as much disdain as one could put in such a short greeting.

"Hi," Catie said back.

"Annie was just asking about how it feels to fly the Oryx," Jason said. "I was telling her how amazing it is to take one up. They're so smooth and powerful, the freedom of being up there with nothing around you."

"Sounds like you're enjoying it," Catie said.

"Well you know how it is," Jason said. "Annie, Catie took me for my first flight in an Oryx; she even let me fly it for a while."

"Oh, so you're a pilot too," Annie said, clearly not happy that Catie had anything in common with Jason.

"She's the best pilot they have," Jason said.

Catie blushed at the praise.

"How many flights have you made?" Annie asked Jason.

"I've only made thirty-five so far, Catie's probably made way more than that," Jason said.

"No, I've only made about thirty in an Oryx," Catie said. "We've got enough pilots now, so I'm not going up much."

"Where are you flying them?" Annie asked.

"Oh, we're just hauling cargo between islands," Jason lied. "But it's a lot of fun."

"Maybe, you could take me up once?"

"I'd have to get clearance from my boss," Jason said awkwardly.

"We have an Oryx that is just finishing ground testing," Catie said. "Maybe you can ask your boss if you can do one of the test flights. Then you could take Annie along, and it wouldn't be such a long flight."

"You think he would let me?" Jason asked, knowing full well that Catie assigned the pilots who did the test flights.

"I bet he would, especially for the second one, you know the high-altitude flight."

"That would be nice," Jason said. "I'll be sure to ask him."

Catie gave Jason a wink, letting him know she'd arrange it. "It's nice meeting you, Annie," she said as she moved on.

Catie wandered around a little, feeling very awkward; eventually, she wound up sitting in a chair by the wall. She was furious with her mom for cutting off her comm because now she was stuck with absolutely nothing to do and bored out of her mind. Forty minutes before the movie.

"You look like you're having as much fun as I am," a voice to Catie's side said. She looked up and saw Artie Gillespie leaning against the wall.

"Hi, I'm Catie."

"I'm Artie."

"I'm not much of a party person," Catie said.

"Me neither. This is my first party, besides birthday parties," Artie said.

"I guess it's my first teen party too," Catie said.

"Well, only thirty-eight minutes until the movie starts."

Catie laughed, "You're counting down the time too."

"Yes, but I am looking forward to the movie."

"You're a Star Wars fan?"

"Absolutely, I've seen them all," Artie said. "I really like space movies. Do you want to play a game on our phones?"

"I can't, my mom blocked my phone for the duration."

"Oh, that's mean," Artie said. "Are you going to be in Sophia's class at school?"

"No, I homeschool," Catie said.

"I wish I could," Artie said, "but my parents teach at the school, so they make me go. I guess they don't want to have to teach school all day and then come home and teach me."

"That would be hard, but my dad doesn't really spend that much time with me on school," Catie said. "I mostly do it on my own, with help from my coach. She checks my work and gives me extra assignments if I seem to be struggling with a subject."

"That sounds good, maybe I can talk my parents into it. Where do you study, at home?"

"Mostly, or in our offices, so I'm usually there anyway."

"Offices?" Artie asked.

"Yea, where we work and hold meetings and stuff."

"What kind of meetings?"

"I don't know, a board meeting every two weeks, but there's always some meeting to coordinate with someone you're working with."

"What kind of work do you do?"

"Coordinate projects and some design work, and help others with their projects," Catie said.

"What company lets a kid do design work for them?"

"MacKenzie Discoveries," Catie said.

"Oh my god, you're that Catie McCormack," Artie gasped.

"That's my name. What's the matter, did someone say something bad about me?"

"No, no, but you're like famous."

"If I am, it didn't help me get out of this party," Catie said.

"Wait until I tell my sister that I met you," Artie said.

"Why would she care?"

"She thinks you're a goddess," Artie said.

"How old is she, like seven?" Catie asked with a shake of her head.

"No, she's sixteen," Artie said. "She wants to be a pilot like you."

"She's old enough to get a license," Catie said. "I'm sure she can find someone to give her lessons. Is she going to school here too?"

"Oh, she's supposed to start college this year," Artie said. "Mom's trying to get her to go to the University of Auckland or Australia National University. That way, she would be closer to visit."

"With the new Lynx we have, you can get there in about half an hour," Catie said. "We have permission to fly to Australia and New Zealand."

"Wow, wait 'til I tell my sister that. She'd be able to come home on the weekend. Are you guys going to run a regular service?"

"To Auckland for sure," Catie said. "Probably to Sydney and Wellington too, but I'm not sure about Canberra. So, your sister skipped a few grades?"

"We both did," Artie said. "I'm in the same class as David, but he and all the kids ignore me because I'm so young."

"I had the same problem, that's why I like homeschooling," Catie said.

"So, what grade are you in?"

"It depends on the class," Catie said. "Another reason I like homeschooling. I'm starting college-level math and science, twelfth grade English, history, and social sciences."

"That does sound cool. Do you mind if I tell my parents about you?"

"Why would I care? Tell them you can use ADI as your coach like I do. They'll know who she is."

"The movie starts in three minutes," Sophia announced. "Popcorn is ready, and candy is now out on the counter if you want any." Mrs. Michaels had kept the candy hidden away until the movie was ready to ensure there would be some left.

Catie looked at her comm for the time, surprised to see it was seven minutes to eight. "Great, just three more hours to go," Catie mumbled.

Artie laughed, "Do you want to sit together during the movie? I can fill you in on anything you might not know."

"Sure," Catie said.

# 23　What Do We Know?

"Okay, everybody's had a week to think about options, let's have them," Marc said as the admiral and the members of the board settled down at the table.

"We now know the carriers that are involved in the exercise," Kal said. "They are the Carl Vinson, the Nimitz, and the Theodore Roosevelt."

"Admiral Morris commands the Carl Vinson," Admiral Michaels said. "I'd put my money on the president tagging him."

"Why?" Marc asked.

"He's a zealous patriot," Admiral Michaels said. "The president pushed for his promotion to rear admiral based on a recommendation from one of his prominent supporters, so there's a history and a bit of debt on the part of Admiral Morris."

"What can you tell us about him?"

"He has a hot temper, he's extremely arrogant, and extremely competent."

"How confident are you that he's the one the president will select for the mission?"

"Ninety percent. With the other two, it's fifty-fifty they would refuse the orders since they would be risking war without proper congressional oversight."

"Okay, let's assume it's Morris."

"Will the president have fully informed him of the mission yet?" Samantha asked.

Admiral Michaels grimaced and tilted his head a bit, "I'm not sure. He might just be telling him where to go right now."

"So, we need to listen in on the admiral's conversations," Samantha said. "If we can catch him issuing illegal orders, or the president instructing him to do so, we can use it."

"I don't see how we can hear conversations between the president and the admiral," Blake said.

"Come on all you geniuses, how do we listen in on the admiral?" Samantha looked around the table at a bunch of blank expressions. Then she settled on Catie. "Out with it, Catie, you've been sitting there playing with that hockey puck and smiling like a Cheshire cat for the whole meeting."

"Well," Marc gave Catie a demanding look.

"We just need to put a couple of these on the carrier," Catie said.

"Don't you think they'll notice a new black puck sticking on one of the bulkheads?" Blake asked.

"Not necessarily," Catie said. She laid the surveillance puck down on the table; flicked her eyes up into her HUD and blinked. The puck took on the color of the table.

"I didn't know they could do that!" Blake exclaimed.

"Me neither," Catie said. "I just read all the specs last night and found out about it."

"So maybe they won't notice them, but how do we get them in place?"

Catie flicked her eyes up and blinked again. The puck started moving, when it got to Blake's edge of the table, it slid around the lip of the table and disappeared underneath. It came back up in front of Samantha and continued down the center of the table toward Marc. When it reached Liz's comm unit that was laying on the table, it grew six legs and carefully walked over the comm unit, without touching the main surface.

"Wow, and I didn't know they could do that either," Blake said.

Admiral Michaels was smiling and shaking his head.

"Okay, how do you plan to get them on board the carrier?" Marc asked.

"On a surveillance drone," Catie said.

"Are you going to make me come over there and squeeze the information out of you, or are you going to tell us?" Marc said. He was both mad and laughing at the same time.

"Too much drama?"

"I think so."

"Okay," Catie closed her eyes momentarily as she organized how she wanted to explain things. "I guess I'll just walk through it. First, you have two Foxes buzz the aircraft carrier at Mach five. They have to approach on the deck below radar and just pop up and buzz each side of the comm tower without their shockwave suppressors on. We'll need to practice the maneuver on the Mea Huli, so we're comfortable with how the planes handle without the shockwave suppressors and to make sure we get the timing down perfectly."

"Just the highlights for now," Marc said. "We'll all be asking questions after!" Marc emphasized the 'after' so everybody understood he didn't want them interrupting Catie.

"Okay, one of the Foxes launches the drone right as they pass the comm tower. I've done simulations, so I'm sure it will work. The drone lands on the tower, up behind one of those communication dishes that they have up there. If the first drone doesn't make it, the second Fox launches its drone. Once a drone is in place, someone just walks each puck into position. I assume one on the bridge and one in the admiral's office or his quarters." Catie looked at Admiral Michaels for confirmation.

"All three, if possible, office otherwise," Admiral Michaels said.

"We have to make a small mod to the drone, but we can send three," Catie said after she checked the design on her HUD.

"Okay, so now we can see and listen in," Marc said. "How do we get them to have the conversation we want?"

Catie raised her index finger.

"Of course, you have more," Marc laughed. "Please, continue."

"With the drone on the comm tower, we can break into their communication system."

"ADI says she can't decrypt fast enough," Marc stopped talking as he saw Catie shaking her head. "Continue."

"Not their encrypted communication, the actual comms, the speakers, the phone itself. We can talk to them; we can hear what they can hear, and we can connect their phone or speaker to another phone or speaker anywhere."

"Oh, low tech, I love it," Blake said. "We grab our info after they decrypt it for us."

"Wait," Samantha said. "You mean we could have your father talk to the admiral over their system as though he were talking over their military-encrypted channel."

"Yes."

"Could we have, say, anyone talk to him, like patching someone's cellphone into the conversation?"

"Sure."

"Ohh, this is what we need," Samantha cooed. "You better get to practicing those maneuvers, I want those pucks on that ship as soon as we're sure which one it is."

"Okay," Catie said as she started to get up.

"Just one minute, young lady," Marc said. "Blake, can any of our other pilots handle those maneuvers?"

"Oh sure, they might not be able to beat Catie in a dog fight, but they all can fly a Fox as well as she can."

Catie pouted and stuck her tongue out at Blake, "Traitor."

"I think it's time for you to learn what it's like to plan a mission and then send someone else on it," Marc said. "Besides, we might need to replan or improvise, so having you here instead of flying would be better."

"Send me your simulation please," Blake said. "I'll get a few pilots training right away."

Catie crossed her arms and continued to pout. But she flicked her eyes in her HUD, sending the simulation over to Blake's comm. Samantha grabbed her hand and pulled her up. "Girl, come with me. We have a few tricks to plan out."

Marc's mouth fell open as he watched Catie and Samantha head out without any explanation to him about what Samantha was thinking.

"Having trouble controlling the troops?" Admiral Michaels said. He was actually laughing.

"Sometimes."

"That daughter of yours is something else. Did I hear right, she's the top dogfighter in your squadron?"

"Yes," Marc rolled his eyes. "She started training on the Foxes before anyone else, and she was relentless. She's also very adept at learning the habits of the opposing pilots and predicting what they're going to do. Blake hates it that she can beat him, he's the second-best."

"Oh, that would be hard to take," Admiral Michaels said. "Do the guys tease him about it?"

"Not if they don't want to be embarrassed the next time they go up," Marc said. "Catie's the only one who's allowed to tease her uncle. Anyone else makes a comment, and she'll embarrass the hell out of them."

"She's that good."

"That good and she plans ahead. If you're on her list, she'll spend days figuring out how to get even."

"I'll make sure to stay off her list then."

"Sound advice."

# 24 They're Coming

The next day it took four practice flights before the pilots could place the drone on the Mea Huli's comm platform. After doing it consistently three times in a row, Blake called it good. The pilots would come in staggered. If the first missed, the second would launch their drone also. It would take two seconds from launch to the drone alighting on the tower, so the second pilot would tail by five seconds, just enough time to launch if the first one failed.

It was 02:00 Thursday when Marc was awakened by ADI, "Captain, the first carrier group has turned south."

Marc rolled over and checked his clock. "Thanks, ADI, put a ten o'clock meeting on the board's calendar. Notify each of them when they wake up, or by eight o'clock."

"Yes, Captain."

Marc rolled over, hoping he could go back to sleep.

"Okay people, the Carl Vinson and her carrier group have headed south," Marc said as everyone assembled in the boardroom. "It seems clear that the admiral was right and the president has tapped Admiral Morris. The group is south of Hawaii and steaming directly at us."

"What ships are with it?" Kal asked.

"The USS Carl Vinson; the guided-missile cruiser USS Lake Champlain; and guided-missile destroyers USS Wayne E. Meyer and the USS Michael Murphy; and the Wasp-class amphibious assault ship the USS Boxer." ADI iterated. "They are traveling at their top speed of twenty-two knots, and are three days away," ADI added.

"Any last-minute concerns, questions, other ideas?" Marc asked. He looked around the room at the collection of somber faces. "Okay, let's begin this thing. Catie, you have a green light to put the drone on the Carl Vinson."

The two Foxes launched from Delphi City at 11:00 on Thursday, August twenty-seventh. They were flown by Liz Farmer and Jaime

Hernandez. The plan was to time their pass on the Carl Vinson for noon. The board was assembled in the meeting room with the display showing the Carl Vinson and the carrier group steaming toward the Cook Islands.

"How are you getting that image?" Admiral Michaels asked.

"Privileged," Marc said.

"Here they come," Catie said, pointing to the second display showing the zoomed-out view. It showed a blip for the two Foxes, and you could just make out the Carl Vinson.

"Fox one, this is flight command. You are eight hundred kilometers out. Adjust speed to Mach five," Blake said into the comm.

"Copy, flight command. Adjusting speed to Mach five," Liz responded.

"Two minutes," Catie said.

Everyone gripped the arms of their chairs as the blip approached the carrier. "One minute," Catie announced.

The first screen started showing a split image, the second image was the view from the nose of the Fox as it approached the Carl Vinson. You could see the carrier now, barely making out the carrier's island since the Fox was flying only ten meters above the water.

"Up they go," Catie said.

"Fox One, you are clear to engage," Blake said.

"Copy, Fox One engaging."

The view suddenly changed as Liz's Fox climbed up to twenty meters and was now above the flight deck. The carrier had two fighters preparing to launch. The Fox's camera showed the crew chief about to signal the first fighter to launch when the siren went off as the ship's systems finally detected the Foxes coming at them. Liz turned her Fox so the wings were perpendicular to the deck and she was by it in a split second. A big green dot showed up on the Carl Vinson signaling that the drone was in place. Everybody in the room cheered.

"That's our girl," Blake said. "Nailed it."

"How did Jaime do?" Fred asked.

"He buzzed the carrier's island on the other side, five seconds behind just like we drew it up," Catie said.

"Great. Were any missiles launched?"

"They only had an eight-second window from detecting Liz to Jamie being by them. They both went vertical just after passing the carrier, so the destroyers didn't have a shot."

"I'll bet Liz is disappointed that they didn't even try to shoot at her," Catie said.

"I don't know," Blake said, "I like not getting shot at."

"When do we move the pucks?" Samantha asked.

"Tonight," Catie said. "We want things to settle down first."

"Okay, call me when they're in place."

# 25    Showdown

## Midnight Friday

That night, it took Catie four hours to get the three pucks into place. The bridge was easy, it was essentially open and with predictable traffic. The admiral's office wasn't as bad as she had feared; she attached the puck to the bucket the cleaning crew used when they cleaned it. They just carried it into the office for her. Of course, nobody was going to be cleaning the admiral's quarters in the middle of the night, so she had to wait until he got his morning coffee. She had the puck waiting on the bulkhead by the door. When the steward went in, she was able to have it crawl around the door jamb while he was struggling with the tray and the door. That was 04:00 since the admiral was still on San Diego time. Catie assumed that Samantha wasn't completely serious when she'd said 'call me when they're in place,' so she told ADI to inform her at 7:00 and she went back to bed to grab a few hours of sleep.

## Friday 08:30

"I told you to call me," Samantha said.

"Oh, you were serious," Catie sat at the breakfast counter where they were meeting.

"No, I'm actually glad you decided on seven o'clock. Did you get any sleep?"

"Two naps, one before midnight and the other after four o'clock when I finished."

"Your note said that they're running on San Diego time."

"At least the admiral is."

"Good, so it's almost eleven o'clock for them. We'll start our call in an hour, I'd like to interrupt the admiral's lunch."

"Ask ADI what time it's scheduled. She probably knows by now," Catie suggested.

"The admiral has scheduled his lunch for one hour and twenty minutes from now," ADI replied.

"Thanks, ADI. God, what I would have done with such an efficient assistant when I was working at the firm," Samantha said.

"She is good."

"Thank you," ADI said.

"But impossible to talk about without her knowing," Samantha giggled.

"Oh, you can tell her not to listen," Catie said.

Samantha cocked her head in surprise, "You can?"

"Sure. Though she mostly figures it out anyway."

"What do you mean?"

"She hears other people talking, so eventually she knows anyway. I ran a few tests; on average, it takes her six hours to know the secret."

"Those were fun," ADI said.

"She has fun?" Samantha mouthed.

"Yes, and I lip read as well," ADI said.

Samantha blushed. "She's just messing with you now," Catie said.

"ADI, no listening or lip-reading on us," Samantha said.

"Yes, Cer Sam."

"Okay, so she has fun, and she's messing with me. How do I get even with her?" Samantha asked.

"It's hard," Catie said. "I'll think about it, and we can come up with a plan."

"Okay, how do I tell her she can listen again?"

"Message her on your HUD."

Samantha sent ADI a message to allow her to listen again.

"I look forward to your attempt," ADI said.

"What, I thought she wasn't listening."

"She wasn't, but she's deduced what you wanted to talk about, and you've just confirmed it."

"Oh, you just wait, ADI." Samantha shook her fork in the air.

"Of course, Cer Sam."

# Friday 10:15

"They just served the admiral his lunch," Liz said as Catie and Samantha entered the meeting room.

"Good. ADI, give him a few minutes to get a few bites, then make the call."

"How many bites?" ADI asked.

Samantha gave Catie a 'is she messing with me look.'

"No, she really is that precise," Catie said.

"Four bites."

Everyone had gathered in the boardroom to watch the show. The display in the boardroom was showing the bridge of the USS Carl Vinson. The communications officer looked surprised after his headset buzzed, and he turned to the captain.

Captain, "I've got a call coming in from a Dr. Marc McCormack for the admiral. It's coming in over our secure channel."

"Well then, I suggest we inform the admiral," the captain said. He nodded to the yeoman, indicating that she should go knock on the admiral's door and inform him.

They watched as the admiral was interrupted in the middle of his lunch. It was apparent that he was deciding whether to make Marc call back while he finished his lunch or take the call. Finally, he said he'd take the call in his stateroom. He was most displeased when the yeoman informed him that the call couldn't be transferred since it was placed on the bridge's secure communication system. He threw his napkin down and followed the yeoman to the bridge.

"Oh good, he's already mad," Samantha said.

When the admiral stepped onto the bridge, everyone came to attention, except the captain. The admiral told them 'at ease' and grabbed the phone from the comm officer.

"Admiral Morris," he said into the phone, not even trying to hide his frustration.

"Good day, Admiral Morris. This is Dr. Marc McCormack, the Mayor of Manuae in the Cook Islands. I've just had a phone call from the White House," Marc lied.

The admiral scoffed when Marc announced his title. "Good for you."

"They informed me that I was to surrender the City of Delphi to you," Marc said.

The admiral straightened up. "That would be best," he said.

"You do realize that any attempt to seize the city would be an act of war against the nation of Cook Islands, and since we are a protectorate of New Zealand, an act of war against them as well."

"I don't care about some shit-hole island nation," the admiral said. "And I doubt very much that New Zealand cares that much either."

"If you don't care about us, then why are you attempting to seize us?"

"We are simply executing a seizure order from the IRS for the assets that you have illegally siphoned off from the United States and hidden there," the admiral said.

Samantha got excited and spoke into her comm quietly. She carried on the conversation for a few minutes while Marc continued.

"Since when has the IRS used the Navy to conduct its seizures?"

"Since you ran off and hid in a foreign country and got yourself appointed mayor," the admiral said.

"You have to know that we can't allow you to violate our territorial waters," Marc said, getting a thumbs up from Samantha.

"And what exactly are you going to do about it," the admiral said. "That little stunt you pulled with your jets yesterday wasn't all that impressive."

"We are considering our options," Marc said. "That little stunt as you call it was just a wakeup call. We would like to avoid any hostilities, but we will not allow you to violate our waters."

The admiral laughed, "Well sonny, you'd best move that little boat of yours because I'm going to dock my ship right where it is, and I might crush it. And if any of your jets get close to my ship again, we're going to shoot them down."

"I doubt that Admiral," Marc said. "We were by you before your ship even knew we were coming."

"I've seen that trick of flying on the deck before; we won't let it happen again."

Catie started raising her fingers one by one as she counted down, "Five . . . four . . . three . . . two . . . one."

The shockwave was deafening as Liz buzzed the bridge of the Carl Vinson.

"I'm sorry, Admiral, I couldn't hear you over the noise of our jet. Did you manage to shoot it down? That was your Gatling gun I heard go off?"

"God damn it," the admiral yelled at the captain.

The bridge was scrambling as they were tracking Liz as she went vertical after passing the bridge. "Shoot that thing down!"

"It's already out of range. We couldn't get a targeting solution in time to fire," the weapons officer announced.

"What about our fighter screen?"

"Their jet is too fast, it was doing Mach five," the radar technician reported. "And we can barely see it on the radar."

"Admiral, is everything okay?" Marc's voice came over the speaker system on the bridge.

"I am going to sink that blasted city of yours," the admiral yelled.

"I would really suggest you consider other options besides starting a war. Congress won't look kindly on you starting one without their approval."

"The war will be over before Congress even knows about it!" the admiral yelled. "Now get that man off my comm system!"

"Perfect," Samantha clapped her hands. "That will be playing on every news channel as their opening for the evening news."

"You have those kinds of connections?" Admiral Michaels asked.

"Pfft," Samantha said. "All you need is the number of one reporter, then the feeding frenzy will start. We'll give him an hour to simmer, then we'll make the next call."

# Friday 12:28

Everybody took the hour break to go to the restroom and grab another drink. Blake and Kal opted for a beer.

When Marc saw Blake with his beer, he gave him a dirty look, "Hey, we're just here for the entertainment," Blake said. "This is Sam's show."

Marc smiled and gave a shrug. Blake was right, only he and Sam, and maybe the admiral, needed to be on their game, everyone else was just watching.

"Okay, ADI, please make the calls."

"Captain, it's the White House," the communication officer on the bridge of the Carl Vinson said in a hushed tone.

"For the admiral, I assume," the captain gave the comm officer a hard glare admonishing him for not announcing that critical piece of information.

"Yes, sir."

The yeoman was already heading to the admiral's office. Thirty seconds later, the admiral was almost running as he came onto the bridge. He grabbed the phone, "Admiral Morris here."

"Why are you calling me?" the president yelled into the phone.

"Mr. President, you called me, sir."

"You called a meeting with me, the Secretary of Defense and the Secretary of State," the president yelled. "How dare you."

Samantha nodded to Marc.

"No, gentlemen, I called you both," Marc said. "I thought you might want to see the evening news. I think the report you'll be interested in is on any of the major news channels. I'll have my assistant put it up on your display, Admiral."

ADI piped the news channel to one of the Carl Vinson's tactical screens.

"Breaking news! Admiral Morris threatens to bomb Delphi City." The news immediately showed the scene where Marc was asking the admiral if he was okay.

"How could you be so stupid," the president's voice rang out. "And where did that video come from!"

"I don't know, but we'll find out!" the admiral yelled.

"Sir, what is going on?" Secretary Palmero was heard saying. "How could you authorize such a mission?"

"Where are you now?" the president demanded.

"We are five hundred miles from Rarotonga," the admiral said. "It will take us thirty-two hours to reach that floating city."

"Now!" Marc said.

On the display showing the bridge, you could see a definite lurch as the Carl Vinson suddenly lost propulsion.

"I think you should revise that estimate," Marc said.

"What the hell happened?" the admiral and the captain yelled together. The bridge crew was frantically checking status.

"Engineering reports we've lost our starboard shafts!"

"What happened?" the president yelled into the phone.

"We've lost some of our propulsion," the admiral said.

"What does that do to the mission?"

"We cannot launch fighter jets, but we can still make it to the target."

"Unless you lose the other two shafts," Marc threatened.

"Sir, the Speaker of the House is on the phone," someone announced, their voice could barely be heard over all the other noise on the channel. "And the Senate Leader is on the other line."

"It seems the president has other matters to attend to," Marc said.

Everyone could hear the president's phone crashing against something. "Damn it, this is a mess."

"Close the calls," Marc ordered. "Okay, Sam, do you have what you need?"

"Yes. We'll send that last video to the president," Samantha said. "Then he can decide how he wants to play this out."

## Friday 17:00 EST

"Today the White House announced the firing of Admiral Morris, saying he had hoped to curry favor with the president by forcing Delphi City and MacKenzie Discoveries to share their jet engine design with the US military. The White House added that the video of the admiral that you saw here on the evening news was during a moment of frustration and anger and that in no way was the admiral intending to bomb Delphi City."

"I guess we can rest for now," Samantha said. "But we need to find a way to keep the Russians and the Chinese from doing something similar."

"Well, at least we can take a break," Marc said.

"Captain, North Korea has just launched a missile."

# Afterword

## Thanks for reading *Delphi Station*!

I hope you've enjoyed the third book in the *Delphi in Space* series. As a self-published author, the one thing you can do that will help the most is to leave a review on Goodreads and Amazon.

## The next book in our series, **Delphi Nation**.

The McCormacks have been trying to keep a low profile so they can complete their plan to bring Earth to the club of spacefaring civilizations without creating a world war over the technology. But it's hard to keep a low profile while building a space station, what with lifting all the material they need, designing new shuttles, and harnessing asteroids. Without any other choice, they go public.

Find out what is in store for them as the nations of Earth deal with the shocking technology and power that having the high ground of space means.

# Acknowledgments

It is impossible to say how much I am indebted to my beta readers and copy editors. Without them, you would not be able to read my books due to all the grammar and spelling errors. I have always subscribed to Andrew Jackson's opinion that "It is a damn poor mind that can think of only one way to spell a word."

So special thanks to:

My copy editor, Ann Clark, who also happens to be my wife.

My beta reader and editor, Theresa Holmes.

My beta reader and cheerleader, Roger Blanton, who happens to be my brother.

Also important to a book author is the cover art for their book. I'm especially thankful to Momir Borocki for the exceptional covers he has produced for my books. It is amazing what he can do with the strange PowerPoint drawings I give him; and how he makes sense of my suggestions, I'll never know.

If you need a cover, he can be reached at momir.borocki@gmail.com.

# Also by Bob Blanton

Delphi in Space
*Starship Sakira*
*Delphi City*
*Delphi Station*
*Delphi Nation*
*Delphi Alliance*
*Delphi Federation*
*Delphi Exploration*
*Delphi Colony*
*Delphi Challenge*
*Delphi League – coming in April 2021*


Stone Series
*Matthew and the Stone*
*Stone Ranger*
*Stone Undercover*